Murder on the Church Council

Karen Berg-Raftakis

TABLE OF CONTENTS

TABLE OF CONTENTS (CONTINUED)

DEDICATION

This book is dedicated to my family: Mom, Dad, Andy, Alex, Jim, Liz, Mark, and Meghan.

ACKNOWLEDGMENTS

I'd like to especially thank my daughter Alex, my brother Jim and my friend Allen for helping me proofread this book and for providing many valuable suggestions. I am very grateful for your help.

And a special thank you to Agatha Christie, whose murder mysteries have kept me captivated from the age of seven to present day.

CAST OF CHARACTERS

Pastor Pete – Minister at St. James Christian Church. Very attractive but has a weak work ethic.

Ron Dorchester – Morbidly obese Chairman of the Church Council. Rules the church with an iron fist and not surprisingly, does not get along well with most people.

Hannah Dorchester – Meek, but surprisingly strong wife of Ron and Vice-Chair of the Church Council.

Dick Anderson – Council Member who comes from old money. Prefers to detach himself from all the hoopla.

Shelley Anderson – Snobby wife of Dick who believes appearances are all that matters.

Bob Grossman – Former Army man who complains about everything.

Sheryl Grossman – Long-suffering wife of Bob who has a plethora of physical ailments.

Thomas Manning – God-fearing, stick-in-the-mud who's on an everlasting crusade against Satan.

Gary Forrester – Friendliest and most outgoing of the Council members. Most consider him annoying but harmless.

Ruth Williams - Long-time church member and grieving widow.

Lorraine Barger – Lonely (SCS) Superintendent. Spends most of her time obsessing over the Sunday School.

Jay Muster - Owner of Jay's Catering and best friend of Ron.

CAST OF CHARACTERS (continued)

Mike Stevenson – Chief of Police of Meadowville and Arianna's on-again, off-again boyfriend.

Sallie Rigelli - Youngest Council member. She's both beautiful and promiscuous.

Arianna Archer (Riann to her friends) - Acquaintance of Sallie's. TV fanatic and bibliophile, currently without employment.

Chapter 1 - St. James Christian Church (Sunday)

"If among you, one of your brothers should become poor, in any of your towns within your land that the LORD your God is giving you, you shall not harden your heart or shut your hand against your poor brother, but you shall open your hand to him and lend him sufficient for his need, whatever it may be. Take care lest there be an unworthy thought in your heart and you say, 'The seventh year, the year of release is near,' and your eye look grudgingly on your poor brother, and you give him nothing, and he cry to the LORD against you, and you be guilty of sin. You shall give to him freely, and your heart shall not be grudging when you give to him.....''

"God is pretty clear here in the book of Deuteronomy, Chapter Fifteen about the importance of being generous to your brothers and sisters," the pastor stated emphatically.

As Pastor Pete droned on and on about the poor, Sallie Rigelli looked down past her matching lipstick at her scarlet red fingernails, for the third time in the last fifteen minutes. God, I can't wait to get my nails done. I wonder if Margie works on Sundays. I guess I'll call when I get home. She squirmed in her seat and pulled her black skin-tight mini-skirt down a millimeter. Sallie preferred skirts that left little to the imagination. She tossed her long shiny black hair back and crossed and uncrossed her long slender legs several times, drawing attention to her silver three-inch high heeled shoes as well as her shapely legs. Many of the married male parishioners were pretending not to notice, but judging by their wives' faces, they were failing miserably. Sallie was twenty nine years old and worked at a high-end department store on Michigan Avenue. She joined the church five years ago, having found God after a bad breakup with one of the dozens of men she had relationships with over several years. Despite her consistent bad luck with men, Sallie fancied herself as being quite intuitive. She would tell whoever would listen about the "gift", which along with flashing black eyes, she'd inherited from her Italian grandmother on her father's side.

A few pews up, Hannah Dorchester, a petite middle-aged woman with red hair and freckles, noticed the pastor had been preaching about giving to the poor quite often, as of late. She wasn't sure if it was just her imagination, but she almost felt as if he was speaking directly to her and Ron. She looked at her husband and sighed. She and Ron had been members of St. James Christian Church of Meadowville for twenty years. St. James Christian was a quaint little church built in the 1930's. It was very simple, displaying only a minimum of stained glass windows depicting the Virgin Mary and the Lord Jesus. A plain wooden cross was stationed at the center of the altar with the pulpit, where the pastor stood for most of the service, directly in front of it. If you were facing the front of the church, next to the pulpit on the right was a baptismal font, and the pastor's office was on the left side of the church. Unfortunately, the congregation had no room for a secretary's office nearby, but the church did boast a huge basement that contained the bathrooms, kitchen, and an enormous dining area, as well as, many small classrooms which were utilized by the Sunday Church School. The basement also contained a room off to the side, which featured a beautiful long mahogany table surrounded by twelve big black comfortable leather chairs, a donation from the Andersons years ago. This was dubbed the Council Room because all of the Church Council meetings were conducted there. On the opposite side of the basement was what appeared to be a not quite finished beautiful library, with numerous shelves containing all types of religious, theological and spiritual books.

Hannah could count on one hand the number of Sundays she and Ron had missed church in all those years. Sometimes I would love to just sleep in, she thought. She began fantasizing about spending a Sunday doing absolutely nothing but relaxing in bed, that is until her husband considerately poked her in the side as the offering plate was being passed around. She sat up with a jolt, hastily threw their envelope into the plate, and with a guilty look on her face, stood up with the rest of the congregation to sing the closing hymn of the day.

Thomas Manning, a widower with two grown sons, who had quit the church as soon as they were able, was deciding whether or not to stay for the Coffee Hour. He and his late wife Wanda, who had died a premature death from breast cancer, had taken an active role in the church for many years. Years ago, the couple was instrumental in both initiating and instituting a strict dress code for Sunday services. Now Wanda's dead and everything has gone to hell in a hand basket, thought Thomas. Ron and that robotic wife of his had gone and done away with the dress code. I'm just glad Wanda can't see this, she'd be turning in her grave right now. People wear just about anything they want to church, I'm surprised half the congregation aren't wearing their bathrobes and slippers to the 10:30 morning service. He glanced over at Sallie in disgust. She looked, as usual, like a trollop. He scanned the rows of pews until he laid eyes upon Ruth. He smiled approvingly. She was wearing a conservative gray dress with a white Peter Pan collar, black stockings and sensible flats. At least Ruth knows what's appropriate, he thought.

Once or twice he had toyed with the idea of asking her out to dinner, but the few times he had a conversation with her recently, all she could talk about was Roger, her husband who had died from cardiac arrest several months ago. Ruth, evidently, had taken his death very hard. The couple had been married many years but had no children. After giving it some serious consideration, Thomas decided to skip the Coffee Hour. He had learned a long time ago that all it did was serve as a vehicle for idle gossip among the ladies, not to mention the fact that the men folk were always playing cards or betting on football or some other sport. Thomas did not believe in gossip or gambling, well-known snares of the devil. You have to be constantly vigilant against Satan, he strongly believed. He frowned, he knew Wanda would have understood. He slipped his arms into his coat, picked up his gray fedora sitting next to him on the pew, placed it upon his head, then quickly walked down the aisle and out of the church.

Ron and Hannah Dorchester were greeting the Pastor after the service. "Nice sermon this morning Pastor," Hannah said politely.

The pastor smiled, "Thank you Hannah," he replied.

Ron smirked and said, "It was....," he paused, "interesting," in a way that clearly meant it was not. The pastor frowned slightly, but said nothing.

As they walked away, Hannah put her hand on Ron's right shoulder. "Do we have to stay for Coffee Hour?"

"Of course we do, why wouldn't we?" Ron asked, somewhat taken aback.

"Well, would you mind if you just went on without me?"

"Of course I mind. What do you have to do that is more important Hannah?" Ron replied, visibly annoyed.

"I, I just thought I would get some housecleaning done," she answered nervously. After seeing the expression on his face, she quickly changed her mind. "You know I can always clean tonight," and continued to walk with him downstairs to the Coffee Hour.

"Fine, just don't bother me during the Blackhawks game," he replied.

Dick and Shelley Anderson were down in the church basement holding court at the Coffee Hour. They always sat at a table situated directly in front of the buffet facing the people, as if they were a king and queen passing judgment on their subjects. Dick Anderson, tall and thin with graying hair and glasses, came from money. His grandfather had been the chief cardiologist at the Mayo Clinic in Minnesota, and his father, a prominent attorney in a wealthy suburb of Grand Rapids, Michigan. Dick had made his own money primarily from buying up properties dirt cheap during the recession of the early 80's, and turning them over for a quick profit a few years later. Semi-retired, he liked to spend most of his time golfing with a couple of his long-time friends, and reading the Wall Street Journal.

Although Dick and Shelley never had any children, Shelley never held a job outside the home. However, she was always busy serving on one important committee or another. She was of average weight and height, with frosted blonde hair piled in a bun on the top of her head. Her voice had a raspy quality to it, like that of an ex-smoker. She was never seen without her expensive dainty pearl earrings and matching necklace. Shelley was a long-time member of both Meadowville's Gardening Club and the Women's Auxiliary Club, and she and Dick had many friends in high places. They could easily afford to move out of Meadowville and live somewhere more commensurate with their financial circumstances, but the couple seemed to like living there. It was rumored that Mrs. Anderson had close family around Meadowville and wasn't blessed with quite as an auspicious upbringing as her husband. Dick adjusted his glasses and wondered, if it was still sunny outside and they ate quickly enough, would he have time for a round of golf. Shelley meanwhile, sat waiting for various church members to approach her. If whoever approached her was someone she approved of, she would bestow upon them the honor of inviting them to sit down next to her. If it was someone she didn't approve of, she pretended not to notice them.

"Well I'll say, haven't seen you two in church for a while!" Shelley frowned distastefully and turned her head in the opposite direction, as Gary Forrester, long-time bachelor and fellow Church Council member, hovered over the couple.

"Yes, well, we've been vacationing in Aspen," explained Dick, as Shelley touched his arm and shot him a warning look. Gary meanwhile, took Dick's response as an invitation to sit down.

"Aspen? Wow, I've never been there myself. Heard it's super expensive, but then of course you two can afford it, right?" he laughed. Shelley grimaced. "Speaking of money, didn't you just love Pastor Pete's sermon this morning about the love of money being the root of all evil?" Not waiting for a response, Gary went on, "Hey Dick, we better start putting more money in the offering plate," as he reached around Shelley and slapped Dick hard on the back. "Did you hear me Dick? We better start putting more money in the offering plate!" he shouted over Shelley's head, effectively screaming in her ear.

Shelley stood up abruptly, "Excuse me," she said curtly, and hurriedly walked away to the rest room.

Gary moved into Shelley's vacant seat, not missing a beat, and began talking to Dick about the cost of cinnamon coffee cake going up $.75 at the local Jewel's Food Store. He let Gary's words filter in through one ear and out the other. Dick chuckled to himself, boy he knew he would get an earful from Shelley on the ride home. She could not stand Gary, thought him very "uncouth". Dick didn't mind him too much, as long as he nodded his head a few times, and muttered "uh huh" or "yes" every couple of minutes, Gary would believe he was listening. In the meantime, Dick's mind wandered, I wonder where Apple's stock will close at tomorrow?

Ron and Hannah Dorchester sat down at the Anderson's table a few minutes later. Dick was not pleased with Ron, as of late. Three months ago, Ron had decided he wanted to start playing the market and asked him for advice. So Dick, out of the kindness of his heart, introduced him to one of his oldest friends Carl, one of the best stockbrokers in Chicago. He even went so far as to set up a round of golf in Somerset Hills between the three of them. Carl, an avid golfer, took his game very seriously, and from the first hole onward, Ron had acted like a world-class buffoon. He complained constantly about the heat, and was sweating buckets, which made it very difficult to look at him without cringing. Ron was a horrible golfer and couldn't even hit the ball onto the green most of the time. He had blamed the north wind first, then the east wind, then the sun. He also ordered their caddy around, who happened to be the grandson of one of Dick's oldest friends. Worst of all, any time Carl would try and give him advice, Ron would talk over him pontificating about, God knows what, thought Dick. At the 9th hole, Carl leaned over and whispered to Dick, "You owe me big time," and unfortunately, Carl meant it.

Consequently, a few nights later, Dick had been forced to accompany him to a strip club on the seediest edge of Chicago, where the "ladies" were long in the tooth and so unattractive, that only sailors fresh from a six month voyage would have any interest. Dick had no idea why Carl liked this place so much. He hypothesized that the cheapness of it all provided him with some perverse thrill he couldn't obtain elsewhere. If Shelley ever found out, Dick thought, she'd shit a brick. Most of the "exotic dancers" had graying hair and sagging breasts, the ones who actually had breasts, that is. Written all over their faces was complete utter boredom and apathy. They slowly swung their skeletal bodies around greasy poles and rolled around on the stage, which was draped in stained purple velvet. A stage that, if the team from the TV show "CSI" ever conducted an investigation on it, they would have a field day with their ultraviolet light. At one point, one of the women stopped rolling around and Dick wasn't sure if she was passed out or dead. Either way, nobody seemed to care. One man, who bore a striking resemblance to Reverend Jim on the TV show "Taxi", was tossing coins on top of her, as if she was the Tivoli fountain in Rome. Needless to say, Dick had taken two showers when he got home that night.

Dick looked across the table and coldly asked, "So how's work Ron?"

"Oh, can't complain," Ron mumbled, while talking with his mouth full, spitting out his food in all directions. After making what he considered the requisite small talk, Dick felt he could go back to concentrating on his food, and proceeded to ignore Ron for the rest of the Coffee Hour.

Shelley turned to Hannah, "Pastor Pete has been acting sort of aloof lately, don't you think? His sermons seem to be getting shorter too, and they're almost always about money."

Hannah responded with a wry smile, "Yes, well Ron and I would have to agree with you there."

Shelley leaned in closer, "You know the pastor at St. John gives forty-five minute sermons, which include a short film AND interpretive dance." Hannah raised her eyebrows in response. "By the way, how's Toby?" Shelley asked.

Hannah replied, "He's doing fine, I miss him though."

"Really?" answered Shelley, "I would think you'd be glad to have the house back to yourselves."

"Well, yes of course, I guess," she replied, looking down at her tea.

Lorraine Barger was in her mid-forties and almost anorexically thin, with short dark brown, straight hair. She almost always wore a knee-length skirt with a white or black blouse, and most often appeared sleep-deprived. She was, at the moment, precariously standing on a stool in the middle school (3rd-5th grades) Sunday School classroom. Lorraine was busy taking down the September-October decorations and putting up the November-December Advent posters, etc. She found herself becoming more and more annoyed, as she watched everyone eating coffee cake and guzzling up gallons of Taster's Choice. Not one of those unappreciative jerks volunteered to help me, she said resentfully to herself. Lorraine believed nobody really cared about the children except for her. She had been the Sunday Church School (SCS) Coordinator for the last fifteen years.

Her husband Ralph did not attend St. James Christian, for he was what they called, a "lapsed" Catholic. Every time she tried to get him to come to church, he would decline and cite his "traumatic Catholic school upbringing" as reason not to go. However, he secretly just enjoyed sleeping in and watching his NFL games in peace. Lorraine didn't mind so much when their two daughters were little, because she would take them every Sunday to church, like a family. However, now that they were just out of college and lived far away, her life had increasingly become more and more lonely over the years. As she and Ralph slowly grew apart, her SCS fanaticism increased exponentially. Every day of her life was devoted to some aspect of the Sunday School. She was constantly planning classes, retreats, Sunday socials, exams, games, sleep-ins, etc. to ensure that the children at St. James Christian got the best Christian education possible.

Lorraine had finally finished, when she spied one of her middle-school teachers, Jean, getting ready to leave. "Hello Jean, can you come over here for a minute?" she asked.

Jean, a woman in her late twenties, with shoulder-length light brown hair and blue eyes, walked over to her reluctantly, "Yes, Lorraine?"

"I was thinking about our next youth service project," Lorraine said.

"Oh, didn't we just have one a few weeks ago?" Jean frowned at her.

"Well, yes but these projects are very crucial, we need to teach the children the importance of service in the Christian community," she replied.

"Okay, well you were saying?" asked Jean pointedly.

"Oh yes, I thought we could have the kids go around and put envelopes in all the pews asking for donations for the local animal shelter. The younger grades can decorate the envelopes with drawings and stickers of animals. Then they can all go to the animal shelter together, and see how our donations make such a difference," she said with enthusiasm.

"Oh," Jean replied, "sounds good to me," as she started to walk away.

Lorraine walked briskly after her, "I was thinking you could head this one up Jean."

Jean stopped, was about to say something, but then thought better of it, "Sure Lorraine, whatever," she replied with an annoyed look on her face.

"Fantastic!" Lorraine smiled and walked away happily.

Pastor Pete, was a very attractive man in his thirties, tall, dark and swarthy, with big brown eyes. He had no idea that most of the ladies in the congregation had a crush on him. After the service ended, he walked into his office and ripped off his collar He would blush if he knew how often his female parishioners fantasized about him wearing just that collar and nothing else. Pete had served at St. James Christian for four years, and prior to that had presided over a large wealthy church in Franklin, Michigan for five years, before moving to Meadowville. He had met his wife up there, while she was visiting friends who attended his church. After dating on and off for a year, the couple decided to get married. Afterwards, he chose to bite the bullet and move to Meadowville, so Susan wouldn't have to leave her steady job as a legal secretary in Chicago. Her work paid decent money, but he made less than half of what he had made up in Michigan.

The pastor was promised if he brought people in to the struggling church, he would receive a pay raise commensurate to those numbers. Within six months, the church gained five new middle-aged female members, and each year that he's been there, the female membership has increased altogether. However, he was denied his raise every year for some stupid reason or another which Pastor Pete believed was due to that blowhard Ron and his lackeys. He hated this little hick church. The pastor had decided that if he wasn't going to get paid what he was worth, then he would put even less effort into his sermons than he usually did. As a result, his sermons were getting shorter and shorter each week, and people had barely enough time at the beginning of his sermon to visit the restroom and get back to their pew before it would be over. He had also shortened his visits to the sick, and was practically never available in his office for spiritual counseling. Instead, he spent a lot of time with his old friends in Michigan, who were mostly doctors and lawyers, and made about five times what he did. His less than appropriate salary didn't seem to bother his wife Susan, but then again Pastor Pete believed, Susan was not very ambitious.

Bob Grossman, an average sized, middle-aged man, with jet black hair and blue eyes was driving his wife Sheryl Grossman, a slightly overweight woman with blond hair and a penchant for babushkas, to Dunkin Donuts in their old white Buick Le Sabre after church. This had been a family ritual for many years. The Grossmans had three children who were raised in the church, but one by one they each dropped out, and eventually, all three had married and moved away. Their oldest was expecting their first grandchild. Unbeknownst to Bob, his kids had less of a problem with organized religion, and more of a problem with spending more than one moment necessary with their father, who could be very difficult. Consequently, all three attended other churches in the Chicagoland area.

As they pulled into the Dunkin Donuts parking lot, Sheryl complained, "Bob, I don't know why we couldn't have stayed for Coffee Hour just for a short while, and talked to the Dorchesters or the Andersons."

"Sheryl, if I told you once, I've told you a thousand times, we are not going to socialize with any of them until we get what I want, I mean, what we want," he hastily corrected himself.

"And what is that again?" Sheryl weakly asked.

"I told you, I want them to play patriotic songs on Memorial Day, Fourth of July, and Veteran's Day. It's a slap in the face to all the veterans out there who served our great country so faithfully!"

"But it's only November, you mean we have to ignore our friends until they play the songs you want in May?" whined Sheryl.

"Sheryl, you just don't get it," said Bob.

On the contrary, Sheryl did get it. Bob had been fighting this battle for years. Many of the ministers and congregation members at St. James Christian had believed that patriotic songs were secular and did not belong in a religious institution. Bob droned on, threatening once again, to start placing less money in the coffers if he didn't get his way. Sheryl put a hand up to her forehead.

"Sheryl?"

"Yes, what?" she asked distractedly.

"What is wrong with you, are you getting one of your migraines again?" Bob asked.

"Yes, I think so, maybe. Just one quick cup of coffee today and a honey-dipped donut please. I'd like to go home and get to bed straight away."

Bob nodded his assent. He worried about Sheryl because she seemed to get sick a lot. Last winter she came down with pneumonia and every spring her allergies flared up. During the summer she usually suffered heat stroke, and every fall brought with it migraines and other various aches and pains. To tell the truth, Bob considered Sheryl's maladies to be very inconvenient at times. She always seemed to get sick at the worst possible moments, usually when he was right in the middle of trying to stage a crusade for or against something important, and could use her help.

Ruth Williams walked home alone after the 10:30 service. Ruth was in her sixties and had cotton-white hair, bright blue eyes and a pleasant face. She was considered quite pretty in her day. It was a beautiful, crisp, sunny fall day, and so she brought only a cream-colored sweater to wear over her knee-length gray dress. Meadowville was a nice quiet, middle-class suburb, with a range of two bedroom, ranch houses to four bedroom, two-story Victorians. Thomas Manning drove by in his old black Cadillac and honked at her. She turned and waved. Ruth lived only two short blocks away from St. James Christian and preferred to walk to and from church every Sunday. She had always despised driving, (it made her nervous) and avoided expressways like the plague. Therefore, most of the time she either walked wherever she needed to go or depended on others for rides. Most people had no problem with this, for after observing her behind the wheel a few times, they considered it a miracle that she ever received her driver's license at all. Consequently, they figured it was their civic duty to keep her off the streets as much as possible.

When Roger was alive, they used to enjoy walking together. Now of course, she walked alone, and it was certainly not the same. The couple used to walk hand-in-hand, and would from time to time, look lovingly at each other. Sometimes she would detect a mischievous glint in her husband's eyes, and knew that meant she should expect an afternoon of "romance" when they arrived back home. Roger and Ruth never had any kids, but neither had wanted any. They didn't really discuss the matter much, it was almost like they both immediately knew parenthood just wasn't for them. They could always read each other's mind and they had quite a lot in common. They were both avid and passionate readers, and were in the middle of building a huge church library for the congregation, when halfway through, Roger suddenly gasped, clutched his upper left arm and collapsed. Thirty seconds later, he took his last breath. That was six months ago and Ruth still couldn't believe it. He was her life and nothing could ever replace him. A couple of well-meaning parishioners had tried to get her out and dating again, but that was not for her. She could never taint Roger's memory by allowing another man into her home, or God forbid, her bed! She unlocked the front door and entered her little white and green Dutch Colonial. Ruth then walked through her living room, over the brown shag carpeting to her bathroom, and opened up the tiny mirrored medicine cabinet above the sink. She reached for the small brown container, popped the cap off and swallowed a couple of Valium that were prescribed by her doctor after she became hysterical at her husband's funeral.

***

Ron Dorchester, a middle-aged man with an excess of both dark brown hair and body weight, sporting a thick mustache and full beard, glanced around his family room and sighed contentedly. Life was good. His son Toby was out of the house, which meant the deluge of boys traipsing through at all ungodly hours had stopped. Hannah misses the boy, and so do I of course, but I'm not going to lie, I love the silence, he admitted to himself. He put his feet up on the camel colored vinyl footstool that matched the over-sized chair he was sitting in. Then he took a sip of his *Pinot Noir* that he had opened with his roast beef dinner that evening, and folded his hands across his enormous stomach, looking very much like Henry VIII. He had it all, he thought. If it wasn't for all the complaining ingrates he had to suffer at church, his life would be near-perfect. Tomorrow night is the last Council meeting until they adjourn for the holidays and resume again in January, and of course Wednesday night's the banquet, he reminded himself. Ron always looked forward to those. The food was consistently phenomenal, since every church function was catered by Jay's Catering. Ron and Jay Muster, the owner, had been friends for years, and Jay was instrumental in Ron landing the CPA gig he currently enjoyed at Palmer Mackinghouse. Therefore, Ron made sure Jay received as much business as possible. *Quid pro quo,* as they say. Ron put his glass down, and after thinking a moment, decided to call Jay on his personal cell phone.

"Yello!" Jay answered cheerfully on the second ring.

"Hey Jay, it's me."

"Hello Ron, what can I do you for?" Ron could hear a great deal of noise in the background.

"You're not still at work, are you Jay?"

"Well you know me, I like to keep on top of things."

"But geez Jay, you gotta sleep sometime," Ron replied.

"Yeah, yeah yeah." Jay had heard it all before. Most of his friends had no idea how much time, energy and work was involved in running a successful business.

"I'm just checking up on things, remember the banquet's in a few days."

"How could I forget?" Jay laughed. "Don't worry, everything will be taken care of, as usual."

"Good! I know I can always count on you Jay."

If Ron were honest, he'd admit Jay was the only person that he considered a friend in this world. Ron did not make friends easily and he didn't tolerate fools gladly. Those who feared him most were usually the recipients of his wrath. However, Jay, to his delight, could dish it out as well as he could take it, which Ron respected in a man.

"One hitch though that I should tell you about Ron," Jay added.

"Yes?" Ron asked warily.

"You know the Culinary Expo I go to twice a year?"

"Yeah," said Ron.

"Well, they moved it up this year so it falls on the same day of the banquet," he explained.

"This isn't going to be a problem, is it?" barked Ron.

"No, not at all," Jay assured him, "I just wanted you to be aware of it. I will be taking care of everything before I leave though, so don't worry."

"Well, I hope so!" Ron gave a hearty laugh, "You know how much the church looks forward to these banquets."

"Of course, I will have everything boxed and ready to go by late morning," promised Jay.

"All right then, I'll let the Council know, in case anything comes up."

"Yes, Kevin can handle any last minute requests," replied Jay.

"Excellent," responded Ron. "Are you and Jeanne still coming over for dinner next week?"

"Yep, got it right here on my calendar," confirmed Jay.

"See you then," said Ron, before he hung up the phone.

He suddenly felt a bead of sweat roll down his forehead, off of his face, and onto his brick-red XXXXL silk shirt. Damn it! Ron thought. Why does Hannah always have the heat set to fricken sauna temperatures? He resolved to remember to chastise her as soon as she was done with her bath.

Chapter 2 - The First Church Council Meeting (Monday)

Gary Forrester threw back his single white flannel sheet and plaid comforter, sprang out of bed, and as he did most mornings, managed to trip over the cat. "Meow!" Snickers screeched, ducking under the bed. Gary was fifty-five years old, with thinning light brown hair and brown eyes. He was of average height and build for the most part, except for his growing stomach, which his shirts never managed to keep covered. Consequently, church members were often treated to the unwelcome sight of an extremely hairy, alabaster pot-belly. He then walked into the kitchen and poured himself a bowl of Lucky Charms cereal with milk. After eating all the cereal, he brought the bowl up to his lips and slurped the remainder of the left over milk, resulting in a milk mustache that he wore for the next hour. Then he sat on his living room couch and watched "Oprah", "The View" and "Regis & Kelly", all in rapid succession. Gary found people in general, fascinating.

Besides TV talk shows, he loved watching the celebrity gossip channels. He enjoyed learning about TV and movie stars' love lives and latest foibles. He was the only one of his friends who could not only name all of Liz Taylor's husbands, but how long she was married to each of them. This talent came in very handy when playing trivia games. In fact, it was only during the playing of trivia games, that Gary could ever recall being fought over to join someone's team. He was certainly ready in case he ever decided to try out for "Jeopardy", which Sallie kept urging him to do. He couldn't wait until the last Church Council meeting of the year, which was to be held that evening. Gary didn't work, so he had a lot of extra time on his hands. He used to have a job as a substitute teacher, and had held many different temporary jobs over the years, but luckily for him, and unluckily for his aunt Florence, she died and left him a considerable amount of money. Not enough to make him rich, but enough that he didn't really need to work. Gary was excited about the Council meeting because he had tons of great ideas. Gary always had a lot of "great" ideas. Unfortunately, Ron and Hannah almost always shot them down. More so Ron, Hannah basically just seconded whatever her husband said, Gary noticed.

***

Ruth Williams had arrived at the church at 6:30 pm. She, along with Hannah, were almost always the first to arrive at their meetings. It was nice, because she felt that Hannah was the only woman in the church she could really talk to, and who understood her. They would often share personal conversations before Ron would come in, and Hannah would immediately clam up. Ruth sat down demurely at the Council Room table. She wore a black pill box hat, which was in fashion fifty years ago, and a formless black dress that resembled a gunnysack. She took her black and white gloves off and placed them next to her small white clutch purse on the table, crossed her legs at the ankles, and waited patiently.

At 6:50 pm, the Andersons exited their 2012 red Lexus, which was parked directly in front of St. James Christian's main doors. Unfortunately, the church did not have a parking lot of its own, and so most of the congregation had to make do with the few spots available in the residential area which surrounded the church. Consequently, many were forced to walk a block or more on Sunday mornings. Dick was, as usual, wearing an expensive tan Ralph Lauren shirt and beige Dockers with brown loafers.

"Thank God this is the last meeting of the year," complained Shelley in her raspy voice, as the pair entered the church. She was matching her husband perfectly, wearing a simple but expensive, light brown dress and taupe colored flats, along with her pearls of course.

"They're really so tedious, aren't they?" she remarked.

"If you find them so tedious, then why do you insist on us serving on the Council each year?" replied Dick sensibly.

"Well, uhh," at a loss for words, Shelley eventually acknowledged, "it's good to have a say in what goes on, to keep the rest of them from doing something foolish, don't you think?"

"Yes dear," Dick commented, patting her arm reassuringly.

The Grossmans arrived at 6:55 pm. They would have arrived sooner, but Sheryl was feeling a bit under the weather, and took longer than usual to get ready. Bob was carrying a heavy black binder notebook, held together by numerous rubber bands, packed so full, papers were falling out left and right. This binder contained all of his "church improvement" ideas, which he was eager to share with the Council. Bob was wearing army green pants and purple suspenders with a yellow plain T-shirt underneath. Bob's unfortunate color choices over the years had convinced most of the congregation that he was color blind.[1] Sheryl wore a dark blue flowered sweater, appropriate for a woman her side of sixty, dark blue polyester pants and a sky blue babushka. Gary was right behind the couple, running to catch up with them.

"Good evening Grossmans!" he greeted them cheerfully. The pair acknowledged him by nodding briefly in his direction.

---

[1] He wasn't.

Lorraine Barger was rushing out of her house, running late because one of her SCS teachers had just called to let her know she had a last-minute business trip scheduled, and she wouldn't be able to teach her Preschool/Kindergarten class this Sunday. Usually, Lorraine would just offer to teach the class herself, but the last time she taught this grade level, she ended up with a run in her stockings, a Kool-Aid stained blouse, and a raging headache. It had required three phone calls to line up a teacher brave enough to substitute this Sunday.

"Ralph, I'm leaving! Your dinner is in the fridge!" she shouted, and not waiting for a response, turned and slammed her front door shut as she raced over to her silver Ford Taurus. Unfortunately, she tripped over the curb, fell, ripped her black stocking, and bloodied her knee. "Oh Shit!" she yelled, then looked furtively around to see if anyone had heard her, while simultaneously rifling through her purse to find a Band-Aid.

Meanwhile, Pastor Pete, wearing a casual, navy blue polo shirt, open just enough to get a glimpse of chest hair, and what looked like brand new Levis, was holed up in his office finishing his Whopper and onion rings. He had gained fifteen pounds since serving St. James Christian's congregation, although you'd never know it, as he still had quite an athletic build. Many late evenings at church forced him to miss a number of healthy, home-cooked meals, and he was starting to become a regular at the Burger King drive-thru. (He had an entire desk drawer devoted to ketchup and mustard packets.) He had locked himself in his office because he knew from experience, that if the Council Members were aware he was at the church early, inevitably they would plead their case to him about why the Council should or shouldn't do something. Pastor Pete didn't like to get involved in these disputes. If it were up to him, he wouldn't even go to these meetings at all, but Ron insisted it was mandatory for the pastor to serve on Council. He wondered if maybe he could take next Sunday off and ask Lorraine to give the sermon. Perhaps, she could make a whole "Youth Sunday" thing out of it. Yes, that's a great idea! Pastor Pete was proud of himself for having thought of it.

At 6:59 pm, Thomas Manning arrived and sat down at the table. He took out his expensive silver Parker pen and his special yellow legal pad of paper that he reserved only for Council business. Even though he didn't hold an official title like "Secretary", it was assumed that he would be the one taking notes each month for the Council. He also had his <u>Robert's Rules of Order,</u> which he never dared open at the meetings anymore, due to "The Incident".   A couple of years ago, Thomas would pull it out and read from it quite often, to the other Council Members' dismay. One unfortunate evening, when Ron was not feeling "up-to-par", he made it very clear to Thomas that if he read from that book one more time, he would shove it up a very private part of his anatomy. Thomas was also responsible for videotaping the meetings, because it was originally his idea last year to record them, just in case there was any confusion about what exactly occurred at each meeting. The church's video camera was very "old-school" - big, black and bulky. It was perched on a tripod, kitty-corner from where Ron Dorchester traditionally sat. Fortunately, all Thomas had to do was turn it on. The church bells chimed seven times as the Council Members took their seats.

"Ahem," Ron coughed, "It's 7:00 and it looks like everyone is here but..," his voice trailed off as Sallie Rigelli dashed to her seat, wearing a dark purple blouse that had the first four buttons undone and a pair of designer jeans so tight, you'd need a crowbar[1] to get them off, leaving a heavily perfumed Juicy Couture trail in her wake. "Sallie," he smiled widely, "you're here, and now we can begin." He cracked his knuckles and motioned to the pastor to start. Pastor Pete opened the meeting with the usual prayer. Ron then asked Thomas to read off the Old Business, which had been tabled last month, from the minutes of the previous Council Meeting.

---

[1] or in many cases, just a charming smile.

"Sunday hymns," read Thomas. "Bob Grossman made a motion that a vote be given on singing patriotic hymns in church, specifically on the Fourth of July, Memorial Day, and Labor Day. Is there anyone willing to second this motion?" He glanced over at the other Council Members, who were all looking at Sheryl Grossman.

Sheryl, realizing she was supposed to do something, said loudly, "I'll second that," as Bob nodded his head approvingly at her.

"Alright, any discussion?" Ron asked.

Bob coughed and said, "Yes, I served my country for eight years in the United States Army, along with thousands of other brave men and women, and it is only right that we pay homage to our veterans by singing these patriotic hymns on or near the requisite holidays; the Fourth of July, Memorial Day, and Veteran's Day. Incidentally, I also think Flag Day, Pearl Harbor Day, and September 11th would be appropriate days to honor them as well."

"I don't see any reason why we shouldn't, if you want my two cents," said Thomas, leaning back in his chair.

Dick spoke up, "I don't know why we always have to bring up patriotism in church, don't we have enough to deal with as it is?"

"I agree with Dick," said Shelley. "If you're so concerned about veterans Bob, why don't you just throw your own private party for them on those days?"

Sheryl, who had a sudden vision of Bob suddenly deciding to throw six parties a year in honor of veterans, panicked and immediately responded, "I hardly think that is reasonable or appropriate."

Sallie, who was busy daydreaming, perked up at the mention of the word party. "Ooh, is someone going to have a party? My calendar is pretty full, but I can see if..."

"Nobody is having any party Sallie," Bob interrupted. "Shelley, it is not my responsibility to do this for the veterans, it would be like throwing a party for myself. It is we as a nation that needs to do this. What kind of message are we sending by not honoring and respecting them on these special days of the year?"

Pastor Pete said, "Bob, I agree we should all pay homage to veterans, just not in church."

"That's right," agreed Ron, "this is a secular matter, does not belong in church at all."

Ruth coughed and said, "Roger would say that it is our Christian duty to do this for the veterans." Bob shot her a grateful look.

A moment of silence ensued, then Gary suddenly broke it with, "I LOVE singing "Onward Christian Soldiers"! I also love singing "Kumbaya"!" He then started singing at the top of his lungs, "Someone's singing Lord, Kumbaya! Someone's singing Lord, Kumbaya!" He stopped, commenting, "Although, that song probably isn't patriotic...." his voice trailed off, as he noticed everyone staring at him with annoyed expressions on their faces, except for Hannah, who was looking up at the ceiling with great concentration, trying not to laugh.

"OK," Ron said, "let's take a vote, all in favor say aye." Five hands shot up including Thomas's, Gary's, Ruth's, and of course, Bob's and Sheryl's, (who originally wasn't paying attention during the vote, as she was busy blowing her nose, and only raised her hand after her husband elbowed her in the ribs.) "All against?" Ron, Hannah, Sallie (who most often voted the opposite of Thomas, out of spite), Mr. and Mrs. Anderson, Lorraine and Pastor Pete all voted nay.

"Seven to five against," declared Thomas, "well, it looks like a no-go on the Patriotic Hymns motion."

Bob Grossman's face was flushed and he sat stone-faced and silent for the rest of the meeting. Sallie, bored again, cracked her gum loudly. Ron and Shelley simultaneously frowned at her.

"Next item up for discussion!" barked Ron.

Thomas spoke up, "This would still be Old Business, I'd like to take the vote we tabled last month for the Sunday Church Service dress code to be reinstated." Sallie rolled her eyes. "As you all know, my late wife Wanda and I had written up a Sunday Church Service dress code, which had been implemented for many years, until it was dismantled a few years ago, for some unknown reason," he stated, glaring at Sallie. Next, he stood up and handed everyone a copy of the dress code, as last implemented. Originally, the Dress Code Thomas and his late wife Wanda wanted implemented was:

No dressing like a street bum or a harlot.

Needless to say, the Council at that time felt it needed a little re-working and clarification; therefore, the Dress Code as last implemented, stood as the following:

No tennis shoes or flip-flops
No blue jeans or excessively baggy pants
No cleavage
No halter tops
Must wear a bra, if female
Must wear underwear
No excessively tight clothing
No excessively short skirts or shorts

Sallie became very nervous, as the Dress Code effectively rendered all of her current wardrobe unsuitable.

Dick, whose only source of pleasure these days was seeing how far Sallie could push the boundaries of good taste, spoke up, "I think this Dress Code infringes upon our personal individual rights to express ourselves." Shelley looked over at him with her "just wait until we get home" face, which brought a shiver down Dick's spine.

"Yeah, what he just said!" Sallie said defiantly.

Ron interjected, "I would have to agree with Dick there. Who are we to impose arbitrary guidelines as to a person's appearance. What is this, Nazi Germany?"

Gary, who was very much afraid he wouldn't be able to wear all of his favorite excessively tight T-shirts anymore, nodded his head vigorously in agreement with Ron. Ruth, who secretly got a kick out of seeing what Sallie showed up in each week, also nodded. Being as there was no further discussion, the Council took a quick vote. The result was only three ayes for the re-implementation of the Dress Code, which came from Thomas, Shelley, and Lorraine, (who felt Sallie's attire often distracted the male members of the congregation away from her SCS programs.)[1] As a result of this unfortunate outcome, Thomas's countenance was considerably darkened, and he joined Bob in silent sulking for the rest of the meeting.

"Now onto New Business," Ron stated. Immediately, Gary raised his hand. Ron groaned deeply, "Yes, Gary?"

In an excited voice, he spoke rapidly, "I think it would be kind of nice if we scheduled like a Council weekend retreat. Maybe in the Dells, or perhaps even Michigan, or maybe even Florida? Disney World would be..."

Ron rudely interrupted him, "thanks Gary. Moving on to other business..." Gary appeared crestfallen, but cheered up a few seconds later when Ruth passed him a handful of red and green wrapped Hershey's Kisses under the table.

Ron asked, "Sallie, where are the decorations for the Autumn Banquet being kept?"

"Oh, I um didn't buy them yet," she answered, biting her lip nervously.

---

[1] Last Christmas, all the men were busy looking at Sallie's cleavage and totally ignored the delightful Nativity Play her SCS children were performing.

"What do you mean you didn't buy them?" Ron snarled, giving Sallie a shaming look, "it's in two days!"

"I guess I forgot, I'm sorry," said Sallie.

"What is the matter with you? The same thing happened last year. Obviously, you can't be trusted to handle any type of responsibility," Ron replied. Sallie looked appropriately contrite.

Shelley interceded, "Ron, I can take over on the decorations, I'll pick some up tomorrow," she offered, giving Sallie a dirty look.

Ron agreed, "Yes, that will be fine, Shelley you take over." Shelley was pleased, for she had been tired of all the tacky decorations Sallie had provided in the past. She was going to make sure that the decorations this year would blow anything the church ever had in the past right out of the water. Ron continued, "I did want to briefly mention that I have started receiving the background checks on the Council Members that we discussed last month, and I should have all of them back by the end of next week. I think that's all, shall we adjourn?"

"Excuse me," interjected Lorraine, who during the entire meeting was still trying to get her knee to stop bleeding, "there's still the matter of next year's SCS budget," she reminded Ron.

"That is actually a Finance Committee decision, and we voted last week that the SCS budget will have to be cut in half."

Lorraine's face fell. "What!?" she asked incredulously.

"Listen," said Ron, "we all have to make sacrifices Lorraine, times are tough. Giving has been down 16% this year and most of our expenses have skyrocketed."

"Yes I understand, but the children are getting short-changed!" she shouted, effectively waking up Dick Anderson, who had been successfully catching up on his sleep. "Just who is on the Finance Committee anyway this year? I want to talk to them!"

"Well," Ron snickered, "you can do just that, as it is comprised of yours truly, Hannah and Pastor." Hannah looked down at the table and Pastor smiled awkwardly at her.

"Oh this is ridiculous, what am I supposed to make do without then next year?"

"Well, maybe you can cut back on paper?" offered Gary most helpfully. "That would save money AND help the environment."

"Oh shut up Gary!" she yelled. Gary sat back in his chair looking sheepish, as Shelley raised her eyebrows at Lorraine.

While all of this transpired, Ruth noticed Lorraine's bloodied knee and had grabbed the first aid kit the church kept attached to a nearby wall. She then expertly cleaned and dressed her wound, which was made all the more difficult because Lorraine's leg would jerk every time she became agitated. "Oh I almost forgot," added Ron, "Jay Muster will be at the Culinary Expo at McCormick Place the day of the banquet, so if there are any problems Wednesday you can just contact Kevin at Jay's Catering instead."

Shelley spoke up, "Ron, I would like to bring up possibly changing the catering company after this year's banquet. I have a number of friends who use Professional Catering Associates instead. They're slightly costlier, but they're more upscale and do a very elegant spread."

Dick agreed, "I think that's an excellent idea."

"Well, I do not think that's an excellent idea," said Ron, pounding his fist on the table. "We don't have any extra money in the budget and Jay's is consistently reliable and provides good quality food."

"Well, shouldn't we at least consider another company?" asked Shelley, sounding frustrated. "I am sure we can negotiate a suitable price."

"Is there anyone else who agrees with Shelley, besides Dick?" Ron bellowed.

Sheryl raised her hand and Gary started to raise his, but then after seeing the look on Ron's face, put his hand down. Lorraine decided to stay out of it because she had many other priorities. She honestly didn't give a flying fuck about the food, for she rarely ate anything anyway. Of course, Sallie was too scared to argue after the whole decorations screw-up. Shelley was looking at Dick threateningly, until he realized he was supposed to raise his hand, and so he did post haste.

"It looks like there's only a handful of people who want to discuss this, so the answer is no, end of discussion," Ron decided. "OK then, meeting adjourned."

As soon as Lorraine stood up, Gary immediately whispered loudly, "Are you okay Lorraine? You seem a little cranky. Do you think you're going through the Menopause?" Pastor Pete, very much amused, started choking on his cough drop, which he had just popped into his mouth a minute earlier. Lorraine opened her mouth and then thought better of it. She left the table without answering him.

As they got up to leave, Ron asked Mrs. Anderson to wait. "I'd like to talk to you for a moment, Shelley."

A flustered Ruth broke in, "Actually Ron, there is something I really need to discuss with you."

Ron put his hand up as if he was directing traffic and brusquely said, "Not now, I want to talk to Shelley alone first."

They walked into one of the Sunday School classrooms together, as Dick looking a little confused, sat back down and immediately fell asleep again. Ten minutes later, they came out, Shelley first, looking livid and Ron right behind her, looking smug.

"Let's go, Dick!" she ordered her husband, as he awoke with a start and dutifully followed his wife out of the church.

Ron looked at Ruth and asked, "What's up, Ruth?" as she stood directly in front of him blocking his path.

Chapter 3 - A Surprise for Thomas (Tuesday)

The next day, Sheryl Grossman was napping on the couch, wearing her pink terrycloth bathrobe and slippers. Bob was sitting in his white undershirt and boxers in his rocking chair trying to read the newspaper.

"The print in this newspaper is way too small. How can anyone be expected to read this? You know why newspapers don't make the print bigger? Because they're cheap, that's why!" Bob didn't seem to notice Sheryl was asleep, but it didn't matter, as he didn't wait for a response anyway.

"Oh, I've been meaning to have a conversation with Pastor Pete about Ron Dorchester. That man has just way too much power in the Church. He practically runs everything. Who died and made him king anyway? I wanted to be on Finance Committee, but HE decided three people were enough. We'll see about that," he paused, "by the way, are we going to have Thanksgiving this year Sheryl?" Bob asked. Receiving no response, he yelled, "Sheryl!"

"Uhh," she moaned and opened her eyes, "Yes?"

"Are we going to have Thanksgiving this year?"

"Well, I suppose so," Sheryl answered, "but none of the kids are going to make it this year, so it would just be the two of us again, I'm afraid." She yawned and said, "I think the kids are all going to their in-laws."

"What?" Bob replied, "that's ridiculous!" "This will be the third year in a row! You'd think they were trying to avoid us or something!" Sheryl closed her eyes and attempted to go back to sleep.

***

Meanwhile, on the other end of town, Pastor Pete was talking to his wife Susan.

"What do you think about Colin, for a boy?"

Susan smiled, "I think that's a fine name honey, what about for a girl? I was thinking maybe Violet or Lily."

"Hmmm, a little old-fashioned, don't you think? I was thinking maybe Pamela?"

Susan made a face in response. "How about Dawn? That's pretty, isn't it?"

"Not bad, I think I'm going to make a few calls to the guys up in Michigan and see if they know of any big churches that are looking for a pastor," he remarked.

"Really?" Susan asked, surprised.

"Well, you know I've been making a lot less money since we moved here, and I'm working twice as hard. It's ridiculous!"

"I know dear," she replied, "and you know I will support you no matter what you decide."

Pete felt very lucky that he had found someone as wonderful as Susan. She was so sweet, loving and patient. He wished he could do right by her and make the kind of money she deserved. If it wasn't for that ass Ron Dorchester, he might just be making that kind of money, he thought furiously.

***

Thomas Manning was sitting on his couch, wearing a pressed

long-sleeved, button down, light blue shirt and dark blue slacks, reading one of his favorite books, <u>Would You Recognize Satan if He Stood Next to You in Line at the ATM Machine</u>? by Dr. Uell Rottenhell. He always believed in dressing formal, even if he was at home alone. Suddenly, his younger son Kenny, tall, blond and blue-eyed, who took after his mother, came walking through the door. He was wearing a black leather jacket with a pack of Marlboros sticking out of one pocket, a tight white T-shirt and old ripped blue jeans, looking as if he stepped right off the movie set of "Grease". Kenny was twenty-three years old and living on his own. He had a job as a bartender at a hot nightclub downtown and made surprisingly good money. Thomas very much disapproved of Kenny and especially Kenny's latest girlfriend, Tabitha who, in his opinion, made Sallie Rigelli look like a nun. Kenny didn't go to college, and frankly speaking, his high school grades didn't lead anyone, least of all his father, to cling to any illusion that there was a chance of that ever happening in this lifetime.

Thomas's older son Glenn, who resembled his father but sans glasses, was the exact opposite of Kenny. Glenn was twenty-five years old and had earned a B.A. in Business Administration. He was hired straight out of college as a financial analyst for a big company located in the Loop. Glenn did not currently have a girlfriend. Actually, Glenn never had a girlfriend, Thomas realized after thinking about it. Well, Thomas figured, there was plenty of time for that. He would love to be a grandfather someday and Glenn would make an excellent husband and father. He was reliable, smart, trustworthy, and respectful towards women. Kenny, on the other hand, would not make a good husband OR father. He had gone through one woman after another, until he settled recently on this Tabitha, a red-headed floozy that he met at work. When dealing with his youngest son, Thomas very much felt like Job, a man struck with undeserved misfortune. He believed that God was constantly testing him in this regard.

"Hey Pops!" Kenny yelled, not bothering to knock and slamming the front door behind him.

"Hello Kenneth," Thomas replied formally, and went back to reading his book. Kenny took a seat next to him on the couch.

"How are things?" he asked his father.

"Fine, fine," Thomas responded curtly.

"How's church? Have you got that dress code reinstated yet?"

"No, no I haven't," Thomas felt his blood pressure rising.

"Oh well, that's a shame," Kenny said, doing his best to commiserate with him. "Hey Pops, I have some good news."

"Oh?" Thomas raised his head from his book.

"I'm getting married!" he exclaimed.

"Married?" Thomas threw down his book. "To whom?"

"To Tabitha of course!" he replied, sounding hurt.

It was times like these that Thomas really missed Wanda. "What? You have got to be kidding! Why on Earth would you marry that bimbo?"

"Hey Dad, you're going to have to start acting more respectful towards her," Kenny told him sternly, while standing up.

"Why? Why son? You're only twenty-three years old, why throw your life away?" he asked, as he stood up and faced his son.

"Dad, you got married to Mom when you weren't much older than me and besides," he paused, "she's pregnant."

And that was the last thing Thomas Manning remembered before he hit the floor with a thud.

Chapter 4 - The Banquet (Wednesday)

As people walked into the basement for the Annual Autumn Banquet, they were struck by the smell of nutmeg and cinnamon, and were floored at how amazing everything looked. There stood a huge *faux* Elm tree in one corner and a giant scarecrow in another. Small pumpkins on piles of hay were spread throughout the basement and there were leaves with fall colors hanging down from the ceiling. Pictures of turkeys, Pilgrims and Indians were all over the walls. Every table was covered with a linen tablecloth of either orange, brown, amber or red. Dishes of candy corn and eye-catching cornucopias were on every table. Shelley obviously spared no expense when it came to buying the decorations.

Gary Forrester, who out of his love for Christmas, was wearing a red reindeer sweater, with a bell on its nose that jingled every time he moved, and dark green pants. It didn't matter that Christmas was over a month away, he believed in celebrating everything early.

As soon as Gary spotted Ron and Hannah, he ran up to them. "Hey Ron, why don't we have a "St. James Christian Adult Movie Night" soon? I know Halloween is over, but we could show "Nightmare on Elm Street" or "Psycho"?" he suggested.

"Gary, use your head! Do you really think that is appropriate for a church audience?" Ron bellowed.

"Well, I did say it would be for adults only," reasoned Gary.

"Still, do you want to give some of these old bags a heart attack?" Ron yelled loudly.

"Ron," murmured an embarrassed Hannah.

Gary, clearly crestfallen, said, "It was worth a shot," and walked away, his shoulders slumped with defeat.

The Banquet began with the usual tradition of the Vice-Chair of the Council making a short introduction, followed by Pastor Pete leading everyone in prayer. Hannah Dorchester, wearing a cute, short-sleeved button down dress, which reflected all the colors associated with autumn, walked up to the microphone that stood in the back of the basement. She smoothed down her bouncy red curls and put her dark-brown, horned rimmed reading glasses on. She then took a piece of paper out of her left pocket and held it out in front of her until it was an arm-length's away. She squinted at it with her big brown eyes.

"Excuse me," she looked around while everyone continued to talk, ignoring her. "Excuse me, may I have your attention please?" she said, in a much louder voice. The people quieted down. "Welcome to our 15th Annual Autumn Banquet. This is the time when we traditionally look back over the year at our accomplishments, and also give thanks for our many blessings. This year, thanks to the Memorial Committee, we got our new roof!" The crowd applauded enthusiastically. "We also purchased a new organ, thanks to a generous donation by Dick and Shelley Anderson!" Shelley tried to look modest, but wasn't too successful at it, as the crowd applauded again. "And most of all," Hannah looked down and read straight from her notes, "a big thank you to my husband Ron Dorchester, for faithfully serving St. James Christian as the Chair of the Church Council for the 15th year in a row!" A smattering of applause was heard after that, which mostly came from Ron himself. "And now, Pastor Pete," Hannah looked up from her notes, "would you do us the honor of a prayer, before we dig into this delicious meal provided by Jay's Catering?"

Pastor Pete who was quite bored, almost missed his cue and stood up hastily. Every female in the room's eyes were fixated on him, but as usual, the pastor seemed to be oblivious to it. "Umm yes, let us bow our heads. Dear Lord, bless us and keep us. Lord make your face shine upon us and give us peace. And... and thank you for this food," he added as an afterthought, "Amen."

"Amen," the church members echoed.

The head table, where traditionally the Dorchesters and the

Andersons sat, began the line for the buffet every year. Ron, for the fifteenth year in a row, was at the head of it. The buffet as usual, included trays of such traditional favorites as roasted turkey, mashed potatoes, ham with pineapple slices, salad, fresh fruit, sweet potatoes, buttery dinner rolls, apple tarts and pumpkin pie, as well as more exotic fare such as; linguini with *puttanesca* sauce, meatballs, and chicken tacos. While Ron was piling his plate up with food, Lorraine, who was wearing a white blouse, long tan skirt and brown flats, took the opportunity to approach him.

"Ron, I received three phone calls this morning from angry SCS teachers!"

"Oh?" he replied, without looking up.

"Yes, they said they received an email from you mandating that they pay for the Sunday School supplies from their own pocket, the only exception being the textbooks," she told him frustrated, her voice steadily getting higher.

"Yes, it's a great idea, isn't it? Now your budget isn't an issue any longer."

"Ron, I have enough problems as it is, with the teachers not showing up on time, many times not even showing up at all, and now they find out they are going to have to pay for their own supplies! Don't you see what trouble this has caused?"

"Well, deal with it, you ARE the SCS Superintendent!" Ron pointed out.

"You haven't shown me any consideration at all! You didn't even copy me in on the email or even discuss this with me first." "This is just, just," she paused, "inexcusable!" as she stalked away angrily. Ron continued to fill his plate, behaving as if nothing had happened.

Sallie Rigelli was wearing a tight, dark-green cashmere sweater with a matching mini-skirt, looking ravishing as usual. She was immersed in deep discussion with Gary, who was shoveling candy corn from his pockets into his mouth, while at the same time telling her all about the fascinating people featured on his favorite morning talk show.

"Sallie, there was this man on Jerry Springer, who was having an affair with his wife's sister, mother, and grandmother at the same time! Can you imagine?"

Meanwhile Bob Grossman, who was sitting between his wife, who was wearing a burnt orange babushka for this special occasion, and Ruth, was in the middle of complaining about the Grace that Pastor Pete had given.

"Don't you think he could have at least mentioned the fact that this is the month of Martin Luther's Birthday?" He looked over at Ruth who, mesmerized by his choice of attire, didn't hear him. Bob had really outdone himself tonight by sporting a deep purple jacket, orange shirt and tie, and what appeared to be, glow-in-the-dark yellow Dockers. Exasperated, he repeated himself, and she quickly nodded. Ruth learned a long time ago it was best to just keep quiet when Bob went on one of his rants.

Ron happened to glance over at the table where the Grossmans were sitting. He took one look at Bob's attire and went searching for Sheryl.

He found her in the nursery chatting with Lorraine, and carelessly interrupting them asked, "What the hell is Bob wearing tonight, Sheryl?"

"What, what do you mean?" she answered, taken aback.

"What do I mean? I mean that monstrosity of an outfit."

"Ron, my husband is a grown man, he can dress however he likes," Sheryl replied defensively.

"Well, don't you have any influence at all? You are his wife, aren't you? It's bad enough that he has to dress like that on Sundays, but on special occasions he could at least try not to dress like a ridiculous buffoon!" He stalked away angrily. Sheryl just stood there, her eyes welling up in tears.

"There, there," Lorraine awkwardly put her arm around her. "Don't let Ron upset you, it's nobody's business but his, if Bob wishes to dress like a mentally ill clown." Unfortunately, Lorraine's kind words did not have their intended effect, and Sheryl burst into full blown "ugly-face" crying, while Lorraine frantically tried to locate a box of Kleenex.

At the same time, Thomas Manning was sitting off by himself. After he had fainted the night before, Kenny called Glenn, and the boys both spent the next hour with him, making sure he was okay. Thomas was not okay. After feeling a splash of cold water, that Kenny evidently had thrown in his face trying to revive him, he remembered everything. He sent them both away soon after, preferring to be by himself while he alternately wailed and prayed for the next two hours. When Thomas awoke this morning, he had decided he was going to pretend like none of this ever happened. Denial seemed to him to be the best course of action in these dire circumstances.

Meanwhile, Hannah was engaged in conversation with Shelley, who was dressed in an expensive black Chanel suit, complete with her signature pearls. Wearing a formal black tie and jacket with white shirt, which was already splattered with a variety of food stains, Ron had gone back up for seconds, this time making sure he got to the linguini, meatballs and chicken tacos. After a couple of minutes, he returned to his seat, and Shelley looked down at the mountain of food on his plate and made a face, silently judging him. Oh the hell with you, Ron thought, as he sat back down next to his wife. I can damn well eat as much as I please. He didn't bother to make any small talk and proceeded for the next few minutes, to eat like there was no tomorrow. Ron thought the food was even more delicious than usual. He made a mental note to ask Jay next week if his company was doing anything differently.

While Ron was finishing his linguini, he didn't feel well all of a sudden, and so he got up without saying anything to anyone, and headed for the men's room. By the time he got there, he was a little out of breath and figured he needed some fresh air. Why do they always have to keep the church so damn hot? he thought. He walked upstairs, planning on standing out in front of the church for a moment or two. Ron couldn't wait to feel the cold outside air on his skin, but after he got to the sanctuary he felt his throat begin to tighten.

At the same time, Lorraine Barger, who had been helping out in the kitchen, excused herself and left the basement. She walked up to the short flight of stairs to the sanctuary and pulled out her cell phone. She wanted to see if she could reach either Tessa or Bethie, her two daughters who evidently had very active social lives. It's still early enough that they've probably not gone out to dinner yet. I may get lucky and catch them, she thought. She started punching in Tessa's number while simultaneously walking up the stairs. When she reached the sanctuary, she heard a ruckus and flipped on a light.

Ron Dorchester was standing in front of her, his face, including all three of his chins, was bright red. He gasped, "Ah, ah, ah," his meaty hands clutching his neck. He fell to one knee and then collapsed on the ground.

"Oh my God, oh my God! Help!" Lorraine cried at the top of her lungs. "Something has happened to Ron!" Dick Anderson was headed to the men's bathroom, when he heard shouts from upstairs and was the first to arrive on the scene.

"My word! Whatever is the matter Lorraine?" He stopped short when he saw Ron. "Well, don't just stand there with your mouth open, woman, call 911!" Lorraine ended the call she was in the middle of making and hands shaking, managed to get the 911 operator on the line.

"Hello, hello, this is an emergency. Ron, someone at our church, was choking or having a heart attack or something, but now he's, he's still!" she stammered.

"Okay," the woman on the line said in a calm, professional voice, "do you know if he is breathing?"

"I don't know!" said Lorraine, panicking. "He's lying on his stomach, I don't think so." "Dick," she asked, "is Ron breathing?"

Dick tried to flip Ron over, but it proved too difficult. Instead, he picked up his wrist and tried in vain to find a pulse. "I don't think so," Dick said, looking at her gravely.

The paramedics arrived five minutes later, but in the meantime, practically the entire congregation had poured out of the basement and were milled around Ron. Unfortunately, there was nothing the paramedics could do, except pronounce him dead at the scene. Everyone except for Hannah and Pastor Pete were shooed away. Hannah, looking very pale, was in shock, appearing to not know what to do without direction from her husband. Pastor Pete, never having been in this type of situation before, felt extremely anxious and panicky. He decided to try and comfort Hannah by throwing out any familiar bible verse at random, hoping one would eventually stick and make her feel better. I wonder if the Old or New Testament would be more appropriate, he asked himself.

Meanwhile, back in the basement, the Council Members were all congregating together. Shelley whispered loudly to Dick, "I bet he choked to death, did you see the piles of food on his plate?"

Dick nodded in agreement. "Lorraine said he did seem to have trouble breathing when he collapsed and his hands were around his neck," he said.

"She did try and give him the Heimlich Maneuver didn't she?" asked Shelley.

"Doubtful, she was busy standing around screaming like a ninny when I happened upon the scene. Also, she would have to be able to put her arms around him to give him the Heimlich and you would need at least two people for that. I couldn't even turn him ov..."

Bob cut him off, "It was probably food poisoning! I never liked that Jay's Catering, but Ron always insisted we had to use them for our banquets. Tonight the food seemed off to me. If only he would have listened, none of this would have ever happened," Bob said, nodding confidently. Sheryl bent over and put her head between her legs.

"Good God man, what is she doing?" Dick barked.

"She's fine. Sheryl starts hyperventilating when she gets excited," Bob explained.

Gary walked over to them and in an incredibly loud voice declared, "I betcha it was a heart attack. He must have been at least 350 pounds." "At least!" he repeated, to emphasize the point.

"Gary please," Ruth whispered.

"Yes please," Shelley agreed, "show some respect for the dead."

Dick said, "Well, we'll know soon enough won't we?" Sallie, who had been quietly sobbing in one of the stalls in the ladies bathroom, came out and unobtrusively joined the others.

Thomas noticed Sallie. "So did your legendary psychic intuition tell you Ron was going to die?" he asked in a smart-alecky way. Sallie shot him a mean look.

"Thomas!" Ruth admonished him.

"Sorry," he mumbled. A couple of minutes later, Pastor and Hannah drove away with the ambulance and everyone else left as soon as all the clean-up was done.

For the first time in many years, Lorraine couldn't wait to get home and crawl into bed with Ralph. What a day! She was finally able to reach Tessa on the phone before she left the church.

"Oh Tessa, Tessa!" Lorraine cried out dramatically.

"Mom, what's wrong?!"

"Ron is dead, he's dead!"

"Wait, Ron who?" asked her daughter, confused.

"Ron Dorchester!" Lorraine said, exasperated.

"You mean that fat ass from church?"

"Yes....I mean, Tessa, that's terrible!" Lorraine admonished.

"Hey mom, I was just about to step out with Tony, we have tickets to a show. I'll talk to you later OK?"

Lorraine frowned, "Oh well, sorry!" she said affronted, "I just witnessed a horrific death, but don't worry I'm fine, don't let me keep you!"

"Oh great, here comes the guilt," Tessa complained. "Listen mom, I'll call you tomorrow and you can tell me all about it." The phone went dead in her hands. Lorraine sighed. Exhausted and irritable, she slipped her coat on and walked out of the church into the crisp Autumn air.

***

Hannah was lying in the California King Size bed that she and Ron had slept in together during the duration of their marriage. She appeared very small and frail amongst the white satin sheets, comforters and several decorative pillows. Their son Toby was in Indiana, visiting a friend on his winter break from college. After Pastor Pete called him, (Hannah just couldn't bring herself to do it,)

Toby assured her that he'd be over first thing tomorrow morning. The doctor at the hospital had said Ron had gone into anaphylactic shock. Hannah told him that couldn't be right, because his only allergy was to shellfish, and he didn't eat any shellfish. The doctor argued that there must have been shellfish at the banquet. She explained that Jay Muster, the owner of Jay's Catering, knew about his allergy and never included any shellfish in anything they made for the church. She was going to add that even if there was, he would have had to ingest an exorbitant amount of it for him to die that quickly.

Hannah had experienced a few of his attacks over the years, when Ron had accidentally eaten a piece of shrimp, and he always had plenty enough time to get to his epinephrine. He used to carry it on his person, just in case. Although it had been years since he had suffered an attack, so he was getting lax about always carrying it with him. He would become aggravated with her if she nagged him about it, so she had stopped. She didn't have the strength, nor the inclination to go into all of this with the doctor, and what did it matter anyway? He was dead, she thought, and nothing's going to change that. As that idiot Pastor Pete so helpfully told her, "God works in mysterious ways." As she drifted off to sleep, Hannah not only felt confused, but she had an uneasy feeling she couldn't shake.

Chapter 5 - The Aftermath (Thursday)

The next morning, phones in Meadowville were ringing off the hook, but Ruth Williams was still in her blue and pink flowered nightgown and pink fluffy slippers, doing her laundry. Ruth let her phone ring, she didn't feel like indulging in gossip, especially when there was a death involved. Death is a serious business, she thought, as she threw all her delicates into the washer, poured the detergent in and slammed the lid down. She turned the settings to cold and hand-wash, and pressed the button. Almost immediately, her doorbell rang. Oh for crying out loud! Ruth grabbed her bathrobe, hurriedly slipped it on, and tied it around her waist. She walked over to her front door and looked out the peephole, it was Thomas. She paused, trying to decide if she should pretend that she's not home or not. Guilt won out and she opened the door, forcing a smile on her face.

48

"Good morning Thomas, please come in."

Thomas in a chipper mood, ill fitting the occasion at hand, said briskly, "Terrible business last night, just terrible."

"Yes, please sit down, would you like some coffee?" Ruth offered.

"No, not for me, can't stay long I'm afraid." Ruth breathed a sigh of relief. "I just wanted to let you know we were all wrong, he died from anaphylactic shock," Thomas explained.

"Really, what was he exposed to?" she asked.

"I heard that it was probably fish of some sort that must have been mixed up in the banquet food."

"Oh, how horrible!" Ruth cried.

"Well you know, Satan works in mysterious ways," said Thomas.

"I thought it was God who worked in mysterious ways?" Ruth replied, puzzled.

Thomas blushed. "It's both of them," he said in response, quickly changing the subject. "Yes, we all knew it would have been one thing or another with Ron. He wasn't in the greatest physical condition, you know," said Thomas, pointing out the obvious.

"I expect Hannah will move into the position of Chair...," Ruth guessed.

"You never know," Thomas said, "she may be in mourning for a very long time. We may have to elect a new Chair, and I don't mind telling you that I think I would be a great interim Council Chair. We could definitely get this church back on track, don't you think?" Thomas said with confidence, as Ruth walked him out.

***

Gary Forrester slipped on his blue Members Only jacket that he'd had since 1987, walked outside and locked his back door. He opened his garage and hopped on his red vintage Schwinn bicycle, complete with basket and bell. Gary had always been a kid at heart, and at the moment, was pouring a giant cherry Pixie Stick down his throat. A few years back, he had suffered a minor heart attack and his doctor prescribed plenty of mild exercise. He decided that he would get his exercise on nice days, by riding his bicycle all around Meadowville. He noticed that most people smiled and waved at him when he rode by ringing his bell with gusto. Nevertheless, strangely enough, when he rode past the Andersons, even though he must have waved and rung his bell at least five times, Shelley didn't seem to notice him at all. He decided that she must have poor eyesight. I'll recommend a good eye doctor at our next Council Meeting, he thought.

Gary was pretty excited, as this was the first death of a church member that actually took place at St. James Christian. Gary always had a morbid fascination with death, even as a child. He loved slasher films and never understood why his older sister would freak out so much, whenever they would watch one together. He was dying of curiosity to find out how Ron died. It was difficult though, because most of the church people clam up when he's around, and to his dismay, he's usually the last person to know anything. Very frustrating indeed, he thought. He wondered who he could visit that would be most likely to talk to him. He decided on the Grossmans, as he rode out of his driveway ringing his bell.

***

Sheryl Grossman woke up that morning with a blinding headache. She slowly managed to get dressed. The events of last night took their toll on her. Her husband Bob, on the other hand, had been on the phone for the last half hour with their youngest, and it had developed into a screaming match. Something about "not knowing how to handle money." Bob had always been an early riser, and Ron's death didn't seem to affect him, at least in that regard. She really needed to go to the bathroom to get some ibuprofen, but didn't want to be seen.

She tiptoed quietly, and almost made it when, "Oh here, your mother's up. Sheryl, tell Joe why he shouldn't be investing in the stock market right now."

"Umm, maybe later honey, please. I need to use the bathroom." Bob sighed and got back on the phone bringing up, in his opinion, yet another brilliant point, when the doorbell rang.

"Listen Joe, I've got to go, we'll continue this discussion later!" He sprang from the couch and walked over to the door.

"Gary, good to see you, come in, come in!" greeted Bob. Before Gary could say a word, he continued, "I know this probably seems premature seeing Ron just died, but I have some ideas on how to improve the church, starting with the music." "Sheryl, bring me my binder!" he yelled.

"Umm, yes well," Gary said uncomfortably, "speaking of which, do you know what actually killed him?" "Was it his heart?"

"No," Sheryl walked into the living room handing Bob his Council binder. "It was anaphylactic shock."

"Anaphylactic shock?" questioned Gary. "Isn't that what happens when you get stung by a bee?"

"Yes, but it can also be caused by an allergy. I think it was something in the food last night," said Sheryl.

"Oh, that's just horrible," Gary squeaked.

"Well, that's another thing," Bob interjected, "if that isn't a valid reason to get rid of Jay's Catering, I don't know what is!"

Chapter 6 - Arianna Receives a Phone Call (Saturday)

Two days later, Sallie paced back and forth in her bedroom, which was pink, gaudy and decorated like a French bordello, complete with mirrors on the ceiling. She had just come home from Ron's wake, which had been held at Meadowville's only funeral home – Riverview. Her face was tear-stained with the non-waterproof mascara that she had on her lashes, which gave her a kind of haunted raccoon look. She had worn a red and black skin-tight leather mini with matching earrings for the occasion, and added extensions to her already long cascading hair, that from the back, made her look like Crystal Gayle. She noticed a lot of appreciative glances from the men and snotty looks from the women, especially from that bitch Shelley. She's probably just jealous that her husband looks at me and not her, Sallie told herself.

Ron had been cremated, many believing that the unlikelihood of finding a casket large enough to fit him on short notice, was a major factor. Sallie was just glad that she didn't have to look at him, as she did not do well at wakes. The story going around was that Ron died of anaphylactic shock from shellfish, specifically clams that were in the linguini sauce. Jay Muster was there crying a lot with his wife Jeanne. They didn't speak to anyone except for Hannah and Toby who both appeared to still be in shock. The rest of the Church Council were busy chit-chatting with each other, acting as if nothing had happened. Sallie felt depressed and anxious. She had a sense that something wasn't right with his death. She knew he wasn't in the best physical health, but she also knew a lot of people who had probably wished he was dead. I just don't know, she thought, I can't shake this feeling that it wasn't an accident. Sallie was blessed with a strong intuition and it came in handy quite often. It's just unfortunate that it never works when it comes to my relationships with men, she thought. Sallie suddenly stopped pacing and smiled, she knew what to do.

***

Arianna Archer was lying in bed in a chocolate ice cream stained t-shirt, and sweat pants covered in dried paint, mesmerized. She was watching the television show "The Mentalist" and had just finished viewing an episode of "Elementary" that she taped on her DVR months ago. Now that she was unemployed, she had plenty of time to catch up on her TV watching. Arianna had worked for twelve years for a book distribution firm that had hit hard times during the recession and consequently, Arianna found herself without a job for the first time since she was fifteen years old. She was not coping well. She had scoured the internet for jobs, but to no avail. When she wasn't on the internet, she was either lying in bed, watching TV or stuffing her face full of food. Right now she was doing all three, for Arianna had always been a great multi-tasker.

It had been five months since she had found herself without work. By the time she was let go though, she had just about had it with the people in her workplace. She was sick of watching supervisors earning twice as much as her, work half as hard. Arianna believed that if she was in charge, she would be an awesome boss, like a smart "Michael Scott" on the TV series "The Office." She also had it up to here with her co-workers, especially Susie, who basically considered work a type of social club. Susie spent half the day on very loud personal phone calls and the other half telling anyone who would listen, her personal business. Arianna would put in her ear buds and listen to her iPod as loud as she could stand it, yet nothing could drown out the sound of Susie's shrill, annoying voice. Arianna wasn't sure what she had done in a previous life, to deserve a Susie in this lifetime, but she was sure it was something awful. If she compared her workplace to the one on "The Office", then Susie was definitely "Kelly", the social nitwit of the office. I certainly don't miss HER, she thought, managing to cheer herself up a little by finding a positive in her current situation.

When Arianna worked there, she was quite often bored, and would lament that she was born way too late. The men and women on the TV show "Mad Men", which was set in the 1960's, were able to smoke and drink at their desks. Not that Arianna smoked or drank, it was just the principle of the thing. It would be nice knowing that you had that freedom, if you so desired. The women seemed to have so much more fun back then, when they weren't being sexually harassed by some male boss that is.

Arianna was tall and curvy with long blonde hair and hazel-green eyes, very much fulfilling the stereotype of her Scandinavian heritage. However, Arianna was never satisfied with her looks. She felt she was cursed with extremely straight fine hair, having had a long traumatic history of receiving bad perms in the early 90's, and during the years the TV show "Sex and the City" was on the air. Arianna, like a lot of women, wanted Carrie Bradshaw's hair. Unfortunately, her hairdresser gave her the hair of Harpo Marx instead.

Consequently, Arianna had always been jealous of women with naturally curly hair. She was also envious, but wary, of women who were naturally thin. She believed it stood to reason that if they were naturally thin, they must be naturally evil as well, you know, having sold their souls to the devil, that sort of thing. Arianna was also thirty-five and STILL single. At least that's how her mother always referred to her. When introducing her daughter to friends, she liked to say, "Hello, I'd like you to meet my oldest daughter Arianna, she's thirty-five and STILL single," to Arianna's chagrin. It was especially frustrating, since her younger sister Emily was thirty and already had a husband and a little boy named Maxwell, Max for short.

The phone rang loudly startling her out of her reverie. She stretched an arm out from underneath the thick purple comforter on her Queen-sized, four-poster bed and answered it.

"Hello?"

"Hi Riann?"

"Yes?" Arianna asked impatiently, desperately wanting to get back to Patrick Jane and his never-ending quest to find "Red John".

"It's me Sallie."

Sallie, she wondered, why would she be calling me? "Sallie! How wonderful to hear from you, how've you..."

"Riann," Sallie interrupted, "I really need your help!"

Uh oh, Arianna thought, I hope this doesn't involve a man. She recalled how they had originally met. They had both been dating a very handsome Greek man named Gus at the same time, unbeknownst to them of course, when Arianna began to get suspicious. She found Sallie's number when he accidentally left his phone at her house and she found her number programmed in it. Arianna then got her address off the internet and drove over to her house. She was hoping to possibly catch the two of them in the act and maybe cut a body part or two off, but fortunately for Gus, Sallie was alone. The two women talked, traded notes, wisely decided they both had enough and broke it off with him simultaneously, to Gus's dismay. Arianna, being a quick study when it came to languages, managed that day to pull out all the Greek swear words she had learned while dating him.

That was almost a year ago, and except for a few short phone calls, they hadn't talked since. The last time they actually spoke was when Arianna was first laid off. She had called Sallie hoping she might have some business contacts. It turned out Sallie had plenty of contacts who might have been in a position to hire her, but for the fact that they weren't exactly keen on Sallie anymore. Evidently, she was the "love 'em and leave 'em" type and most of her relationships didn't end well.

"OK then, what can I do for you?" asked Arianna.

Sallie bluntly stated, "You have to come to my church."

"Your church?" Arianna asked, sounding shocked. "I don't even go to church," she started to add.

Sallie quickly interrupted her and said, "That's OK, but I need you to meet me at St. James Christian Church in Meadowville at 10:00 am Sunday morning." Arianna hesitated. Sallie didn't even strike her as the religious type, how odd, she thought.

"Riann!" Sallie raised her voice.

"Huh, oh yes, sorry what did you say?" she asked.

"I asked you if you were going to come," said Sallie.

"Well, yes I guess. OK, but can't you even give me an idea about what this is all about?" Arianna inquired.

There was a pause and then Sallie whispered, "murder" and abruptly hung up. Arianna looked incredulously at the receiver in her hand. Murder, she thought, as she threw off her blankets, this could be worth getting out of bed for.

Chapter 7 - Arianna Attends Church (Sunday)

Arianna, dressed in a dark blue, long-sleeved sweater and matching skirt, felt extremely awkward. She had not stepped into a church in ages, since she was twenty-one, to be exact. She distinctly recalled telling her parents, "Now that I'm twenty-one, I'm old enough to decide if I want to go to church or not, and I don't!" Her parents had basically thrown up their hands and Arianna had not attended church since. For a small town, Meadowville had more than its fair share of churches. Methodist, Presbyterian, Lutheran, Episcopalian, Catholic, Baptist, as well as Greek Orthodox, all called Meadowville their home. She had also gone to a small Christian church like St. James, and couldn't for the life of her, remember what people wore to church. All she could recall was the incredibly strong stench of Emeraude perfume on every middle-aged woman's coat, including her mother's. She spent most of the winter months every year trying not to gag, Arianna recalled, frowning at the memory. She hoped she looked presentable. It was extremely windy outside, and her hair was all over the place. It was still early, so there were very few people around. Everyone who noticed her, basically ignored her, which was fine with Arianna, not being a people person herself. She wondered where the nearest bathroom was so that she could fix her hair.

A couple of minutes later, Sallie sailed through the arched, double front doors of the church, which were held open that morning by a set of very heavy, gray ornate doorstops.

"Hey Riann!" she gave her a big hug, "Sorry I'm a little late, you look great!" she gave Arianna an approving look. You're the one who looks great, as usual, thought Arianna. Sallie was wearing a one piece, skin tight, denim jumpsuit circa 1978 and from the looks of it, sans any undergarments to speak of, with denim-blue, three inched spiked heels to match.

"Come with me," she said and took Arianna's hand. She walked her over to a balding middle-aged man with a T-shirt that was way too small on him which read, "What Would Jesus Do?" in bright orange letters. "This is Gary Forrester. Gary, this is my friend Arianna."

"Oh, nice to meet you." He grabbed and shook her hand so enthusiastically, she was wringing it out for a couple of minutes afterward. "So how long have you been friends with our Sallie?"

Before she could respond, Sallie grabbed her and said to Gary, "Sorry, we've got to go," and pulled her away.

Arianna asked, "What did you do that for, he seemed like a nice man?"

"You don't know Gary, he'll talk your ear off and I have other people for you to meet." She whispered in her ear, "I'll explain the situation I mentioned over the phone after the service. For now, I just want to quickly introduce you to everyone I serve with on our Church Council." Council? Arianna wondered. Wow, it was hard enough picturing Sallie going to church, but actually serving on the Church Council? She felt like her brain was about to explode. Just then, a somber looking woman with white hair and dressed in black nodded at Sallie.

"Oh Ruth, please stop for a minute, I want to introduce you to my GOOD friend, Arianna." Arianna raised her eyebrows but said nothing.

"How do you do?" said Ruth politely.

"Hello, nice to meet you," Arianna responded. Ruth nodded at her and walked briskly away.

Sallie whispered in her ear, "she's a little weird, but nice enough, I suppose," and pulled her into one of the pews in the back of the church. "So Riann, how've you been?"

Before Arianna could answer, a voice called out, "Good morning Sallie, who is your friend here? I believe introductions are in order," said a thin, little man with black greasy hair and glasses, dressed in a split-pea green colored suit and matching tie. He extended his right hand towards her. After Sallie introduced her to Thomas Manning, he said pointedly, "I'm glad *someone* knows how to dress appropriately for church," and turned on his heels. Sallie grunted and stuck her tongue out at his back.

"What an old fuddy-duddy. Riann, we can meet the rest of the Council later, the service is about to begin."

There were, she guessed, about sixty-five people in attendance at the worship service. The service was not noteworthy except for the announcement that today's Coffee Hour was hosted by Hannah Dorchester in honor and memory of her husband Ron. A few congregation members bowed their heads reverently during this announcement. Arianna wondered if this was the "murder" Sallie had been referring to on the phone. The pastor's sermon revolved around the idea that it is easier for a camel to get through the eye of a needle than for a rich man to get into Heaven. After the service, the two women walked into the pastor's office, where Sallie made the introductions.

"Thank you for coming Miss Archer, we hope to see you again soon," Pastor Pete said, while sitting at his desk, barely looking up at her. Arianna had noticed the pastor seemed to just be going through the motions, exactly like he did during his sermon. He also reeked of "Drakkar Noir", a cologne Arianna was very familiar with, as her high school boyfriend used to wear it religiously, so to speak. As they left his office, she peered into the pastor's garbage can and noticed it was filled with Burger King wrappers.

Sallie then took her down a short narrow staircase that led into the church basement. There was already quite a crowd of people gathered. The two women walked up to the table filled with coffee cakes, danishes and bagels. A cute petite woman with red hair and freckles stood behind the table. Arianna assumed this was Mrs. Dorchester. She smiled awkwardly at Arianna when Sallie introduced her.

"Welcome to our church Arianna, please help yourself we have plenty of food here," she gestured generously at the trays of food. As Arianna began to load up her plate, a skinny woman with very short brown hair, who seemed quite frazzled, ran up to Sallie.

"Sallie, we have a couple of teacher openings for the junior high Sunday School grades, if you're interested."

Sallie quickly answered, "No, thanks though for offering, I have too much on my plate right now Lorraine. But I don't think you've met my friend Arianna Archer," answered Sallie, obviously wishing to change the subject.

A disappointed Lorraine looked over at Arianna and muttered, "Hello." Then her face brightened and she asked, "Say, you wouldn't want to teach Sunday Church School now, would you?"

"Umm, no sorry," answered Arianna, as she quickly tried to find an open seat at one of the long brown rectangular tables in the room.

As the two women sat down, Arianna said, "I can't believe I've been to one church service and I've already been approached to teach SCS."

"Well Lorraine IS pretty desperate, oh I'm sorry Riann, I didn't mean...I just realized how that must have sounded," Sallie apologized.

"Don't worry about it," grinned Arianna in response, "I honestly wasn't offended."

Sallie continued, "I just meant, teachers are always quitting on her. There's only so much torture they can take," Sallie explained.

"How so?" asked Arianna.

"Well, the children of this congregation are pretty ornery, not to mention the fact that Lorraine is a massive pain-in-the butt. She's the SCS Coordinator and is pretty much a control freak about everything."

They ate for a few minutes in silence in which Arianna, who was blind as a bat without her contact lenses, but was compensated by having the bat's exceptionally good hearing, cocked her head to one side and attempted to eavesdrop on the conversation the people at the next table were having. She overheard them discussing how Ron Dorchester's gargantuan weight must have contributed to his unfortunate demise. Arianna was starting to become extremely curious as to why she was called here in the first place. As she lifted a cinnamon raisin bagel loaded with low-fat raspberry cream cheese to her mouth for a second time, reminiscing how elaborate church coffee hours can be, she suddenly noticed four people openly staring at her. She wondered if she had cream cheese all over her face and tried to subtly lick off anything that might be there, which unfortunately produced the effect of making her look like a demented dog.

Sallie must have noticed them staring too, because she suddenly announced, "Arianna, this is Dick and Shelley Anderson and Bob and Sheryl Grossman." "This," she pointed at Arianna, "is my friend Arianna, I decided to invite her to church this morning."

"Oh how lovely," said Shelley, "welcome." Dick looked down at her briefly through his spectacles and then went back to reading his Wall Street Journal. Bob Grossman slid down a couple of seats until he was sitting next to Arianna.

"Young lady, are you searching for a church?"

"I uhhh," she looked over at Sallie for help.

"Well, search no further," Bob continued. "St. James Christian is the best Christian church around these parts," he confidently added. Sheryl Grossman smiled weakly as she sipped her hot chamomile tea, which she was told was good for her stomach. "Now of course, we're not perfect. The Council minutes are never distributed to the congregation in a timely manner and Pastor Pete's sermons really should be a lot longer. We're not really getting a lot of bang for our buck there, if you know what I mean."

Arianna didn't know what to say to that, so she murmured "oh?" in reply. Bob took this as a sign of encouragement and launched into a ten-minute rant about how St. James Christian does not advertise enough, and then shared his ideas about bringing more people into the church. It was a little difficult to take someone seriously who appeared to be wearing a blinding fluorescent orange T-shirt and neon green sweatpants, she thought. Arianna wolfed down the rest of her bagel and slugged down a half a cup of coffee, which unfortunately, was scalding hot and she ended up burning her tongue and throat in the process.

"Sallie," she gasped, "we have to go, don't we?" Arianna looked pleadingly at her. Luckily, Sallie took the hint and hastily excused them both from the table.

"OK," Sallie said, "I'll tell you everything, come with me." Arianna followed her into a small room, which appeared to be the nursery school classroom, judging by the amount of toys on the floor and the colorful Jonah and the whale mural on the walls.

"Have a seat, Riann," Sallie offered. Arianna sat down on an incredibly small uncomfortable chair while Sallie elected to sit cross-legged on the burgundy carpeted floor besides her.

"Ron Dorchester died the other night of anaphylactic shock at the church's Annual Autumn Banquet. He was allergic to shellfish, and it was discovered there was a mix-up between the *puttanesca* and the red clam sauce at Jay's Catering, which provided the food for the banquet."

"OK," said Arianna, "go on."

"The sauces actually look very much alike because the clams resemble the black olives in the *puttanesca* sauce. Jay's Catering, which caters every church function, was very much aware of Ron's allergy and says there was a mix-up with the order."

Arianna waited for Sallie to continue and when she didn't, she said, "I see, well I don't understand, you said something about murder on the phone?"

"Well," she blushed, "I don't believe this was an accident."

"Why not?" asked Arianna, "did you hear anyone threaten Ron?" "Is there a police investigation going on?"

"No, not that I know of," Sallie answered.

"Well it seems like a clear-cut case of accident to me, besides..."

"Listen, Riann!" she interrupted, sounding quite adamant. "I just know in my gut his death was NOT an accident, and I need someone to take me seriously and investigate this. I'm getting bad vibes about the whole thing. Like, you know, 'psychic vibes'," explained Sallie.

Arianna knew better than to question "psychic vibes", for she had seen every episode of the TV show "Medium", and so she simply asked, "but why call me?"

"Well," Sallie said, "You were so clever the way you figured out about Gus and me, and I remember how you had the entire Agatha

Christie mystery collection at your house, and and…you're always watching those crime shows on TV."

"But that's fiction Sallie, it's not the same thing," she tried reasoning with her.

"Riann," she cried plaintively, "you're the smartest woman I know!" Arianna knowing Sallie, didn't think that was saying much, but still, she'd take her compliments where she could get them. "And besides," Sallie continued, "you don't have anything better to do now, do you?" she asked pointedly.

Arianna sighed deeply, "I guess not," she answered.

Chapter 8 - Jay's Catering (Sunday)

After Arianna left church that afternoon, she was filling up her gas tank at the local Speedway when she heard someone behind her exclaim, "Riann, how's it going?"

It was Susie, her ex-coworker, or as Arianna used to like to refer to her, "the bane of my existence". What the hell was she doing out in Meadowville, doesn't she live way up north someplace, she thought. She forced a smile on her face as she turned around. Susie was short and stocky, with medium-length black hair, brown eyes and an olive complexion. She was dressed as if she was on an expedition team to Antarctica, wearing a very heavy, gray winter coat with a hood, scarf, and huge bulky mittens.

"Oh hi Susie. I'm…,"

Susie cut her off and spent the next fifteen minutes boring Arianna to death with a blow by blow description of all the latest tragedies which had befallen her family. Only by reminding herself that she would not do well in prison, was Arianna able to keep from strangling her. Arianna was convinced that in jail she'd probably wind up as somebody's bitch, for she could be quite cowardly at times. Sometimes, she actually did feel sorry for Susie. She would be the last person on Earth who'd she'd want to trade places with. Susie had married her husband straight out of high school and her whole life since then, revolved around her two sons, who were now both in high school. Susie's life consisted of one disaster after another. Physical illnesses, financial woes, kids with bad grades and worse friends, etc. However, Susie was under the misimpression that her Greek tragedy of a life was somehow interesting to people other than herself.

"Aren't you warm in that outfit?" Arianna interrupted her.

She ignored the question. "You're probably wondering what I'm doing all the way out in Meadowville," she was saying, but Arianna had all she could take.

"Hey Susie, I really have to leave, sorry. I'm babysitting my nephew and I can't be late." she fibbed and drove out of the gas station, as though she were in a drag race. Arianna had developed a splitting headache and she silently thanked God that her destiny did not involve a husband nor kids.

Five minutes and three tablets of ibuprofen later, Arianna decided her first course of action would be to drive over to Jay's Catering and ask a few questions. Jay's Catering was only about a mile away from the church on the outskirts of Meadowville. It was a large establishment that had been thriving for many years with a giant blue neon sign out front that flashed the name of the restaurant, and an ample parking lot When she walked through the door, there were many workers milling about. She took a deep breath and marched over to the counter.

"Excuse me," she asked a tall, good-looking blond man with green eyes and very developed forearms, wearing tight blue jeans and a white T-shirt that said "Jay's Catering" in red letters, "may I speak to Jay, please?"

"You're looking at him, beautiful!" The man's eyes twinkled at her. "How can I help you?" he inquired.

"Hi, I'm Arianna, my friend attends St. James Christian and I heard about Ron's sudden death..." her voice trailed off, as his face immediately darkened.

"Yes, it was a very unfortunate incident," Jay said shortly.

"Well," Arianna lied, "the reason I'm here, is that my niece will be graduating high school next June. I want to throw a huge party for her with over 100 guests, and I've heard such great things about your business."

Jay's face brightened, "Yes, we have done many, many graduation parties," he said proudly, "I can give you a bunch of references if you like."

"Umm, maybe later. The reason I wanted to talk to you specifically about this, is I do have a cousin with a severe shellfish allergy and, I don't need to tell you, I was a little worried when I had heard about what happened with Ron Dorchester," said Arianna.

"Yes, well let me assure you nothing like that will ever happen again," he replied.

"But how can you be so sure?" Arianna asked.

"Listen," he walked out from behind the long shiny white counter towards her. "Let's sit down," he gestured towards a small square table in the corner with an Aloe Vera plant on it.

"I was very good friends with Ron," Jay said, his voice cracking. "Everyone knew that for any St. James Christian function, I and I only, was to arrange, cook and box the order. That afternoon I already had everything made and boxed up. Every year for the last fifteen years, we provided the same food order for the Annual Autumn Festival. Kevin, who's been with me a couple of years now, received a phone call from a woman at the church asking him to change the *puttanesca* sauce to a red clam sauce. I, as circumstances would have it, happened to be in Chicago at a Culinary Expo that day at McCormick Place. Not knowing any better, he unpacked the *puttanesca* sauce and substituted our red clam sauce. Our red clam sauce resembles our *puttanesca* sauce so much, that unfortunately, Ron didn't notice the difference."

"How is that possible?" she asked. "Even if they looked the same, wouldn't Ron or anyone else notice the difference in taste?"

"First of all, Ron used to be a chain smoker until he quit several months ago because of health concerns, and his taste buds had pretty much desensitized over the years. Also, from what I had heard, the congregation loaded up so much on the traditional favorites we provided, that very few people had actually gotten around to sampling the linguini. There was a lot left over. Besides, not everybody knew about Ron's allergy, it's not something he would just bring up in casual conversation," Jay pointed out.

After thinking a moment, Arianna said, "You know what this means don't you? Someone deliberately wanted to cause Ron Dorchester harm, maybe even his death."

"What?!" he exclaimed, "where do you get that idea?" "Obviously, the person who called had no idea that Ron had this allergy, and probably just preferred the clam sauce." He leaned over the table as if trying to control himself.

"Maybe so, but what if you have a killer working for you? How do you know this Kevin didn't just make up the story about the phone call?" demanded Arianna.

"Because," explained Jay, as if he was talking to a four year-old child, "we have Caller ID." "Besides, he's a good kid, what possible motive could he have for killing Ron?"

"Maybe he didn't need a motive. Maybe he's a serial killer who kills at random?" Arianna countered, knowing she sounded ridiculous even before she finished her sentence. Jay looked at her incredulously, his arms crossed over his chest. "Can I talk to Kevin, is he here now?" asked Arianna.

"Sure, but why are you so hung up on this? You didn't even know Ron, did you?"

"Umm," answered Arianna, thinking rapidly, "I just want to make sure before I place my catering order, that you don't have a deranged killer working for you."

"Look here," Jay said, while waving his finger at her, "most of my staff has been with me for twenty years and I can vouch for all of them." "I would even trust some of them with my life, and I won't have you throwing around wild false accusations!"

"Kevin, come over here please!" he barked. A short scrawny kid about nineteen years old, with sandy brown hair and freckles walked over to the table smelling of cigarette smoke.

"Yes boss?"

"This lady here would like to ask you some questions about the," he paused, " 'linguini incident' the other day."

"Oh," his face blanched, as he shot her a worried look.

"Don't worry," Arianna said, "you're not in trouble, I just wanted to know about the phone call you received." "Jay said it was from someone at St. James Christian, do you know that for sure?"

"Yes, that is what the Caller ID flashed when the call came in, so it had to have been made from there," Kevin replied, nodding.

"And it was definitely a woman?" asked Arianna.

"Well yes," he replied haltingly, "I guess so."

"What do you mean, you guess so?" Arianna asked, sounding mildly frustrated.

"It sounded like a woman, they didn't tell me their name, but to tell you the truth, there was a lot of background noise here in the kitchen." "Also, the connection wasn't that great, but I would say yeah, I'm pretty sure it was a woman unless," he thought, "it was a dude with a girly type of voice."

"OK, thanks," said Arianna, "that's all the questions I have." Kevin got up and walked back behind the counter into the kitchen. "He seems to be legit," she said. "But one last question. Who called in the original banquet order?" Arianna asked Jay.

"That one's easy, I took it myself, and like every year for the last fifteen years, that would be Hannah Dorchester," Jay replied. Arianna picked up her purse and coat and started to walk out, when Jay called after her, "Hey, wait, don't you want to talk about your niece's graduation party order?"

"Umm, I'll come back at another time, gotta go." She turned, waved and yelled, "see you later!" as she ran out the door.

Arianna drove home and noticed when she got out of her car, that the "For Sale" sign which had been up on her neighbor's lawn three doors down, now had the word "SOLD" emblazoned across it. Yay, she thought, the economy is slowly turning around. She entered her house, threw her purse and jacket on the kitchen counter, and made a phone call to her "on again, off-again" boyfriend Mike, who also happened to be the Chief of Police in Meadowville.

He picked up the phone on the first ring. "Stevenson."

"Hey Mike, it's Riann," Arianna greeted him.

"Hi sweetie, how've ya been?" he answered enthusiastically.

Mike Stevenson was sixteen years older than Arianna at fifty-one years of age, divorced - no kids, and six feet tall with graying beard, mustache and blue eyes. Mike and Arianna had known each other since Arianna's early twenties. He was a nice guy and Arianna was very much physically attracted to him, but unfortunately, they had little in common. The thing that really wrecked the possibility of a long-term relationship for Arianna was that Mike was not a TV watcher. He even refused to watch "Reno 911" on Comedy Central with her, which Arianna believed was the best TV show about cops that she had ever seen. The only time he watched TV, was when there was a football game on. For Arianna, that was a deal breaker. Without TV, there was no point of reference between them. He missed a lot of her references, most of her funniest jokes,[1] and her constant comparisons of people they knew to popular TV characters. To be frank, she just didn't trust people who didn't watch TV. Something had to be wrong with them. Maybe a defective chromosome, she guessed. Her sister Emily thought this was utterly ridiculous, but what would she know, she's not a TV watcher either. Arianna felt she had learned tons of important things from watching TV.

For example, she learned from "Homeland" to never fall in love with a marine turned traitor.[2] She learned from "24" to never trust your co-workers.[3] Lastly, she learned from "Breaking Bad" to never cook or sell drugs. However, if you do decide to choose this as a career, you would do well to pay attention in your high school chemistry class.

Incidentally, one of her biggest pet peeves was people who say they don't have time to watch TV. In her opinion, that would be as ridiculous as saying they don't have time to pee. Much of the time, especially now, Arianna's life revolved around television. Arianna even had her own TV related blog on Tumblr.

[1] And they were hilarious, if she did say so herself.
[2] Way too much drama.
[3] Most of the time they turned out to be working with the enemy.

Her latest blog, which received a lot of likes and reposts, was her "Top Ten Ways You Know You've Been Watching Too Much "Criminal Minds" List", which was comprised of the following:

1. *As soon as any flight you're on leaves, you feel strangely compelled to repeat an obscure quote from some famous person.*

2. *You start calling that woman in the IT department "Baby Girl".*

3. *You begin avoiding all white males between the ages of 25 and 29.*

4. *You don't let your children out of your sight, which becomes somewhat awkward, since your children are over 18.*

5. *When someone in your house doesn't replace the toilet paper, you're ready "to give a profile"!*

6. *Your wardrobe suddenly includes lots of pinks, greens, and feathers, and you're contemplating putting some crazy highlights in your hair.*

7. *You annoy your friends by interrupting their conversations with long, boring, detailed histories of whatever they're discussing.*

8. *You accidentally call your boss "Hotch".*

9. *Even your own mother starts to look like a potential "unsub".*

10. *You begin keeping a packed carry-on close at hand, so you can be ready to leave in 20 minutes.*

Truth be told, Mike had found her TV addiction quite irritating at times, especially when she'd insist on watching TV during certain "romantic" occasions. Arianna never could understand why it would upset him if she watched "Criminal Minds" at the same time. She admitted she probably should have worn ear buds and kept the sound down, but as mentioned before, she was a great multi-tasker. The couple were currently on "off again" status; however, Arianna still had feelings for him, and also felt free to call on him for favors when the need arose, which unfortunately happened quite often.

"Good. Say Mike, do you think you could come over soon?"

"Oh baby, I wish I could, but we are swamped right now. Lots of home burglaries and store robberies, you know with Christmas coming up and all. Can I have a rain check?"

"Of course Mike, it's nothing important."

"Can you at least tell me what it's about?" he asked.

"I'd rather not," she replied, "it's kind of a mystery I'm trying to solve, that's all."

"Ohh a mystery huh, I hope this doesn't have to do with any of those crime shows you're always watching, like "The Demented". Please Riann, leave the detective work to the professionals."

"It's "The Mentalist" she snapped, very much annoyed at him for calling it that for the hundredth time, "and it has nothing to do with any TV show." "While I have you on the phone though, you know everyone in town, have you heard any rumors about Jay Muster and Hannah Dorchester ever getting together?"

"Nope. Why?" he asked suspiciously.

"I'll tell you later. Thanks Mike, give me a call when your schedule frees up."

"Will do sweetheart, don't be a stranger," he said, and hung up.

A few hours later, Arianna was making dinner when the phone rang. "Hello?"

"It's me Sallie, have you made any progress?"

"Not really," said Arianna with hesitation. Arianna knew from all the mysteries she ever read, that everyone is a suspect in a murder investigation and not to rule anyone out. Even though, to be honest, she couldn't imagine Sallie cleverly planning out anything, unless it was what lingerie to bring to a rendezvous with her latest fling. Still, it was probably good to keep her cards close to her chest right now.

"By the way, how many people knew about Ron's allergy?" she asked her.

"Oh," Sallie pondered, "I don't know."

"Do you think all the Council Members knew?" asked Arianna.

"Hmm, hard to say. I knew about it and of course, Hannah did. I would guess most of them did, but I don't think the subject ever came up in a Council Meeting," she answered.

"One more question, who helped set up and prepare everything the day of the Banquet?"

"The Church Council always handles everything in regards to the Annual Autumn Banquet, nobody else. Ron was always very adamant that the Council is responsible for the set-up of any special Church function," explained Sallie. "He especially felt that way about the Banquet. That was HIS baby."

"I see," Arianna said. "Do you remember if every member showed up that day?"

"Yes, actually everybody was there early, including Ron. He would never do any of the hard work though. Ron liked to 'delegate' a lot. That used to piss a lot of the people off," Sallie added.

"Interesting, would you do me a favor?" she asked.

"Sure, anything," Sallie replied. Arianna explained what she wanted her to do and Sallie readily agreed.

"Thanks Sallie, you've been very helpful. I got to go eat, talk to you later." She hung up the phone before Sallie could get in another word. For now crime can wait, but my stomach can't, thought Arianna, as she bit into a tasty beef taco.

Chapter 9 - A Visit from Arianna's Family (Monday)

The next morning, Hannah received a phone call as she was making her son an omelet for breakfast. It was wonderful to have him back home for a while, even if it was under these troubling circumstances.

"Hello?"

"Hi Hannah, it's Jay."

"Oh hello Jay, nice to hear from you, Toby's here!" she informed him enthusiastically.

"Great, tell him I said hi," replied Jay.

Hannah covered the mouthpiece and whispered, "Jay says hello, honey." Toby, a tall good looking boy with a blond crew cut, who thankfully did not take after his father in terms of build, nodded at her as he gulped down his glass of orange juice.

"Listen Hannah, I just want you to know a woman came into the restaurant yesterday asking a few questions about Ron's death."

"Oh?" Hannah raised an eyebrow.

"I just thought you should know, I have a feeling she suspects foul play. Actually, I know she does," he elaborated.

"But why?" asked Hannah, confused.

"She told me she wanted to place a big catering order, but she had a friend who went to St. James Christian and told her about what happened, so she was concerned."

"What did this woman look like?" asked Hannah.

"Mid 30's I'd say, tall, long blonde hair," answered Jay.

"Hmm, that sounds like Arianna Archer. Sallie Rigelli is friends with her and she brought her to church Sunday morning."

"She's got me worried though Hannah," said Jay.

"Why is that?" Hannah asked. She flipped the finished omelet onto Toby's plate, as he mouthed the words "thank you" to her.

"Maybe she's right, maybe someone did want to harm Ron."

"I highly doubt that," replied Hannah, "what would anyone have to gain by Ron's death?"

"Do you think we should at least ask the congregation if any of them had made that phone call?" he asked. Hannah looked over at her son and walked out of her kitchen, carrying the phone into her living room.

"Let's say we did, and we find out who made the call, but that person honestly didn't know about Ron's allergy. Then he or she would feel horribly guilty for the rest of their life. Now say somebody did intentionally mean to harm Ron. Do you think they would actually admit they made the call? Even if they did, they could always just lie and pretend they didn't know about his allergy. So what's the use of stirring things up?" reasoned Hannah.

He sighed, "You're right Hannah, I just don't want you to be in any danger at all."

"Don't worry Jay, I really don't think I'm in any danger, this looks like the will of God to me."

"Well then," said Jay, "I better let you go."

"Thanks for calling." Hannah hung up the phone, walked back into the kitchen and smiled at her son.

***

Arianna's front doorbell rang, she walked over to the door, looked through the peephole and died a little inside. She braced herself and tried to put on a brave front.

"Hi, Mom!" she exclaimed, a big fake smile plastered on her face. "How are ...." she started to ask, as her mother sailed right past her into the living room.

"Good morning Arianna, do you have a job yet?"

A flustered Arianna replied, "No mom, I told you there's nothing out there right now," as she sighed and locked the front door.

"So what are you going to do, just lie back and rake in the unemployment checks?" Sandra Archer demanded. She was sixty years old, tall and trim, with blond-grey hair and the same hazel-green eyes as her daughter. Today she was wearing a simple, but elegant, black dress with matching slingbacks.

"Mom, you make it sound like I hit the jackpot by getting laid off or something. Like now I'm living on Easy Street!" Arianna complained.

"Arianna," her mother said, as she walked into her living room and sat on the flowered Victorian-era sofa, "why can't you be a go-getter like your sister Emily? You really do take after your father." Arianna's dad, John Archer, a handsome, quiet and pleasant man, died five years ago. He was twenty years her mother's senior and had died in his sleep. What a perfect, guilt-free way to escape from mom, she often thought.

"Mom, I'm the doing the best I…," her voice trailed off as her doorbell rang again.

Terrific, Arianna wondered, who is it now? "Excuse me," she told her mother and went to answer the door. Looking out her peephole, she saw her sister Emily who appearance-wise, was a shorter version of Arianna, and was dressed just slightly more casual than their mother with a beautiful lavender angora sweater and slacks, and Emily's son Max. Arianna looked up towards the ceiling, and in a loud voice wailed, "Oh God, why hast thou forsaken me?!"

Her mother called from the living room, "Is that you praying Arianna, have you gone back to church?" She ignored her mother and opened the door.

"Emily and Max," she reached out and tousled her nephew's mop of blond curly hair, "what a nice surprise!"

"Hello Arianna, we thought we would come visit you. I figured you'd be available, since you're not working anymore." They walked through the doorway.

"Why do you guys act like I've been unemployed forever and that I'm not going to get a job anytime soon?" Arianna asked.

Her sister ignored her. "Mom, you're here too, what a coincidence!" she cried, as she ran into the living room. The two women hugged like they hadn't seen each other in years. "Let's all go shopping!" Emily suggested cheerfully.

Arianna's mother and sister were two peas in a pod, and very effectively drove Arianna crazy on a weekly basis. Emily's husband Bill was almost always away on business, so Arianna very rarely had to deal with him at all. In Arianna's opinion, he was pretty forgettable, having virtually no personality to speak of. Consequently, even though Bill had told her several times what he did for a living, Arianna inevitably would forget a minute later. Meanwhile, their son Max, dressed in a blue t-shirt that said "My Grandmother Went to Bloomingdale's and All I Got was This Lousy

T-Shirt" and blue jeans from The Gap, toddled over to Arianna's coffee table and began grabbing everything and putting it all in his mouth. So far he had accomplished this with a candlestick, a ceramic figurine of an angel, and a bottle of hand sanitizer, all in the space of a minute.

"Sorry Arianna, Max is in an oral fixation phase," Emily explained. Arianna hoped to God he didn't wander off into her bedroom, then she would have a LOT of explaining to do.

"Arianna!" her mother raised her voice sharply.

"Yes," said Arianna, distracted.

"Are we going to the mall or not?"

"Umm, mom you know I'm not into shopping."

"Oh Arianna seriously, you don't have anything better to do, do you? It's not like you're dating anyone, are you?" her sister asked.

Arianna groaned inwardly. She wasn't really sure why none of the men she dated ever "stuck". She guessed that some of them might have been put off by her independence but it was more likely due to her TV mania. She just really enjoyed her space and a lot of men, take Mike for example, tended to be clingy. Arianna relished her alone time and loved to just sit quietly re-reading an Agatha Christie or zoning out to one of her many favorite TV shows. There was nothing wrong with that, she told herself. She also wasn't what you'd call a "talker". She didn't care for long phone conversations, and when she came home from work, she didn't want anybody around to barrage her with questions.

She also liked sleeping alone. If her boyfriend at the time wanted to sleep over, he could do so in the guest bedroom. A few she guessed, might have taken offense at this, but she didn't care. "I like to be able to stretch out when I sleep," she would usually offer up as an explanation. Anyway, she really didn't miss being in a relationship. The only times she did, to be honest, was when there was a big bug in the house or when something was wrong with her car. Unfortunately, since she owned a ten year-old Chevy Cavalier, something was wrong quite often.

Arianna had gone to college in Chicago right after high school, but dropped out after a couple of years. She had moved in with a narcissist and his three year-old son, and basically played house for a while. She learned a lot from that relationship, mainly that she never wanted to be married or have kids. In her mind, marriage and kids were severely overrated. When she was a waitress during her college years, Arianna was forced to deal with enough bratty screaming kids to last a lifetime. Why wreck her life, she thought. Plus, she didn't really like to cook, and most often ate delivered pizza, Chinese take-out, or her favorite standby, Spaghetti O's with meatballs.

Her family had no idea that she and Mike had periodically continued their relationship throughout the years. She learned never to expose her boyfriends to her family anymore, as the last time she did, it was a total disaster. Her father had still been alive then, and when she introduced her family to her ex-boyfriend Steve, he shook Steve's hand, said the usual polite things and then retired into the other room. Her mother, on the other hand, spent about an hour reciting every "favorable" trait that Arianna had to him, as if listing the best features of a horse at auction. Even more embarrassing, her sister asked him point-blank how many women he had slept with, and if he considered himself a "ladies' man". Needless to say, Arianna learned her lesson, and for the most part, effectively kept her personal life to herself.

"No, I'm not dating anyone, but I'm actually very busy helping out a friend," Arianna replied.

"With what?" her mother and sister asked in unison suspiciously.

"Never mind," said Arianna, as she sat down in one of her two high-backed Victorian-era chairs that matched her sofa, and surrounded the chess table that sat in front of her fireplace.

Arianna had bought the house a few years ago when it was a buyer's market and she was able to get it, admittedly a fixer-upper, for a steal. It was built in the early 1900's though and so every year, inevitably something needed to be fixed. Her sister handed Max a sippy cup filled with, what appeared to be apple juice, which dripped out onto her furniture, as he walked around turning it upside down. She also gave him a small plastic bag filled with Goldfish crackers, which Arianna noticed, he had devoured within seconds. Her mother put her hands on her hips.

"Oh Arianna, I hope you're not mixed up with something 'illegal'." She whispered the last word, as if she thought her house might be bugged or something. Her sister was looking at her skeptically as well. Arianna was making a valiant effort to hold her tongue.

"What? Oh brother, no, my friend Sallie just asked me to look into a church matter for her."

"Sallie, is she the one who dresses like a tramp?" asked her mother.

"No!...um, well, I guess so," Arianna answered resignedly.

"SHE goes to church?" asked Emily incredulously.

"Not only does she go to church, she's on the Church Council I'll have you know," replied Arianna, in a self-satisfied tone.

"What type of church matter?" her mother demanded to know.

"What kind of church?" her sister asked.

"Oh my God!" Arianna threw up her hands. "What is this, the Spanish Inquisition?" At that precise moment, all eyes turned to Max, who had just vomited bright orange-colored puke all over Arianna's burgundy carpeting. Arianna panicked, ran into the kitchen to get a towel and some water.

"Maxie, are you OK sweetheart?" Emily cooed to her son.

Arianna came back, "Is HE all right? What about my carpeting?"

Emily waved her hand as if she couldn't be bothered with such nonsense, and went back to comforting her son. Arianna got on her hands and knees to clean up the vomit, which only seemed to seep into her carpet more. The smell was getting worse, if that was actually possible.

"Guys," Arianna whined, "I'm really not feeling up to this, please why don't you go without me." Her mother and sister gave each other a look and then began walking towards the front door.

"Alright, we're going," said her mother, "but please get dressed and DO something today," she implored.

"Goodbye Arianna," her sister said, while dragging her son out the door.

After they both left, Arianna sat down wearily on her couch. Note to self, NEVER answer the door again.

Chapter 10 - Mike (Tuesday)

Shelley woke up on Tuesday morning at 8:00 am to the sound of the doorbell. The Andersons lived in the biggest and nicest house in Meadowville. It was also one of the newest as well, containing all the modern amenities. Jacuzzi tubs and heated floors in the bathrooms, marble counter tops, not to mention, an in-ground pool in the backyard. Damn, she thought, Dick was out golfing, so it must be the housekeeper forgetting her key again. It is so hard to get good help these days. She threw on one of her silk robes over her nightgown, stormed over to the front door and yanked it open.

"Hello Ethel," she said crankily.

"I'm so sorry Mrs. Anderson, I don't know where my head's at. I'll get started right away."

Shelley ignored her and went back into her bedroom. She had an appointment for a manicure at 3:00 pm, but she did have one stop to make before then. It was very hard for Shelley to go back to bed once she's been woken up, and so in her mind, her day was effectively ruined. She showered and got dressed and was leaving the house while Ethel, a tiny gray-haired woman in her early sixties, was in the middle of dusting the bookshelves.

"Goodbye Mrs. Anderson!" she waved a feather duster at her.

Shelley grumpily made a "humph" sound and shut the front door. She drove about a mile until she reached a small brick bungalow. She walked up a small flight of stairs, opened a white screen door, took out a key and let herself in.

"Mom?" she called. A white haired elderly woman, wearing pink quilted pajamas and sitting in a wheelchair, rolled herself out into the living room.

"Hello Shelley, how nice to see you." Shelley went over and gave her mother a hug.

"Hi Mom. Have George and Paul come to see you lately?"

"No dear, your brothers are busy I'm afraid."

"Busy? They can't make time for their own mother? Ridiculous!" Shelley was livid.

Shelley and her mother were very close, as her mother had a difficult life after Shelley's dad left. Shelley made a vow to herself that she'd never end up in the same position as her mother, saddled with children and barely making ends meet. She dropped off money on a weekly basis to help her mother out. Her two brothers, who were both married and had grown children of their own, rarely visited their mother at all, only doing so on major holidays. This very much infuriated Shelley, as their mother, who had severe rheumatoid arthritis, was deteriorating at a rapid rate. Shelley was even paying for a private nurse to come in once a day to check up on her and she really resented her brothers' apathy. Her mother took Shelley's hands in hers.

"You're here now sweetheart, that's all that matters." Shelley nodded and smiled at her.

***

Pastor Pete was sitting at home in Meadowville, eating breakfast with his wife in their modest brick bungalow.

"How are you holding up Peter?" asked Susan, a very pretty woman with shoulder-length blonde hair and blue eyes. Wearing one of her husband's over-sized T-shirts and stretch pants, she laid a hand on his shoulder.

"You mean with Ron dying?" He put down his Chicago Sun-Times, "He wasn't one of my favorite people as you know, but of course we're all suffering the loss." He thought for a minute. "I should probably call an emergency meeting of the Council, we need to vote on the new Chair and Vice-Chair, and settle some unfinished business before the end of the year." Susan sipped her coffee out of a "St. James Christian Church" mug.

"Poor Hannah," she said sympathetically.

"Honey, you shouldn't worry about other people so much, you have other things to think about now," as he laid his hand on her belly. She smiled and laid her hand on top of his.

"Yes, you're right, we do have other things to think about."

Later that day, each Council Member received the following email:

To: <Member of the Church Council>

As Pastor of St. James Christian, I would like to invoke my right in calling a special meeting of the Council tomorrow evening to fill the positions of Chair and Vice-Chair in the wake of Ron's passing, and to discuss my salary for next year. This meeting, barring anything unusual, should be relatively short. These are the two items on the Agenda. Please let me know if you have anything to add before the meeting.

1.   Filling of Chair and Vice-Chair positions

2.   Pastor Pete's salary for 2014

Yours in Faith,

Pastor Pete

***

Sallie Rigelli sat on the edge of her bed with her laptop, opened up the email from Pastor Pete, and started weeping. Whatever was the matter with her, she thought, I need to pull it together. Sallie hadn't been feeling well the entire day. She felt that something very bad was about to happen, but she couldn't say what exactly. This was the downside of being "intuitive", she believed. Most of the time you couldn't do anything about it, change anything that was about to happen. Sometimes this "gift" she inherited, was actually a curse. She wiped the tears from her face and sat still for a few minutes thinking. She then shut down her computer, got up and walked over to her huge walk-in closet. She tried to decide what she should wear to the special Church Council meeting. She eventually narrowed it down to either her fire engine red dress with the plunging neckline or the tight hot pink sweater and matching skin-tight skirt. After a few minutes looking in her mirror, she had forgotten why she was crying in the first place.

***

Arianna arrived home to find a package on her doorstep. She reached down to pick it up and ripped off the brown paper wrapper. "What the hell?" she exclaimed out loud. It was a book entitled, <u>How to Pull Yourself Up by Your Bootstraps and No Longer be a Leech</u>. She shut her eyes and inhaled deeply. After she managed to cool herself down, she pushed the front door open. As she walked into her living room, she noticed her answering machine blinking red. She had two new messages. The first one was from her mother.

"Hello dear, I dropped by this morning but you weren't home, so I left you a little something from your sister and me, knowing how much you love to read. I hope you like it, goodbye."

What a shocker, she thought sarcastically, it's from my mother and sister, who incidentally, did not work. Emily did have a job until she became pregnant with Max, but as far as Arianna could remember, her mother never worked. Therefore, she very much resented the both of them acting so high and mighty and butting into her business. She played the second message.

"Hey babe, things are a little slow at the station right now, how about I stop by later and bring a bottle of wine and a movie or TV show, whatever you want. I know you like "24", I can stop and pick that up at the video store or whatever, just call me."

Oh boy, she thought, she did want to talk to him about the case, and she did like wine and "24", but was it worth it to start this whole thing up with Mike again? Eventually, her love of "24" won out and she called Mike back, letting him know she was free at six.

Arianna appreciated "24" because of its tendency to constantly kill off main characters, so whenever she would get sick of someone, she didn't have to worry, because sooner or later they would die. The only exception unfortunately, was Kim Bauer, the lead character Jack's, daughter, who stupidly got herself kidnapped every five minutes. This was much too often for Arianna's taste, and so she frequently wished for Kim's demise. She also found it amusing how Jack Bauer would both yell and whisper at the same time throughout the entire show, especially when torturing suspects, which seemed to occur on an hourly basis. Also, his tendency to scream, "Dammit" every other minute, made her chuckle, as it did thousands of other fans. At 6:00 pm sharp, Mike rang the doorbell. He knew how much Arianna appreciated punctuality, or conversely, how much she despised tardiness.

"Hey Mike," she said, greeting him warmly.

"Hey Riann, how are you doing?" He reached down to give her a peck on the cheek.

"Oh not bad, come in. I see you brought pink *Moscato*, nice!" she exclaimed. "How about we watch "24" first and then I'll fill you in on what's going on with me, OK?"

"Sounds good to me babe," he answered, as he made himself at home in her living room. "Umm, just one small problem though."

"Yes?" Arianna stopped in her tracks.

"The video store was out of "24"."

"What? All eight seasons?" she asked suspiciously.

"Yes, I swear! Stop looking at me like that."

"Well what's in the bag then?" She pointed at the small bag he was carrying that said "Cary's Videos" on it.

"It's a DVD of the 1985 Chicago Bears road to the Super Bowl," he said sheepishly.

"What? You know I don't like that football crap," she said in an irritated tone.

"I know Riann, but honestly, I didn't see anything you'd like," he replied. Arianna found that highly doubtful and continued to fume.

"and besides, I brought wine...." he said batting his eyelashes, trying to make her laugh.

"Whatever," she sighed. "How about we watch that and then I talk to you about what's been happening lately, OK?"

"Sounds fine to me sweetheart," he agreed.

After she retrieved two wineglasses from the kitchen, they proceeded to watch the DVD. Mike immediately began to provide a running commentary throughout the film, going on and on to Arianna's annoyance.

"Oh Riann, this is great! Do you remember that NY Giants game, when the wind in Chicago was so powerful, it suddenly came up, forced Sean Landeta to miss his punt, and Shaun Gayle ran it in for a touchdown? That was unbelievable!"

"Umm, Mike do you not realize I was practically a fetus in 1985," she said pointedly. He made a hmmph sound in response. She decided she would rest her eyes during the remainder of the DVD.

An hour later, he continued his commentary, "Riann, not only was the famous 1985 Bears lineup superb, but there were other, more obscure players on the team, who were practically just as awesome. Guys like Keith Ortego, who did a good job returning punts that year, and their offensive lineman back-up, Kurt Becker. Even their defensive linemen backup was great. They had people like Tyrone Keys or punter Maury Buford step in when they had to, in order to help keep the defense strong." Suddenly Arianna's head dropped heavily on Mike's shoulder, weighing him down and making him extremely uncomfortable.

Within a minute, she began snoring like a freight train. Mike sighed and turned the DVD player off. He pushed her head gently off of him, stood up and pulled down her body into a prone position, placing a handmade quilt that was laying over the arm of the couch on top of her. He went to her bedroom to get a pillow for her head, and then turned off the TV and lights. He left a note and took his leave. The next morning, she woke up a bit disoriented, but soon realized she had fallen asleep on her living room couch. Mike was gone, but there was a note left for her on the coffee table. "Sorry we didn't get to talk babe. I think you must have really needed to sleep, see you later." Well, I guess the universe is just letting me know it's not the right time to talk to Mike about all this, she thought. Arianna frowned and went to make herself a cup of coffee.

Chapter 11 - Sandy's Diner (Wednesday)

The next day Sallie, in a cute plain yellow T-shirt and jeans, and Arianna, extremely overdressed in an expensive black dress, spiked heels, gold necklace and earrings, with her long hair in a *chignon*, planned on splitting a hot fudge sundae at Sandy's Diner and discussing the case. Arianna, tired of being shown up by Sallie, wanted to look her best, but instead ended up looking slightly ridiculous, even if Sallie did say she looked nice. Sandy's Diner was one of the little gems of Meadowville. It was an exact replica of a 1950's diner complete with jukeboxes and obnoxious, gum-popping waitresses, wearing old-fashioned soft pink and baby blue uniforms. It was very popular and they carried all the traditional soda fountain favorites. As soon as Arianna and Sallie were escorted to their booth, Sallie confronted her.

"So, why didn't you tell me about you and Mike getting back together?" she asked, grinning mischievously.

"Who says we're back together?" replied Arianna.

Sallie said, "Oh come on, I saw Mike's police car over at your house late last night when I was driving to Jewel."

"We're just friends. I fell asleep on my couch when we were watching TV, and then he went home," explained Arianna.

Sallie said, "OK whatever, your business is your business," which implicitly implied, she wanted Arianna's business to be her business.

Arianna changed the subject, "Do you have that list of Council Members I asked you for on the phone?"

"Sure," Sallie said, "it's right here," as she dug into her purse and handed a piece of paper to Arianna. "I did exactly what you asked for, I wrote down everything I knew about each of them." Arianna's eyes scanned the page.

Pastor Pete – Hot! Unfortunately, has a wife. Seems nice the few times I met her. Was pastor of a church up north somewhere before St. James Christian. Always asking for a raise.

Bob Grossman – Must be color blind! He was in the Army for like, eight years. He'll tell you all about it, when he's not complaining about the church. He and Sheryl have three kids who never come to church, not even on holidays.

Sheryl Grossman - Takes a lot of naps. Every time I call over there to ask her about Council business, she's sleeping. Has a lot of migraines, sick all the time.

Shelley Anderson – Snooty cold bitch!

Dick Anderson - Is totally loaded. He's always looking at my legs. Gets embarrassed easily.

Gary Forrester – Annoying at times, but always happy and friendly. Likes eating candy. Can be a lot of fun – loves gossip.

Lorraine Barger- Always fighting with the SCS teachers. Doesn't talk about anything but SCS. Sometimes I feel sorry for her. Never met Ralph, her husband. Her daughters are very pretty. I was introduced to them once last Easter. I think they live in California.

Thomas Manning- Stick in the mud. Hates me, always going on about the devil. Wife Wanda had breast cancer. Once she found the lump and went to the doctor she was Stage III, and within a couple of months, she was at Stage IV and died quickly after that. Has two sons, met the older one once I think, looks just like his father unfortunately.

Hannah Dorchester- Not very talkative. Cute enough, I suppose. Has good relationship with Toby. We used to like to call her "Ron's Robot".

Ruth Williams – Pretty quiet and serious. Went a little nuts after her husband Roger had heart attack right in front of her while they were in the middle of putting together the Church Library.

After a minute or two, Arianna folded the piece of paper in half and looked up at Sallie. "Thank you, this is very um...helpful. I did notice though, you didn't mention Ron at all."

"Ron?" Sallie asked, "but he's dead."

"Yes, but sometimes you can learn a lot about the killer by knowing what kind of person the victim was," explained Arianna, happy that watching all those episodes of "Criminal Minds" finally came in handy.

"Well, he was nice looking, a little fat." (Arianna thought that was probably an understatement from what she overheard at Coffee Hour, but nonetheless.)

"Go on," she prodded Sallie.

"He could be a little bossy and arrogant sometimes, but he was really smart. I thought he was a pretty good Chair, all in all. Ummm, he was some sort of accountant, oh and of course he and Jay were good friends."

"Did he mistreat Hannah?" Arianna asked.

"Hmm, I don't know, I don't think so. I mean she's a grown woman, you'd think she could take care of herself, you know?" said Sallie.

"Why did you say Dick embarrasses easily? He didn't seem the type when I met him," asked Arianna.

"Oh, he was bitching a few months ago about Ron's behavior. I asked Ron about it later and he said that Dick 'got his panties in a bunch' because Ron supposedly embarrassed him at his hoity-toity country club. I guess he told Ron that he had made a fool out of himself in front of Dick's best friend. When I asked Ron what he did, he said he had absolutely no idea, and that Dick was just being a snob."

"Hmm, interesting," responded Arianna. "Sallie, if you don't mind, can you tell me everything that happened at the last Church Council Meeting Ron attended, and at the one you said Pastor Pete had just called?"

"Oh Riann, I'm afraid I have an awful memory. Couldn't you just ask Thomas for the notes? He's the official record keeper."

"I'd rather not, it would be kind of suspicious if suddenly out of the blue, I asked him for that. I don't even belong to this church," Arianna explained.

"Yeah, you're right," agreed Sallie. "Oh!" her face brightened, "you could just watch the videotapes."

"Videotapes?" asked Arianna.

"Yes, I had forgotten that Thomas videotapes every Council Meeting. He's kind of anal that way," explained Sallie. "When we're done here, we can drive over to the church and I'll let you in. They're kept right outside Pastor Pete's office."

"That," Arianna, said smiling, "would be most excellent!" "Oh, I almost forgot, did you follow Jay like I asked?"

"Oh yes I did, he's a cutie by the way. Anyway, he didn't go anywhere near Hannah. He was at the restaurant for like twelve hours every day and then went straight home. I talked to some of my friends about him, and they all say he's a workaholic," explained Sallie.

"Thanks so much Sallie, let's get going," said Arianna, anxious to leave.

"Wait, while we're here and you look so nice, let's take a 'selfie'," Sallie said, as she reached into her purse.

"A selfie? What the heck is that?" asked a confused Arianna.

Sallie pulled out a camera and explained, "It's when you take a picture of yourself, or in this case, we're taking a picture of ourselves. Get it? "self/'selfie"."

"Got it," replied a wary Arianna. Arianna never liked pictures taken of her. No matter what she was wearing, what her hair looked like, or what weight she was, she always managed to look terrible. Therefore, she rarely ever posed for pictures anymore.

"Smile!" Sallie ordered, as she extended her right arm in front of the two girls, attempting to hold the camera straight. Arianna begrudgingly moved her mouth slightly upward and she took the picture. "Cool, thanks," Sallie said, returning her camera to her purse.

"Could we go now?" asked Arianna impatiently.

"Sure," Sallie replied. "Check please!" Sallie tried in vain to attract the attention of their waitress, a gum-cracking wise-ass named Bernie, who Arianna thought resembled to a remarkable extent, the waitress Flo from the television show "Alice".

After Bernie ignored Sallie's gestures three times in a row, Arianna told Sallie, "I'll handle this, c'mon let's go." She got up with Sallie and walked over to the manager who was standing at the register. "Thank you SOOO much Sir, we very much appreciate it!" she gushed.

"I'm afraid I don't understand," the short, bald pudgy man replied, confused.

"The free meal you gave us, I mean, I'm assuming it's free since every time we asked for the check, Bernie just ignored us," Arianna said, wide-eyed and innocent.

He frowned, "Wait here a minute." "Bernie!" he growled, as he stalked away. A few seconds later, he returned with the disgruntled waitress.

"Here's your check honey, so sorry about the wait." She sheepishly handed the check to Sallie. Sallie paid for the meal and looked at Arianna with amazement.

"I always knew you were brilliant Riann," Sallie said admiringly, as they walked out the door.

Later, when the pair arrived at the church, Sallie warned Arianna, "Our meetings are not real exciting, in fact most of the time they are major snoozefests, I'm just warning you."

"Don't worry Sallie, I'm not watching them for entertainment you know, I'm looking for clues." "By the way," she asked, "why are you on the Council in the first place?" "It doesn't seem to be your type of thing."

"Yeah, well no, it probably isn't, but Ron asked me to, and I guess I have trouble saying no," admitted Sallie ruefully.

Arianna tilted her head from one side to another, cracking her neck. It felt rather stiff this morning, probably from falling asleep on the couch, she reminded herself. She said, "I think I need to spend some one-on-one time with all of the suspects, I mean Council Members."

"I think that's a good idea," Sallie agreed, "that way you can see what they're really like."

"But how do I do that?" Arianna mulled it over and said. "I don't want to raise any suspicions."

"Boy, I don't know," said Sallie, shrugging her shoulders.

"I got it!" Arianna clapped her hands. "I'll 'accidentally'," she said using air quotes, "run into them and just start talking to them about Ron."

"But how will you know where they'll be?" Sallie asked.

"Good question, I may need to follow them," she answered.

"Follow them? Oh, can I come along Riann?"

Arianna considered having to deal with Sallie tagging alongside her for days, and quickly decided she'd better think of an alternative plan. "You know what's even better Sallie?"

"What?" she asked.

"We find out what their daily routine is, and then I go to the same places they're going to go to," suggested Arianna.

"Ooh, that's a good idea, how are you going to find out their daily routine?"

"That's where you come in, my dear," Arianna explained, smiling at Sallie. "I'll give you a call tomorrow morning, and we'll talk then."

A few minutes later, Sallie took her leave and Arianna perused the rows of videotapes, located in a small bookcase, right next to the door of the pastor's office. She noticed that they went back about three years. She decided to watch six month's worth, which meant she was at the church for several hours, watching them on a television set with a built-in VHS player, in one of the SCS's classrooms in the basement. Sallie was certainly right, most of it was excruciatingly boring. At the Council meeting immediately preceding Ron's death, the only person who really seemed to be paying attention was Ron himself, and he was now dead, she reminded herself. Had she not known it was the shellfish, she would have guessed he died of terminal boredom, with a two day delay.

It became obvious to her that Ron was pretty much a loudmouthed bully who took pleasure in saying no to people. Hannah seemed to be a Stepford wife. Gary, was annoying, but appeared relatively benign. Shelley was unequivocally, a bitch. Dick was in his own little world. Bob was a total whack job and his wife, a sickly person with little personality. Ruth seemed to be serious and meek about everything except the church library, and Lorraine, stressed out and obsessed with the SCS. Sallie, predictably came off as vapid and vain, but she was right, Thomas acted anal about everything. Pastor Pete; however, was hard to get a read on. He seemed competent enough, but he also appeared to have an air of discontent about him. What a bunch of characters, thought Arianna. She sat in the classroom for an additional hour, mulling over her thoughts. When she drove back home, her sister Emily and nephew Max were on her front door step waiting for her. Uh oh, she thought, as she parked her car in the driveway.

"Well hello there, to what do I owe this pleasant surprise?" Arianna asked her sister. "Hey kiddo!" she bent down and gave her nephew a kiss on his cheek, which he promptly wiped off with the back of his hand. "You don't want a kiss from your Auntie Riann?" He shook his head and hid behind his mother.

"Don't worry about that," Emily said, "he's reaching that 'no' phase right now, it's nothing personal."

"No offense taken," she reassured her. "Now, why are you two here so late in the evening? We didn't make plans that I forgot about did we?"

"No, we just got here a minute ago, perfect timing. Bill just got home from a work trip, and we really would just love to go out for a late dinner by ourselves. Do you think you could watch Maxie?" She looked at Arianna with pleading eyes.

"Sure, no problem," Arianna replied.

"Great!" Emily exclaimed. She swung a huge bag off her shoulder onto the ground in front of Arianna. "This bag has diapers, juice boxes, his sippy cup and a few snacks and toys. There are also a couple of storybooks and a Sesame Street DVD."

"This is only for a couple of hours, right?" she asked worriedly.

"Of course! His bedtime was over an hour ago, so he'll probably sleep the whole time, but it doesn't hurt though to be prepared. Bye Max." She bent down and gave him a big hug.

"Mommy and Daddy will be back soon. Be a good boy!" She thanked Arianna profusely and then drove off in a hurry.

"Looks like it's you and me kid," she told her nephew, as she took him by the hand and led him into the house.

An hour later, Arianna was going out of her mind. Max kept whining and crying, and so she was searching frantically through the giant bag for a pacifier. Of course, Emily packed everything but that it seems, she thought, irritated.

"Aren't you tired Maxie?" she asked in a soothing voice, "don't you want to go sleepy sleepy now?"

"No no sleepy!" he shouted.

Damn, Arianna thought. She suddenly cheered up. Maybe I can hypnotize him into sleeping, I think I have something that could work as a pendulum around here somewhere. She started looking in her desk drawer.

Max walked over to her. "Book!" he cried.

"Book? You want me to read you a book?" Arianna asked, delighted.

"Yes, book now!" he yelled.

"OK OK, jeez Louise, hang on," she told him, as she felt around in the bag her sister brought, and came up with a small book of fairy tales. "Yes, success!" she declared triumphantly.

She sat down on the floor, put Max in her lap, and proceeded to read the book. When she was finished, he cried, "Again!"

"Oh, you want me to read it again? OK, sure." She re-read the book to him. "The End," she said as she finished, and shut the book.

Having been quiet the whole time she was reading, he started crying, "Again! Again!" Arianna rolled her eyes. This is EXACTLY why I don't want kids, she thought. Who has the patience for this?

Arianna, reading the book for the fifth time said tiredly, "And he huffed, and he puffed, and he blew the house down!" Suddenly, there was a knocking on the door. Oh thank God, she thought. She got up hastily and went to answer the door with Max.

"Well hello my little Maxie!" Emily bent down to hug her son.

"Mama!" he cried, laughing.

"Did you and Bill have a good dinner?" Arianna asked her sister.

"Yes, it was awesome, thank you. How about you guys? Did he behave?"

"Oh he was fine. A little cranky, but then I read him the fairy tale book, and he was OK."

"Oh yes, Maxie loves his fairy tales, don't you Maxie?" She lifted him up, "Oh phew, Maxie you smell," she sniffed his diaper. "Did you make a poopsie?" She peered into his diaper. "Ugh, you sure did!" Maxie obviously thought this was hysterical, because he began laughing and clapping his hands simultaneously, while shouting "poop!" at the top of his lungs. "Arianna, couldn't you smell that he needed a diaper change?"

"Oh that's what that smell was!" Arianna said with a look of sudden understanding.

"Arrgh, I'll change him in the car," said Emily, mildly annoyed.

"Goodbye!" Arianna waved to Max, as he peered over his mother's shoulder on the way to her sister's car. She walked back into her house and was sitting down on the couch, when she heard a loud squeak.

"Ahh!" she cried, and then moved her butt over to reveal a squeaky toy mouse. She looked at it and threw it on the floor. She put her hands up behind her head. Now, maybe I can think about this case in peace, she thought. She sat there for about twenty minutes, and then got up, changed into her pajamas, and went to bed. Totally exhausted, she fell asleep as soon as her head hit the pillow.

Chapter 12 - Pastor Pete (Thursday)

Arianna woke up around nine the next morning. She carried her laptop over to the kitchen table, and while making herself a vegetable omelet, she powered it up. After logging in and getting on the internet, she checked her email. No new emails, which surprised her. I guess my ex-coworkers have forgotten about me, she thought, feeling a little sorry for herself. She finished cooking her omelet, grabbed the Tabasco sauce out of the fridge, and sat down at the kitchen table. While she ate, she decided to log onto Facebook. She had one notification, which was that Sallie Rigelli had "tagged" her in a photo.

"Oh my God!" she cried out loud.

When Arianna pulled up the photo, she was horrified. It was the "selfie" that Sallie had taken of them at Sandy's Diner yesterday. Sallie looked if possible, more beautiful than ever, while Arianna appeared menacingly hideous. Her head was about twice the size of Sallie's. I can't believe I never noticed how huge my head was before, she thought. Besides her head being the size of a medicine ball, her bangs were brushed aside revealing her bare forehead. This had the unfortunate effect of making her forehead look like the size of Montana. I can't believe how long my face is, she thought. To top it all off, what Arianna had believed was a half-hearted smile at the time, turned out to be in reality, a threatening scowl. She felt extremely depressed.

She picked up the phone and called Sallie. "Hello Sallie?" she said.

"Hi Riann! Did you check your Facebook yet? I have the picture I took yesterday of us up on my timeline. We look so cute!"

"Uh, yes I have, and YOU look cute, emphasis on the you. I, on the other hand, look like an evil conehead," whined Arianna. "Can you please untag me, it's extremely unflattering."

"What?" replied Sallie, sounding a little hurt. "I thought we both looked adorable." There was silence on the other end of the line. "Oh, OK, I'll do it as soon as I hang up with you. I don't know why you have such a negative view of yourself."

Arianna sighed and said, "Thank you, I appreciate it." "I'm also calling because I think I want to talk to the pastor one-on-one first," she told her.

"Now remember Riann, he is married," she reminded her teasingly.

"Uh, no thanks, not my type at all!" Arianna wanted to make it clear that she definitely was not interested. "I did notice from the wrappers on his office floor, that he eats a lot of Burger King."

"Oh yeah, all the time," Sallie confirmed, and then yawned loudly.

"Am I keeping you up?" asked Arianna.

"Nah, I just had a late night last night," she replied.

"Well, you can tell me about it later, if you want. What if I ran into Pastor Pete at Burger King?" suggested Arianna.

"Yeah, he goes there before every Council Meeting, you can go tonight," she said with excitement.

"Good idea. When do his office hours end at the Church?"

"5:30 pm," Sallie replied.

"OK, I'll stake out the Burger King parking lot, beginning at 5:30 until 6:30 or so. What kind of car does he drive?" Arianna asked.

"A grey Honda Civic, with a couple of dents in it," she answered.

"Alright thanks, go get some sleep Sallie," she said, hanging up the phone.

That evening, Arianna drove over to the Burger King, which stood on the border of Meadowville and Somerset Hills. She parked in the lot right across from the drive-thru window. She was hoping and banking on the fact that the pastor was too lazy not to use the drive-thru. After waiting about fifteen minutes, Arianna got lucky and noticed his grey Honda in the drive-thru. She waited until he was driving to the second window to pick up his order, and then she was planning on turning her head, pretending to recognize him, and then flagging him over with some religious question. Unfortunately, she timed it a little too late, and she ended up walking right in front of his car. Pastor Pete was forced to slam on the brakes and turn his wheel sharply, to avoid hitting her.

"What the hell?" he shouted out the window. Arianna walked over to the driver's side of the car and bent down.

"Oh Pastor Pete," she said in a high, fake voice, "fancy meeting you here."

He glared at her, "Why did you walk right in front of my car?"

"I'm so sorry, I guess I wasn't paying attention," she replied, trying to look contrite.

"I guess not," he responded sarcastically.

The teenage girl at the drive-thru looked confusingly at Arianna, who was standing right in front of the window. She tried to give the pastor his order, but Arianna intercepted it and handed it to him herself. "Have a nice day!" the girl exclaimed, while they both ignored her.

"But seeing as you're here and all, can I ask you a question?" she asked.

He sighed and said, "Hang on, let me pull over." He pulled into the nearest parking spot while Arianna followed on foot. "Yes?" he impatiently asked.

"Well, umm," she hadn't thought this out all the way, and had no idea what her question was going to be. "Uhh, I'd like to make a confession!" she blurted out.

The pastor stared at her and said, "We're Protestant, we don't 'do' Confession."

"You don't? Well, why not?" she answered belligerently.

"I'm sorry, ummm what is your?" he started to ask.

"Arianna," she answered.

"I'm sorry Arianna, I don't have time to go over all the intricacies of our Faith right now. I have a Council Meeting to go to and I'd like to eat my dinner." He pointed to his take-out bag.

"I'll only be a minute, I promise," she assured him, as she walked over to the passenger side of his car and got in.

"What are you doing?" he asked, obviously appalled.

"I, I just, I'm afraid of death now, because of what happened with Ron Dorchester," she said, making up this story on the fly.

"Why?" he asked, "are you allergic to shellfish?"

"No, it just brought the whole subject of mortality into my head," she said, trying to appear sincerely upset.

"Yeah, well death is a fact of life," he replied, then added as an afterthought, his face contorting into a fake smile, "God works in mysterious ways."

"Well, do you think Ron went to heaven?" she asked.

"Probably not," he answered matter-of-factly.

"What?" She acted shocked, "Why not?"

"Ron was the type of man who only cared about himself. A man like that will never get into heaven," he said firmly.

"Why is that?" asked Arianna. "Just curious," she hastily added.

"Well for one, Ron loved to say no. To refuse people, just for the hell of it," he explained.

"There has to be somebody he was nice to, someone who he cared about. What about women or old people?" she asked.

"He was especially nasty towards women. Young, old, it didn't matter, he didn't care. Now, I must insist that you leave my car Arianna!"

"Sure," she stepped out of the vehicle and started to say, "thanks for..." when he reached over, pulled the door shut and immediately locked it, speeding away so fast, his tires squealed. Well, that was rude, thought Arianna.

Chapter 13 - The Second Church Council Meeting (Thursday)

All eleven remaining members of the Church Council sat in the Council Room in the church basement, waiting for the clock to strike twelve. It was the first time all the members were there before 6:55 pm, in the history of the Council. At 7:00 pm, Pastor nodded at Thomas to start the video camera, and then led the Council in a customary short prayer.

"Now then, I think before we go any further, we need to decide who is going to be Chair for the rest of Ron's term," Pastor Pete announced. "Hannah," he said, nodding at her, "traditionally the Vice-Chair would take over that role, but given the unusual circumstances at hand, no one would blame you if you decided not to accept the position." All eyes turned expectantly to Hannah.

She hesitated, and then responded softly, "I guess, yes I will agree to take over as Chair to fill Ron's term until the end of 2014. However, after that I would like to step down, as I'd really like to pare down as much as possible, my church activities." There were many surprised, but understanding, murmurs heard around the table.

"Thank you Hannah. OK then, let's take a vote. All in favor of Hannah stepping into the Chair position, say aye." The vote went as expected. "It's unanimous," said Pastor Pete, "the ayes have it!" "And now we need to nominate someone to be Vice-Chair to fill Hannah's position. Any takers?"

Lorraine looking harried as usual, quickly responded, "No, I have my hands full already with the SCS."

"I don't think anyone asked you Lorraine," Shelley considerately pointed out.

Lorraine looked miffed, but kept silent. Dick wasn't paying attention, as he was immersed in deep thought about whether or not he should diversify his funds from his mutual account or move more into his options trading. At the other end of the table, Sallie was playing with her hair and wondering if she should get chestnut brown highlights the next time she paid a visit to her hairdresser. She made a mental note to remember to ask Allen his opinion. Meanwhile, Sheryl Grossman was looking extremely pale, as she had just suffered an egregious bout of projectile vomiting and explosive diarrhea.[1] Sheryl told everyone it must have been food poisoning from a local pizza place that they ordered from the night before. That made little sense; however, because Bob ate two-thirds of the same pepperoni pizza, and suffered no ill effects.

Bob nudged Sheryl. "Oh uh, I nominate my husband for Vice-Chair."

Before anyone could react, Bob hollered, "I'll second it!"

"Is it really proper for someone to second their own nomination?" asked Shelley.

[1] Coincidentally, Bob Grossman's attire that night looked as if it had been the unfortunate target of projectile vomiting and explosive diarrhea.

"Yes, I'm afraid it is," said Thomas, "and actually, I'm going to nominate myself."

When nobody said anything, Ruth spoke up timidly, "I'll second it." Thomas smiled at her.

Pastor Pete inquired, "Is there anyone else interested?" There was no response from the rest of the Council members.

"Wow, this is exciting, Bob versus Thomas!" exclaimed Gary, rubbing his hands together. "This is going to be quite the horse race."

"OK, well we would usually have a silent vote now," explained the Pastor.

"God," groaned Shelley, looking at both Bob and Thomas with disgust, "this is like Sophie's Choice." she complained.

"Oh shut up!" snapped Ruth, totally out of character to everyone's surprise.

Pastor Pete stood up, left the table, and went to grab some copy paper and scissors from one of the classrooms. He came back and sat down. He cut out eleven squares of paper, then distributed one to each member, keeping one for himself.

"Folks, please write down your vote for either Thomas or Bob for position of Vice-Chair."

Thomas, when writing down his vote, put his hand over his paper, shielding it like a third grader taking a math exam. He looked suspiciously over his left, then his right shoulder, oblivious to the fact that everyone knew who he would be voting for. Everyone else quickly wrote a name down and then folded their paper up. The Pastor went around and collected each paper, sat back down and mixed them up. The results were, six votes for Thomas, five for Bob.

"Thomas, it looks like you're the new Vice-Chair, congratulations!" Thomas beamed. "Good try Bob," said Pastor Pete. Bob sat rigid and stone-faced and Sheryl had a resigned look on her face for the rest of the meeting, knowing she was sentenced to hours of listening to Bob complain about his defeat over the next couple of months.

"Now," Pastor Pete began, "one item I wanted to bring up was my salary for next year. As many of you know, I have not had an increase in three years." Most of the Council Members nodded. "I would like to request a salary increase of 6% and reduced office hours - three hours less a week."

Thomas interrupted, "I thought Ron had made it clear that there was no money in the budget for that."

Pastor Pete's face darkened. "Ron isn't here obviously, and we need to take a vote. My salary is low, compared to other churches of this size. Besides, Susan is pregnant and we need that money now, more than ever."

"What? How wonderful!" Exclaims of congratulations went up around the table.

He blushed. "Thank you very much, but let's get on with the vote. I'll excuse myself and retire to my office upstairs. Please call me when a decision has been made," he said, as he quickly left the room. They all looked at each other.

Lorraine was the first to speak. "6% and my SCS budget was cut in half?"

"Ridiculous," said Thomas, "Ron would vote no."

Hannah suddenly stood up straight in her seat. "As Pastor Pete reminded us Thomas, Ron is not here now, and I vote yes."

The result of the vote was eight yeas and two nays. They sent Gary upstairs to call the pastor back in and relay the good news. Nobody had any other business they wanted to discuss, so the Council meeting was quickly adjourned.

Afterwards, Ruth approached Thomas timidly. "Do you have a minute?" she asked, her hands clasped together below her stomach.

"Of course I do," grinned Thomas, "what's up?"

"You know how important the library was to Roger, right Thomas?" she said, looking at him gravely.

"Oh, of course," he replied, and tried to look appropriately respectful.

"Well, as you know, the library remains unfinished. I would like to request that church funds be used to hire someone to finish building and sanding the shelves, and then I'll ask Lorraine to have the SCS shelve the remaining books."

"Oh, I see no reason why that can't be done," replied Thomas.

"There's one more thing," she added, shaking slightly. "I would like to request that the church purchase a memorial plaque for the library and dedicate it to Roger, would that be OK?" She continued on, without waiting for a response. "I've asked for a sample from Engravers, Inc., and this is what they came up with." Engravers, Inc. was a trophy and plaque shop in Westminster, a small town a couple of suburbs away from Meadowville. She reached into a large tote bag and pulled out a very nice plaque that stated, "This library is dedicated to the honor and memory of Roger Williams". "Of course, the real thing would be in gold," added Ruth.

"Well," said Thomas, "Roger was certainly a stand-up guy, and he did a lot for this church." "All of this is OK by me, but the Chair would have to approve it. I think Hannah's still here, hang on, and I'll go find her." Ruth stood there patiently until a couple of minutes later, when Thomas returned with Hannah. Hannah felt sorry for Ruth, as she reminded Hannah of her mother. When her mother lost her husband, Hannah's father, a part of her died as well, and things were never the same. It was as if Hannah and her younger brother Jonathan didn't exist anymore, their mother was lost in her own little world.

"Hello Ruth, Thomas told me of your request, and it is certainly fine by me. It can come out of Memorial money," said Hannah, smiling. "All the contributions given in his name this year will be enough to pay for this."

Ruth's face lit up. "Wonderful, I'll call both the handyman I know, and Engravers, Inc. right now," she exclaimed, as she scampered away quickly to use the church phone. The handyman Ruth hired, readily agreed to come out and start work the following morning. She had also ordered the plaque, which would be ready in a couple of days. When she got home, she called Lorraine and asked her if the SCS kids could help shelve the remaining books. Lorraine, as Ruth expected, loved the idea and immediately called her teachers and had them arrange for the kids to come to the church Saturday morning to complete the project.

Chapter 14 - Sallie Learns Something Surprising (Friday)

The next day, Sallie received a call from Arianna.

"Just checking in, did anything interesting happen at the meeting? she asked.

"Well, Hannah is now Chair and Thomas is Vice Chair. It was a close race between Thomas and Bob, but Thomas got one more vote and won. Boy, did Bob look pissed! We voted to give pastor a raise, oh and his wife is pregnant. Ruth told Shelley to shut up, that was pretty funny!"

"Why did she tell her to shut up?" Arianna wondered.

"Because Shelley was just being her bitch self, as usual. Other than that, nothing else too interesting happened. Listen Riann, I don't want to scare you, but I'm getting a vibe that something bad is going to happen to you."

"What? Bad like death, dismemberment, what?"

"No, nothing like that," Sallie quickly assured her, "just watch your step."

Arianna, trying not to appear too rattled, changed the subject. "Unfortunately, I didn't get very far with Pastor Pete. He was actually pretty rude. I think I want to talk to Ruth alone next, do you know where she spends most of her time?" asked Arianna.

"That's easy, the library," Sallie answered.

"The library, of course. What days does she go there?" she asked.

"Every day except Sunday, when they're closed."

"Perfect, now I just have to figure out what time she goes there, I'm guessing morning," said Arianna.

"Why morning?" asked Sallie.

"Old people are early risers," she explained. This is one of the main things Arianna learned about old people from her waitressing days, that and the fact that they're always cold and they love soup.

"Oh..." Sallie nodded her head comprehendingly.

***

"Bob, you have a phone call!" Sheryl shouted from the kitchen. Bob put down the TV remote control, and picked up the phone in the living room.

"Hello?" he asked.

"Hey tough guy, how's it going?" said a deep, booming voice.

"Mac, how've ya been?!" Bob exclaimed. Bob was very happy to hear from his old Army buddy, and incidentally, so was Sheryl. She knew he'd be on the phone for at least an hour, which not only kept him away from her, but tired him out enough afterwards, that his incessant complaining was cut down to a bare minimum.

"Well, the wife and I went up to Minnesota a couple of weeks ago, and I did some fishing," he replied.

"You catch anything?" Bob asked.

"Eh a few trout, not bad, how are things by you?"

"Well, I've been fighting with the church again. It's really disheartening how nobody seems to care about veterans, especially on days when they should be on the forefront of everyone's minds."

"I hear ya. You're absolutely right Bob, these young people have no respect today. They take everything for granted, including their freedom. They don't even realize it's because of us that they're free," agreed Mac sympathetically.

"No, no they don't. I'm not backing down though, I'm cutting my contributions in half until they play a patriotic song."

"Good for you Bob, say, speaking of your church, I heard Ron died."

"Yeah, what a way to go - death by clams," responded Bob.

"What kind of person is allergic to fish anyway? What a wuss. That church of yours is going downhill fast. You should think about going to our church, Salisbury Presbyterian. We play "Onward Christian Soldiers", "God Bless America", and "Star Spangled Banner" on all patriotic holiday weeks."

"I'll think about it Mac. The Council also voted in Thomas Manning as Vice-Chair over me. What a disaster! Plus, the pastor we have now stinks, Pastor Dave was so much better."

"You and Sheryl need to get away. Why don't you buy yourselves a Winnebago and see the country, you'd love it," suggested Mac.

"That's not a bad idea, but unfortunately, Sheryl's stomach can't take long trips."

"Yeah well, we gotta keep them womenfolk happy, I guess," Mac replied.

***

Allen, who was a few years older than Sallie, had strawberry blond hair and blue eyes. He sported a small gold hoop in his right ear and was currently visiting Sallie at her condo. He was dressed in a bright pink polo shirt and very tight, designer blue jeans with navy Louis Vuitton shoes.

Sallie and Allen had bonded one day at Trader Joes, when Sallie was loading her cart with *Moscato d'Asti* and Allen looked over and whispered, "I love *Moscato d'Asti too,* it's just so sweet and fabulous isn't it?"

Sallie turned around and said, "It is! I won't drink anything else."

"Oh honey, where is that scarf from, is that Gucci?" he said, pointing to the fabric draped around Sallie's neck. As soon as Sallie nodded affirmatively, they both knew they had made a friend for life.

He asked Sallie how everything was going.

"Oh fine, except that idiot Thomas tried to get the Church Dress Code passed again," she answered him, in a depressed tone of voice.

"No!" he cried sympathetically.

"Yeah, I am just so sick of him. He always acts so, so, holier than thou!" She sat down on her bed, her shoulders slumped.

"Wait a minute, he didn't get the Code passed did he?" Allen asked, confused.

"No, luckily he didn't," said Sallie.

"Then I don't understand, why do you look so down in the dumps?"

"It just got me thinking Allen, maybe I do dress a little," she paused, "inappropriately."

"Now honey, don't even start with that. You have the greatest taste sweetie, don't let that jerk try and change who you are!" he told her adamantly, as he sat down beside her and put his arm around her shoulders.

"Thank you, you're so sweet, but I should probably buy some clothes that are a little less revealing though..." she said, looking off into the distance.

Allen's eyes lit up. "I smell a ....shopping spree!" he declared, his voice rising excitedly.

"Yes, I definitely think one is necessary," Sallie stated, perking up, "and we'll use my store discount to get some fabulous earrings," she added enthusiastically.

"Such a shame about Thomas though, especially considering the fact that his son is so much fun." Allen stated.

"What do you mean, his son?" she asked confused, "which son?"

Allen answered, "Glenn, the older one, he's a riot at the clubs."

Sallie stared at him blankly for a minute, then it dawned on her. "You mean Thomas's son is gay?"

"Yes darling, that's what I'm trying to tell you."

"Get out!" Sallie shrieked. "How long have you known this?"

"Hmmm, maybe about five months I suppose," he replied.

"And you didn't tell me? What's the matter with you?" she asked, annoyed.

"I guess I forgot," Allen admitted apologetically, "I'm so sorry sweetie."

"Aargh!" Sallie said in response, "Thomas doesn't know, does he?"

"No honey, Glenn is pretty much buried in the closet."

"Wow! Karma is going to kick Thomas in the balls," Sallie said cheerfully. "He's in for a rude awakening one of these days."

Allen stood up. "Enough about that weasel, Sallie. We're going shopping now!" he willfully declared.

Chapter 15 - Ruth (Saturday)

The following morning, Arianna walked into the Meadowville Library. The library was a hangout mostly for the elderly and the unemployed. They'd sit there for hours reading newspapers and magazines. In the evenings, students could be seen there doing their homework, and the homeless would come in and stay until closing time. The library was pretty big for a small suburb like Meadowville. They had many laptops for rent, as well as, CDs, DVDs, the latest best-sellers, and everything else libraries typically had available to their patrons. Saturdays were primarily dominated by families with small children, as the Youth Library always had story time and other special events for kids.

Arianna spent most of her childhood here in this library, so even though there were other newer and bigger libraries around, Meadowville Library would always hold a special place in her heart. This is where she was first exposed to Nancy Drew books, not to mention The Happy Hollisters, Encyclopedia Brown, and Trixie Belden mysteries. She would dream both day and night about being locked inside this library overnight, allowing her to be able to read to her heart's content. Back then, they only allowed kids to take four books out at a time, and because Arianna was such a voracious and speedy reader, that just wasn't enough for her. This library was also responsible for her first introduction to Dame Agatha, as they carried all eighty of her murder mysteries.

She was pleased to see her favorite librarian, Tim at the check-out desk. He called out to her, "Hey Riann, any luck yet on the job front?"

"Unfortunately not, but thanks for asking," she replied. Tim was a chubby little guy with a thin mustache, in his early 20's. She liked him because he was not only a fellow bibliophile, he was also an avid TV watcher – two pluses in Arianna's book.

"So, what did you think of "House of Cards?" he asked.

She walked up to the desk and enthusiastically replied, "Oh you were right Tim, it IS an awesome show. I watched all thirteen episodes in two days!"

"House of Cards" was a TV series exclusive to Netflix. Arianna did not have a Netflix account, but she didn't let something as inconsequential as that, stop her. Her sister Emily had an account which Arianna broke into from time to time. Her sister was incredibly predictable, and her passwords were always some derivative of her son's name with the number 1. Right now, it was "Maxie1". Luckily for Arianna, her sister was so busy taking care of her son, that she never became suspicious.

"I knew you'd like it," he said, with a self-satisfied smile.

"Talk to you later," she replied, walking away from him and towards the reading area.

Arianna had planned to scope out the place first, and if Ruth wasn't there, she'd find a comfortable chair to sit in and pick out a murder mystery to read. She walked into the Reference section, which was filled with encyclopedias, maps, almanacs, and dictionaries. It also contained computers, in which you could look up on the library's website, if it or other libraries in their network, had the book, magazine, CD, or DVD you were looking for. She immediately spied Ruth, sitting at a small table with four chairs, reading a book. Today must be my lucky day, she thought. When she got closer, she noticed the book she was reading was Agatha Christie's, <u>Cards on the Table</u>. It doesn't get any better than this, Arianna said to herself.

"Hello Ruth," she said. Ruth looked at her quizzically. Arianna added, "I'm Sallie Rigelli's friend."

"Oh yes, yes of course, forgive me, nice to see you," she replied with a smile. Ruth was wearing ruby red lipstick and looked much happier than the last time Arianna saw her.

"I noticed you're reading, <u>Cards on the Table</u>. That's one of my favorite Agatha Christie books," Arianna informed her.

"Really? It is one of mine as well. I'm afraid I read them over and over."

"Me too!" Arianna yelled, as several patrons of the library glared at her. She took a seat across from her. "I'm a major Poirot fan, are you?"

"Well, I'm more of a Jane Marple fan, but I do enjoy Poirot books from time to time," she answered.

"Oh, I love Miss Marple too. My favorite is probably, The Mirror Cracked. My favorite Poirot is Curtain, have you read that one?"

"Oh yes, of course. I've read all her books."

"Me too!" Arianna yelled again, and even Tim shot her a warning look this time. "I mean, me too," she whispered. "Sorry, I get a little excited when I meet a fellow Christie fan."

Arianna, since she was a small child, had always dreamed about being a famous detective. She didn't want to be a Nancy Drew though, she went for the big guns instead. She desperately wanted to be a Hercule Poirot or a Sherlock Holmes and receive all the accolades they received. She would daydream about people pointing to her on the street and commenting, "Look, there goes that clever Arianna!" or "Wow, Riann is a genius!" Then she could also have an arch nemesis like James Moriarty. The closest thing Arianna had to it nowadays, was Susie, but unfortunately, Susie wasn't smart or interesting enough to be a Moriarty.

"That's all right dear, I understand," Ruth replied. Arianna almost forgot why she was there in the first place. She decided she better get down to business.

"So, have you been a member of St. James Christian a long time?" she asked.

"Yes, Roger and I had been worshiping there for forty years."

"Forty years? Wow, then you must really like it there, I guess," Arianna surmised.

"I do now that the library is almost finished and Roger will have his tribute," she replied candidly.

"Oh, did the library take a long time to build?" Arianna inquired. "It seems like it could have, it really is an awesome library."

"Well, it was hard to get the help to finish it, and the necessary funds approved, but thank you for your kind words," answered Ruth.

"I heard about Ron Dorchester, I'm so sorry, were you two close at all?"

"No," she shook her head, "not really."

"Oh well, that's good," she said. "I mean it's good that you two weren't close, because his death might have been devastating for you," explained a flustered Arianna.

"Oh dear, if you knew Ron, you'd know his death was not devastating to anybody," Ruth replied.

"Oh? Was there any particular reason?" "I don't mean to be nosy," she said hastily.

"Some people are just not very nice, dear," said Ruth.

"That's a shame, I guess," Arianna replied.

"Well upward and onward, as they say," Ruth answered.

Arianna wanted to prolong the conversation, but she got the distinct impression that Ruth really wanted to get back to her book. Therefore, she said goodbye and left, but not before she checked out a book from the "New Mystery" section.

When Arianna got home, she wrote down what Ruth said, as much as she could remember, anyway. She certainly hoped Ruth wasn't the killer. She shook her head, it would be such a shame to see a fellow Christie fan arrested.

Chapter 16 - Arianna Receives Some Bad News (Saturday)

Arianna got home and called Sallie, but she wasn't picking up her phone, so she left her a voice mail. A few hours later, Sallie called back apologetic. "Sorry, I was out shopping, what's up?"

"I've talked to Ruth."

"Well, what do you think?" she asked.

"I think she's a nice lady and I doubt she is the killer, but I'm not going to rule anyone out, this early in the game," Arianna answered.

"Did you learn anything significant?" Sallie asked.

"I don't know, maybe a couple of things. I'm keeping a notebook like detectives do when they're investigating a case, and recording my impressions."

"Ooh that sounds cool. Maybe I can be like the Watson to your Sherlock?" Sallie suggested.

"Maybe...." Arianna replied, not really sure what she thought about that, especially since Sallie was still a suspect. If she's cleared, maybe in my next case.... Oh my God, listen to me, in my next case? What am I thinking? Arianna was so busy daydreaming, that she missed what Sallie was saying.

"I'm sorry, can you repeat that?" she asked.

"I asked you who you're going to talk to next," Sallie repeated.

"Oh I don't know, maybe Lorraine or Shelley I guess," she said.

"Oh, Shelley's an easy one, she's always shopping at the Somerset Hills mall. I'd say she's there every other day at least."

"Do you know what stores she shops at?" Arianna asked.

"Yep, either Macy's or Neiman Marcus."

"How am I supposed to know though in advance, what day and time she's going to go?" Arianna asked, wrinkling her forehead.

Sallie thought about it and answered, "Good question." "Oh, I know!" her face suddenly brightened. "I'll tell Shelley on Sunday that there's a huge sale at Macy's, but only between 9:00 am and 10:30 am on Thursday. That way you could be at the mall right when it opens and wait for her," suggested Sallie.

"Sallie, that's a great idea! OK, let's do it."

They hung up and Arianna thought, geez that Sallie is smarter than she looks sometimes. I still don't know about her being my Watson though. At that point, Arianna just happened to look out her living room window, when she saw something, something wearing a grey winter coat carrying a large box. She hid behind her curtain and peeked out. Oh my God, it's Susie! What the hell is she doing here? She's passed my house already, so she's obviously not visiting me. Arianna opened her door slowly, walked out on to her front porch and took a peek. It looked like Susie was visiting someone a few doors down, now she was coming back again. Oh My God, oh no, it couldn't be! Her face blanched. Sallie's premonition has come true! The worst possible luck has befallen me!

"Hi Riann, what a surprise!" Susie, now holding a small box in her hands, stopped in front of Arianna's house.

"You, you you.. bought the house?" Arianna stuttered.

"Yes, that's what I was going to tell you the other day, that we had moved into 808 Butterfield Lane. We wanted a smaller house because we couldn't afford the payments on our last house anymore, and besides, the kids will be moving out soon anyway. I didn't know you lived on this block too. Wow what a coincidence, how cool, we're going to be neighbors!"

Arianna smiled wanly, standing there frozen, watching her walk away. Fifteen minutes later, she was on the phone with Mike, who was sitting in a squad car on the other side of town watching some young men who had too much time on their hands, and if his instincts were correct, up to no good.

"I don't know why you let her upset you so much. Look on the bright side, at least you don't have to work with her anymore," Mike said reassuringly.

"Can't you do something about this?!" Arianna cried half-hysterical.

"Like what? Tell her it's illegal to move into the same neighborhood as you?" he laughed.

"You don't understand, she is extremely annoying!" she replied.

He laughed again and said, "Oh, well why didn't you say so? Now that I know that, I'll just go bust her for extreme annoyance!"

Arianna promptly hung up on him and decided now was a good time to take a nap. She sat on her bed, took off her shoes and socks, and laid down on her back. Soon after, she fell asleep and was dreaming. In her dream, she was in the St. James Christian Church basement surrounded by all the Church Council Members standing around glaring at her.

Ron suddenly appeared out of nowhere and was shouting at her, "Help me! Help me! Help me!" In the dream, Arianna opened her mouth, but nothing came out.

Then Mike appeared in full formal policeman's attire, including his cap, carrying a plate of linguini with clam sauce with one hand, and a giant fork wrapped in linguini in the other. He was coming closer and closer to her yelling, "Eat this!"

Arianna was screaming, "No!" louder and louder. Suddenly, he was forcing her mouth open with the fork and she released a blood curdling scream, "No!!!"

She suddenly woke up and when she opened her eyes, her mother's face appeared inches away from hers. Arianna clutched her chest and made a noise. "Mom!" she squeaked, "Oh my God, you scared the shit out of me! What the hell are you doing here?"

"Arianna, language!" Sandra Archer replied, while shaking her head at her, appalled. "You weren't answering your phone or your door and your car was in the driveway. What am I supposed to think? I thought you might be dead. I was concerned you may have taken your own life, so I used my key," she explained.

"Why the heck would I do something like that, besides the fact that I have a mother who is insane, of course?" she asked.

"Because the majority of suicides are people who are unemployed," she replied, then added, "I saw it on "Nightline"."

Arianna sat up. "Seriously Mother? That key is only supposed to be used in emergencies, like if I'm not home and the house is on fire and you need to run in and save Tony and Carmela!"

"Oh really? If your house was on fire, you think I would risk my life to grab a couple of stupid cats?" she asked incredulously.

Arianna decided to ignore her mother's insensitive comment. "Do you make a habit of using your key when I'm not around?" Arianna replied, crossing her arms over her chest.

"No, I most certainly do not, and you needn't take that tone with me young lady!" said her mother.

"I just don't appreciate my privacy being violated like this. What if I had happened to be with someone when you just barged in?"

"What do you mean 'be with someone'? You mean a man? Oh Arianna, you're dating someone!" she exclaimed happily.

"No, I'm...," she paused, "never mind." "Why are you here in the first place?"

"Tomorrow night I am going ballroom dancing, and I was wondering if you'd like to come along."

"Ballroom dancing? Do you not know me at all? Why are you going? Do you even know how to dance?" Arianna asked, confused.

"I've taken lessons in the past. Listen, there are a lot of men there, Arianna," her mother told her.

"Your point being? Aren't they all like seventy-five years old, anyway? Oh by the way, thanks for the book," she said sarcastically.

"You're welcome, I hope you find it helpful," her mother replied, the sarcasm obviously had gone right over her head. "No, there's actually some very attractive men there, men in their forties."

"I'm guessing they're probably gay." Arianna laid back down and turned over on her side, with her back towards her mother.

"Why do you have to be so negative, Arianna? I'm leaving," Sandra Archer said angrily, and walked out of her bedroom.

"Make sure you lock the door on your way out!" Arianna yelled.

A minute later, she heard the front door slam. Arianna sighed and got up, well this has proven to be a fantastic day so far, she thought. She decided she needed to get some fresh air and walked out her back door to sit in the yard. It was already dark outside. It wasn't too cold out, but she did need to go back in and retrieve her heavier coat. After doing so, she sat on one of her patio chairs and gazed at the full moon, which was big, beautiful and low that night.

Then a familiar, high-pitched voice rang out. "Riann, hi! I've just finishing moving in most of my smaller boxes," Susie called out to her, looking a little tired and worn out. She was standing in her new backyard facing Arianna.

"Oh?" Arianna replied, not wanting to say anything that might encourage a longer conversation.

"Yeah, what a day I've had. Did I tell you I have bacterial vaginosis?" she shouted, while leaning over the chain link fence.

"Uh, uh.," Arianna stammered.

"Oh the itching Riann, my God and the smell, it smells like some wild animal crawled up there and died!" "Oh," she continued, "and the discharge, it looks like..."

Arianna tried to think of anything but Susie's bacterial vaginosis to no avail. She was trying desperately not to dry heave until she got safely back into the house. After a few minutes, she couldn't take it anymore, for she knew she was precariously close to vomiting.

"Umm, oh, I think my phone is ringing, see you later!" she ran into her house, tripping as she stumbled through her back door.

A half hour later, Mike drove by in his squad car and saw Arianna sitting on the front porch, her arms hugging her knees rocking back and forth, while smoking a cigar. He parked the car and walked over to her. "What the...? You don't smoke cigars Riann."

"I do now," she responded. Mike tried to keep from laughing.

"Why Mike? Why? Am I a bad person?"

"Yes, you are," he told her with a straight face, "and you need some serious rehabilitation." "I think you require a couple of nights in the slammer!" He couldn't keep it together any longer and started chuckling.

She gave him an icy stare. "You didn't have to suffer through ten minutes of Susie talking about her bacterial vaginosis."

"What is that? It sounds disgusting," he replied.

"Trust me, you don't want to know," she answered, while puffing on her cigar.

"Riann, you look ridiculous," he said, taking it from her and puffing on it himself.

"Hey give that back!" she cried. "Do you want me to start smoking cigarettes?"

"Riann, you're too cheap to start smoking cigarettes."

She thought about it for a minute and replied, "true."

"C'mon get up, you're going to freeze out here."

"Oh well, it doesn't matter now anyway. My life as I know it, is over," she said dramatically, placing the back of her hand up to her forehead.

"Boy, are you a drama queen," Mike replied. At that point, his radio went off. "311 D&D on 21st and Main," a man's voice boomed.

"I know 'D&D' is drunk and disorderly but a '311'?" she asked.

"Indecent exposure," Mike explained. "Damn, I have to go, we're really short on men tonight. I'll talk to you later." Mike smashed the end of the cigar out on one of her front steps and handed it to her. She watched him walk back to the squad car, frowning and wondering just how much houses cost in Florida right now.

Chapter 17- Arianna Attends Church for the Second Time (Sunday)

The next morning, Arianna arrived at St. James Christian, wearing a simple, conservative white blouse with a black, knee-length skirt, accompanied by Sallie, who coincidentally, happened to be wearing practically the very same outfit. Arianna sighed, I can never win, she thought. The two women immediately ran into Lorraine.

"Hello Lorraine, I'm so glad I ran into you. Would it be alright if I gave you a phone call soon, in regards to the Sunday Church School?" asked Arianna.

"Of course," she replied, "I'm always available when it comes to the SCS." "Do you have my number?"

Sallie interrupted, "I'll be sure to give it her."

"Sounds good, I'll talk to you later," Lorraine replied, as she sat down in the first available pew.

Arianna and Sallie gave each other a conspiratorial grin. They were in the middle of trying to find a seat, when Arianna spied Ruth walking by and stopped her. "Hi Ruth, did you happen to catch "Masterpiece Mystery" on PBS last night?"

"Yes, I did," she replied, "David Suchet is wonderful as Poirot, isn't he?"

"Oh yes, he is!" Arianna gushed, "much better than Peter Ustinov or those other actors who looked and acted nothing like Agatha Christie envisioned Poirot to be."

"I would have to agree with you there. You do know Suchet played him for twenty-five years?"

"I know!" Arianna exclaimed excitedly.

Sallie interrupted, "Riann, the service is about to start." As Ruth walked away, Sallie said, "You get so excited when discussing Agatha Christie, don't you?" Arianna nodded, slightly embarrassed. The two women found a pew and quickly sat down, seconds before the service began.

The service was uneventful, except for the fact that a happier looking Pastor Pete announced to the congregation, that he and his wife Susan were expecting a baby. It was also announced that the St. James Christian Library, which Roger and Ruth Williams had started together several months ago, had now been finished and a gold plaque was erected there, in Roger's honor and memory. After the service, she and Sallie walked downstairs for the Coffee Hour and helped themselves to another extravagant feast. This mystery Sallie has brought me into, is really going to wreak havoc on my figure, Arianna thought ruefully.

After the pair sat down, Sallie spied Shelley over by the coffee. "I'll be right back, I'm going to go tell her about the 'sale' at Macy's on Thursday," she said, giving Arianna a large wink. Arianna smiled. A couple of minutes after Sallie left, Hannah Dorchester, who was looking quite pretty in a soft pink sweater dress and matching shoes, with her red bouncy curls restrained by a pink and black barrette, walked over to their table and confronted Arianna.

"Miss Archer, I hear you've been questioning employees at Jay's Catering?" Noticing Arianna's surprised look, she said, "Yes, Jay called me. Listen, I would appreciate it if you would not harass him about Ron's death. He feels badly enough already."

To Arianna's chagrin, Sallie had come back while Hannah was talking, and leaning across Arianna, whispered loudly, "Hannah, Ron's death was no accident and the truth should come out."

Hannah raised her voice, "It is really none of your business Sallie, I was his wife. Please stop getting your friends to snoop around for you. Jay's Catering got the orders mixed up. Some other party requested linguini with clam sauce, and one of their employees boxed it in the wrong order - case closed!"

"That's not what Arianna heard, it sounds like someone from the church called and specifically asked for that clam sauce," rebounded Sallie. The women were arguing so intently that they didn't notice Gary Forrester, wearing a T-shirt two sizes too small that said, "Don't Worry, Be Happy!" standing right over them looking uneasy.

"Well well well, three lovely ladies all in a row, today must be my lucky day!" he said with a somewhat faked enthusiasm. Sallie and Hannah both gave him a look of annoyance. Gary got the hint and walked briskly away, while Arianna wondered how long he had been standing there.

"Hannah," Arianna interrupted, "we mean no disrespect." "As far as I'm concerned, let sleeping dogs lie, it was an accident, plain and simple. C'mon Sallie, we have to get going." Arianna practically dragged Sallie away and pulled her into the women's bathroom.

"Riann, you know his death was no accident, why did you say that?" Sallie asked.

After first checking under the stalls, making sure no one else was in there, Arianna admonished her, "Sallie, it does no good to get other members of the Council angry at us, and we don't want to set off a potential killer."

"What do you mean, do you think that "Hannah?..." she let the sentence hang.

"All I'm saying is, let's keep quiet about this for the time being," Arianna answered firmly.

"Listen, do you think you would be able to lay your hands on the background checks of the Council Members? At the Council meeting before the banquet, Ron mentioned receiving them."

Sallie frowned, "That would be hard to do, Ron kept all his Council business in a locked cabinet in Pastor Pete's office."

In response, Arianna said, "I'm sure I can distract him long enough for you to get them for me, do you know where the key is?"

"I'm sure Ron's key is at his home," Sallie replied, "but Pastor Pete keeps the spare key on his key ring, which is almost always on top of his desk."

"Awesome!" responded Arianna. "Come, and follow my lead." They left the bathroom and ran upstairs to Pastor Pete's office.

Seeing that his door was open, Arianna poked her head in and whispered, "Hello Pastor, may I talk to you for just a quick second?"

"Yes?" Pastor Pete asked irritably, looking up from his book.

"Would you mind giving me a quick tour of the church, I'm thinking about possibly becoming a member."

"Can't Sallie help you with that?" he replied impatiently.

"Yes, but I had some specific questions about SCS, since I have a small nephew that I might want to enroll, and I think Lorraine Barger has left already." Arianna couldn't help but notice his garbage can was, once again, overflowing with fast-food wrappers. The pastor groaned and then stood up and walked around his desk.

"Sure, follow me," he said to her, as he walked out of his office and towards the stairs to the basement.

Sallie, standing nearby, grabbed the opportunity to sneak into his office and locate the tiny key on the key ring that was lying on top of his desk. She unlocked a small filing cabinet nearby, and pulled out a file folder labeled "Background Checks" that was in a green hanging file folder entitled "Church Council Business - Ron Dorchester". She slipped it into her large, bright red purse and quickly left his office. She walked downstairs and saw Pastor Pete showing the Sunday Church School classrooms to Arianna. Sallie nodded at her, and Arianna suddenly stopped and looked at her watch.

"Oh my goodness, look at the time, well thank you Pastor, but I forgot I had made a lunch date. I have to go, thank you so much!"

While Pastor Pete was left standing there alone with a confused expression on his face, she quickly walked over to Sallie and they both ran up the stairs and fled the church. When they were outside, Sallie looked around her to make sure nobody was watching, and then pulled the file out of her purse and handed it to Arianna.

"Here you go Riann, knock yourself out." All of a sudden, Sallie got a weird look on her face.

"What? What's happening?" Arianna asked, worried.

"Nothing, I just, I just feel something awful is going to happen."

"Not with me again, I hope! You were right the last time."

"Really? What happened?" Sallie asked.

"Ah, never mind," she replied.

"Well, I just feel something real bad is going to happen, but I don't know to who. I don't think it's us though."

"Okay, keep me posted. In the meantime, I want to go check out this file," Arianna informed her.

"Alright, see ya!" Sallie waved goodbye.

Arianna got in her car, raced home and eagerly pored over the file. All of the Council Members' background checks were in there, including Ron's. At first she found that surprising, but then she realized it wouldn't look right if he had the checks done on everyone but himself. She spent about an hour reading them, and when she was finished, came to the conclusion that only one or two of them might have some bearing on this case. Very interesting indeed, she thought, as she put all the papers back in the file folder and placed it on her dining room table. Arianna took a deep breath and realized that she was truly enjoying herself. She felt like she actually might be doing something worthwhile. With a big smile on her face, she sat down on the rug on her dining room floor, and called her two long-haired black cats, Tony and Carmela, over to her. She spent the next half hour petting them both simultaneously, until all you could hear was one big, loud, contented purr.

Chapter 18 - Lorraine (Monday)

Arianna woke up Monday morning, intent on having an in-depth conversation with Lorraine as planned, by appealing to her Sunday Church School fanaticism. She dug into her purse until she found Lorraine's number on the back of a pew envelope that Sallie had slipped her in church. As soon as she finished her daily hygiene routine, she gave her a call.

"Hello?"

"Hello, is this Lorraine?" she asked.

"Yes, who's calling please?"

"This is Arianna Archer." There was silence on the other end of the phone. "Uh, I'm Sallie Rigelli's friend."

"Oh yes, how can I help you?" she asked cheerfully.

"Well, I had been asking around about your Sunday Church School, because I have a nephew who is pre-school age, and I wanted to know more about St. James's program."

"Oh, well I can tell you anything that you need to know. I'm sure Sallie's told you, I've been the SCS Superintendent at St. James for fifteen years."

"Yes, you had already left on Sunday, so Pastor Pete gave me a short tour of the classrooms, but he really couldn't give me much information on the SCS," Arianna said.

"Well of course not, what does he know?" Lorraine sounded irritated. Afterwards, she realized how that must have sounded and hastily corrected herself. "I mean, he has enough to deal with," she paused, "with pastoral duties, you know." "You really need to be talking to me."

"Yes, that's what I figured," she agreed. "Do you have a few minutes? I thought we might have a cup of coffee at Starbucks and discuss it," she asked Lorraine.

"Sure, that would be fine," she replied.

"Great, how about the one in Somerset Hills in an hour?"

"OK, I'll see you there," she said, and hung up. Arianna felt badly about deceiving her, but that's the sacrifice one has to make when there's a killer on the loose, she reminded herself.

An hour later, she walked through the door of Starbucks. Lorraine was already standing there in line, so she walked right up behind her.

"Hello Lorraine."

"Hi Arianna, doesn't look like it's too busy today. We lucked out, there's plenty of places to sit."

"Yes, you're right." Arianna looked around her, there seemed to be only a few college-aged kids with laptops or IPads, sitting in the low brown stuffed chairs, drinking espresso.

The barista asked Lorraine what she wanted and she responded, "tall coffee, black please." Arianna admired her resolve. When it was her turn to order, she asked for a grande frozen chocolate mocha latte with whipped cream and chocolate sprinkles, which had a higher caloric content than Lorraine consumed in one entire day.

Arianna followed her to a small table which sat two, and made herself comfortable.

"So, you have a young nephew?" Lorraine inquired.

"Yes, Maxwell, he's almost three."

"Maxwell, what a nice name," she exclaimed. "Well, our Pre-K through Kindergarten class is for three to five year olds, and we presently have two teachers who alternate teaching that class."

"Oh, can you give me some idea of the curriculum?" Arianna wanted to play the role of the doting aunt to perfection. Unfortunately, she was forced to endure fifteen minutes of a non-stop explanation of the curriculum, and how it surpassed every other SCS's curriculum in the state of Illinois.

"Uh, not to change the subject but," she finally had to interrupt her, "Sallie told me that Ron died right in front of you." Arianna hoped she wasn't being too forward, but Lorraine didn't seem to mind.

"Oh yes," Lorraine's eyes grew very big, "that was horrible, just horrible!"

"I can imagine," said Arianna sympathetically. "Were you two close?" she asked.

"Me and Ron? No, not really." She looked off into the distance, as if in deep thought.

"I heard he was, uh, a little hard to get along with?" Arianna prodded her.

"Ron was," she leaned in closer, as if she was going to tell her a secret, "well, I don't mind telling you, quite difficult at times."

"Oh?" she replied.

"He did not understand how much money it takes to run an efficient, above par SCS." She then proceeded to talk her ear off for the next ten minutes on what it costs to run a Sunday Church School. Arianna was beginning to understand why teachers were always quitting on her. She didn't seem as if she had any intense hatred for Ron though. "Ron was very frugal, way too frugal for my taste," Lorraine was saying, as she carefully sipped her hot coffee.

"Well, now that Ron's gone, will Hannah be Chair?" she asked.

"Yes, that's right," Lorraine answered.

"Well, maybe she'll be less...," she paused, "frugal?" Arianna suggested.

"Hmmph, we'll see, I'm not going to hold my breath," she replied.

Ten minutes later, Arianna thanked her for her time and told her she'd need to discuss the subject with her sister Emily, but that she'd contact her with any other questions she might have. Arianna got into her car, pulled out her notebook from her purse, and starting writing down her impressions from their meeting.

Chapter 19 - Arianna Goes Shopping (Tuesday)

The next day, Arianna was doing her weekly grocery shopping, wearing what she liked to call her, "trying to hide from the paparazzi" clothes, which consisted of a black Led Zeppelin sweatshirt, dark blue pajama pants and white gym shoes. She also had on a very old "Late Night with David Letterman" baseball cap, worn backwards, with a long ponytail. Arianna was wheeling her shopping cart through the Jewel's Food Store in Meadowville and had stopped at the feminine product section. She was trying to decide whether she was going to buy the Super Size or Super Plus Size tampons, when all of a sudden, she heard a loud voice behind her.

"Hey there, you're Sallie's friend right?" She turned around to find Gary Forrester standing there in a tight T-shirt and jeans that were at least two inches too short.

"Oh yes, hello," she replied, quickly dropping both boxes into her cart.

"Well, do you plan on visiting St. James again?" he inquired, smiling brightly.

"Um, sure I guess, it seems like a nice church."

"Yes, I've been attending St. James for years and any friend of Sallie's, is a friend of mine!" Gary magnanimously declared.

"Are you and Sallie close?" inquired Arianna, somewhat surprised, and taking the opportunity to steal a glimpse inside Gary's cart. His cart contained a bag of watermelon Jolly Ranchers, the latest National Enquirer, a bag of mini Baby Ruth's, a box of chocolate covered graham crackers, a jar of marshmallow Fluff, and a case of Coca-Cola. Hmm, looks like a well-rounded diet to me, mused Arianna.

"Oh yes, we're kindred spirits, me and Sallie yup!" he answered, nodding his head vigorously.

She lowered her voice, "I'm so sorry about what happened at your church with Ron Dorchester."

"Yes, it was a terrible situation," Gary quickly replied, seeming suddenly strangely subdued at the mention of Ron's name. "But I really don't know anything about it, sorry but I have to go."

"Well, nice to see you then.." Arianna replied politely, as Gary suddenly wheeled his cart away, acting as if he was in a hurry all of a sudden.

A couple of minutes later, Arianna was trying to decide between sanitary pads with or without wings, when someone came around the corner fast and pushed their cart into the back of her legs hard.

"Ow!" cried Arianna, turning around.

"My goodness, I'm so sorry," mumbled a woman in a nasally voice with big black Jackie O glasses and a leopard print babushka.

"Oh, that's all right," she started to say, when she recognized Sheryl Grossman. She hastily threw both packages of sanitary napkins into her cart. "Say, you're Sheryl from St. James Christian. I'm Sallie's friend Arianna."

"Oh yes," she replied weakly. "Nice to see you again," Sheryl added politely.

"Sallie told me about your friend Ron suddenly dying, I'm so sorry for your loss."

Sheryl took off her sunglasses, and in a much stronger voice, firmly stated, "Ron certainly wasn't my friend, but thank you for your kind words."

"Oh?" Arianna was surprised.

"Ron created a lot of problems within the church. He liked to stir up trouble and didn't care about the fall-out." Sheryl leaned in angrily. "Still," she quickly added, "it leaves their son Toby without a father, which is sad."

Arianna nodded. "Well, it just seems so tragic, because anaphylactic shock is so preventable, isn't it?" she asked Sheryl.

"Oh I don't know," Sheryl's voice sounded shaky. "Death is always around the corner, isn't it? One day we're here and then the next we're gone and there's nothing we can do about it," replied Sheryl fatalistically.

"Yes," Arianna nodded, unsure of what to say to that.

"Goodbye Arianna." Sheryl maneuvered her cart around her and continued towards the checkout aisle. Arianna watched her leave and then started walking towards the feminine hygiene section, when she thought better of it, and turned in the other direction. With my luck, I'd run right into Pastor Pete, she thought, frowning.

Chapter 20 - Gary (Wednesday)

The next morning, Gary Forrester's housekeeper knocked on his front door three times, waited a few moments, and then took out the key from the pocket of her white apron, which she always wore over her simple housedress, and let herself in. She decided today she'd start with the living room. She walked over in her comfortable white nurses shoes to the hall closet, pulled out an old Hoover vacuum, turned it on, and began vacuuming. As usual, she began whistling a tune as she moved into the dining room. Mr. Forrester was a whistler too. Many times if he was home while she cleaned, he'd whistle along with her. Sometimes they would even whistle "The Andy Griffith Show" theme song together. She smiled at the memory. Mrs. Cruxmore was very fortunate to have worked for Mr. Forrester the last five years. He was so cheerful all the time and always managed to brighten her day.

Suddenly, she dropped the vacuum cleaner and screamed, "Oh my God! Oh my God!" Gary Forrester was lying on his back on the newly refinished, hardwood dining room floor, his body cold and stiff, his glassy eyes staring off into nowhere, seeing nothing. After frantically feeling for a pulse, she had determined he wasn't breathing.

Five minutes later, after a hysterical Mrs. Cruxmore called 911, the ambulance arrived. Within a half-hour, it seemed as if most of the town of Meadowville learned that poor Gary was dead.

***

Hannah was in the Master Bedroom pulling clothes out of Ron's closet, not really sure what to do with all of them. She doubted there was a big need for XXXXL suits at the Salvation Army, but she felt badly about just throwing them away. Toby had already left. His break was over and he was driving back to school. The first few days after Ron's death were strange for her. She wasn't used to being able to do whatever she wanted. Last evening she started shivering, but then she remembered she could turn up the heat without any complaints.

Another thing she noticed, was that in the past it was incredibly difficult to watch her figure, because Ron insisted on keeping the house stocked with junk food. She realized she was sick and tired of having to resist the temptation of chocolate chip cookies, BBQ potato chips and any other carb you could name. The first thing she did the morning after Ron died, was to go through the refrigerator, freezer, and pantries, and throw away all of Ron's food. She didn't find out until a week later that Ron had secret stashes all over the house. She really had no idea the extent of his food addiction. I mean seriously, she thought, Ho Hos in his winter boots? That's just crazy. She was wondering if maybe she should surf the web to find some big fat men who were looking for used clothes. She had heard there was a specific homosexual subclass, who were very attracted to big fat burly men.

"I think they're called "Bears," Sallie Rigelli once told her. Maybe if I Googled "Gay Bears" I could find some people who could help me with this, she was thinking, when the phone suddenly rang, startling her. She reluctantly stopped what she was doing and picked it up.

"Hannah, it's Thomas Manning," she heard, his voice sounding urgent. Hannah hoped Thomas wasn't calling about the Church

Dress Code vote. She wasn't in the mood to listen to his histrionics today.

"Yes?" she asked.

"It's Gary, he's dead," Thomas said, with nervous excitement in his voice.

"Gary Forrester?" she asked, shocked.

"Yes, I just heard it on the Meadowville police scanners." Hannah wondered how and why he was listening to police scanners, but after imagining the lengthy explanation Thomas might give, had decided she didn't want to know that badly.

"How? What happened?" she asked, as she sat down on the bed, very upset.

"All I know, is his housekeeper found him and the paramedics came."

"Oh my God, this is terrible!" exclaimed Hannah.

"Yes," said Thomas, "it leaves us with quite a hole in the Church Council."

Hannah chose not to address his blatant insensitivity. "Thomas, this is a shock. I need to get off the phone, thank you for letting me know."

He answered, "of course," but Hannah hung up the phone before she could hear him.

She lowered her face in her hands and cried. Then once she collected herself, wiped her tears, and blew her nose, she began weeping all over again. The first time she cried because of Gary's death, the second, because she realized she cared more about Gary dying than her own husband.

***

Lorraine was sitting at home in her living room with her husband, watching sports on an old, big heavy television set. Ralph, a short, clean-shaven, middle-aged man with light brown hair, was drinking beer with his feet up on the coffee table.

"You know Hannah Dorchester just called to tell me that Gary Forrester from church died of a heart attack yesterday," she said.

"Oh that's a shame," he commented, not taking his eyes off of the TV, as he took another gulp of beer.

"Well, yes it is, and now Pastor Pete and the rest of the Council will be preoccupied with all the funeral arrangements, which means nobody will be focusing on the Christmas Pageant," she complained.

"Yes, well, I'm sure that won't be the case," Ralph replied, trying to both cheer and shut her up at the same time.

Lorraine was struck by an idea. "Ralph, why don't we go to California and visit the girls?" Lorraine suggested, as she sat forward eagerly.

"You know I don't like to fly Rainey, plus airfare is astronomical right now."

"Yeah, I guess you're right," she said, as she sat back dejectedly. "Well," she brightened up, "how about we go to a movie later?"

"Nah, they cost an arm and a leg nowadays. Besides, we have movie channels right here on the TV, why would we want to go out?" Ralph said. Lorraine sighed. Maybe she could call another Christmas pageant rehearsal for this evening, she thought. She got up and began searching for her SCS contact list.

***

Sallie was at home, dressed only in her white lace Victoria's

Secret bra and panties, checking to see how many replies she received in from her online profile on the hottest new dating website, "LustMatch". Her friend Allen had suggested it, after Sallie had run through her latest string of losers. Yesterday, she got eight, but today she got ten! She was pleased, her profile seemed to be very popular, even without a photo. She didn't post her picture, because she wanted men to appreciate her for her brains, not her beauty, Sallie told everyone. The last time she did something like this, it was a disaster. She had noticed a lot of these profiles had women comparing themselves to famous people, so that the potential suitors would get a better idea of what they looked like. Now Sallie was a major "Sex and the City" fan, and she considered herself a "Carrie".[1] She loved Carrie's hair, her body, her clothes and her shoes. Because she didn't feel she really resembled any specific famous person, she put down in her profile that she was a Sarah Jessica Parker (the actress who played Carrie) look-a-like. She ended up getting ZERO replies, despite having her profile up for two whole weeks.

She had absolutely no idea why, until her friend Allen, laughing hysterically, told her, "Oh honey, I'm gay and even I know, that men do not find Sarah Jessica Parker attractive!" he declared, wagging his finger at her.

"They don't?" asked a shocked Sallie.

"It's like being a guy and telling women you're a James Carville look-a-like."

"A who?" Sallie asked, confused.

Allen sighed, "OK, how about a Steve Buscemi look-alike?" Noticing Sallie's blank stare, he added, "Tony Soprano's cousin, Tony?"

[1] despite the fact that everyone knew she was a "Samantha".

Finally understanding. Sallie replied, "ohhh," then she said, "ewww." She immediately changed her profile, upon Allen's advice, to state, "Tyra Banks look-alike, but sexier". Therefore, she actually owed her newfound luck on "LustMatch" to Allen. It was times like these that she thanked God for her gay friends.

She was trying to decide who to reply to first, when she realized she still hadn't given Gary back the book he insisted she borrow entitled, <u>Men with Venereal Disease and the Women who Love Them</u>. Sallie shuddered. All she knew, was that after reading it, she couldn't even think of a penis without shaking. She meant to give it to him at church Sunday, but had forgotten to put it in her purse, before she left home. Sallie only lived a couple of blocks away, so she was planning to drop it off at his house. She slipped on a one-piece purple velour jogging outfit with matching socks and gym shoes. She decided to walk, as she needed to keep in shape for the marathon of dating she was hopefully about to embark on.

When she arrived at his two-story, rose-colored Victorian, there were two ambulances and a police car in front. Oh my God, I hope Gary's house wasn't robbed, but then why would the ambulances be here? she wondered. Well, maybe Gary caught the robbers in mid-theft and they roughed him up. Oh poor Gary, Sallie thought. She was almost in tears imagining all the bruises and broken ribs he must have suffered in the assault. Sallie always did have an over-active imagination. As she approached the front door, a middle-aged woman with facial features similar to Gary's, came out of the house and stood there with red-rimmed eyes.

"Can I help you?" she asked.

"I just wanted to return this book to Gary, is he OK?" Sallie asked anxiously, as she held out the book to her.

"No dear, I'm sorry," she paused, "he's dead." <u>Men with Venereal Disease and the Women who Love Them</u> fell face down on the front porch, as Sallie dropped to her knees, openly sobbing.

***

Arianna meanwhile, was sitting up in bed, wearing one of Mike's old football jerseys that he had given her years ago, and which came down to her knees. She was composing a letter to the producers of the TV show, "Homeland", desperately urging them to eliminate the character of Nicholas Brody's daughter Dana. She annoyed Arianna so much, that she was forced to mute her lap top computer and place her hand on the screen over her face, every time this character was featured in an episode. Arianna had composed many letters in her lifetime, expressing her dismay about various subjects, to numerous TV writers, producers and executives, and she was quite good at it.

Arianna especially became irked when she would get attached to a new show, and then after a year or two, the network would cancel it. Woe to anyone in the television industry who made a decision she didn't agree with. So far she had written, "Dear Homeland producers: For the love of God, please! For the sake of humanity and my sanity, get rid of Dana!!!![1] Then she had considerately listed various ways they could "off her", which included among other methods; a devastating typhoon, a shark devouring her limb by limb, and spontaneous combustion.

Arianna also came from the school of thought, that you can never have too many exclamation points, and so she was in the middle of adding additional ones to the end of every sentence in her diatribe, when the doorbell rang. She got up feeling rather annoyed. Goddammit! I was in the zone, she thought. She walked over to her front door and peeked through the peephole. It was Sallie, of course. Arianna swore under her breath, as she yanked open the door.

"Oh my God, Riann!" she cried, sailing past her into the house. "Oh my God, my premonition came true!"

---

[1] Arianna especially liked the fact that humanity and sanity rhymed.

"Here, sit down." Arianna directed her to the dining room, pulling out a chair for her to sit on. "Now, what happened?" she asked, with a concerned look on her face.

"Gary, Gary from church is dead!" Sallie cried, lowering her head into her hands.

"What? How?" asked a confused Arianna, "I just saw him at the grocery store yesterday!"

"They don't know yet, I just talked to his sister. His housekeeper found him on the dining room floor. They think it might have been a heart attack or a stroke or something. I guess he did have heart problems. This is just too much to take, especially right after Ron's death and everything," she whined. "Oh God, maybe I could have done something!" she added.

"What could you have possibly done to prevent this Sallie? You didn't even know your premonition was about him specifically. Don't beat yourself up," Arianna told her in a reassuring voice. Sallie looked a little less guilty, and wiped the tears from her face. At the same time, Arianna paced back and forth, with a concerned look on her face.

After a minute, she stopped suddenly. "Hmmm," Arianna said, a suspicious tone to her voice.

"What?" asked Sallie.

"It's a little too coincidental that within a few weeks, two members of the Church Council die unexpected deaths, don't you think?"

"What are you saying Arianna?" Sallie asked, her eyes opening wide, "that it was murder?"

"I don't know, have you ever watched the TV show "1000 Ways to Die"?" she asked.

"I don't think so," Sallie thought about it, "what's it about?"

"1000 ways to die, that's what it's about obviously," replied Arianna, irritated. "Anyway, if you watched the show, you'd know there are many different ways to die, most of which you'd never think of in a million years. It might look like a heart attack or some other natural cause, but literally it could have been anything, wasp sting, poisonous blowfish, etc. Who says this isn't murder? Maybe Gary Forrester knew too much, who knows? I just need time to think."

Sallie said, "Ohhh yeah, like on "Seinfeld", when George's fiancée, Susan, died from licking envelopes that had old cheap toxic glue on them."

"Yes!" Arianna nodded, pleased. "Exactly!"

She sat down next to Sallie on one of her straight back dining room chairs, which was upholstered in a beautiful rose colored fabric. However, like almost everything she owned, it unfortunately had been frequently used as a scratching post by Tony and Carmela. The two women sat in silence for five minutes before Arianna broke it.

"Sallie, can you get me a copy of the church financial report?"

"Sure, but why?" she asked.

"I don't know, in Agatha Christie's mysteries, her detectives often point out that murder is always committed because of love or money. If there's a second killing, I've often noticed that it's usually because of fear. I don't know if there's any money motive yet in regards to Ron's death, but the Church finances may hold a clue."

"No problem, I'm on it," replied Sallie.

"Thanks *mon ami*, right now though, I think I need to be alone. You know, to uze 'zee leetle grey zells' " she said, in her best French accent. Sallie looked at her confused.

"Why are you talking in a German accent?"

"It's not German, it's French," she explained, annoyed. Sallie looked at her blankly. "Never mind! I'll talk to you later."

Sallie asked, "I'm a little upset about Gary, Riann. Can I stay here for a while?"

"What do you mean for a while?" she responded warily.

"Just like a couple of hours," Sallie replied.

"Oh," Arianna said with some relief, "sure, no problem."

"Well," she said, feeling somewhat awkward, "I was just about to watch a "House" re-run I've never seen."

"Oh great, I love "House"!" Sallie replied. Arianna was afraid of that, but she felt obligated under the circumstances, being there was a death and all, to be as kind as possible.

"OK, well I have it on my DVR, so I'll just start it now." The two ladies sat on the couch, with Sallie moving uncomfortably close to Arianna. Arianna wasn't sure how to tell her she was invading her personal space, so she just blurted out, "You're invading my personal space."

"What? Oh sorry," Sallie replied, as she moved a millimeter over to the right. Arianna sighed and pressed play.

Within two minutes Sallie started talking, "Do you know I heard Dr. House is really British. Not that House himself is, but the actor who plays him," she explained.

"I knew what you meant," Arianna said shortly. Dr. House had just ridiculed one of his colleagues, and she missed the insult because Sallie was talking. Five minutes later, Sallie got up and started wandering aimlessly in the house, which was distracting Arianna.

"Sallie, did you need anything?" she yelled.

"No, I'm fine, but thanks," she answered, as she walked into the dining room and started petting Tony and Carmela. "What cute cats you have!"

"Thank you," Arianna said curtly, turning her attention back to the T.V.

"I always wanted cats, but my condo association doesn't allow them," said Sallie.

Arianna was thinking, God I wish she would just shut the fuck up. If I take off my shoe and throw it at her, how much trouble would I be in? Would our good relations be irrevocably ruined?

"How old are your cats?" she asked.

"OK," Arianna said, incredibly irked, "I guess I'll try to watch "House" later." She stopped her DVD and turned off the TV abruptly with the remote.

"Oh I'm sorry, I didn't mean to get in the way of your TV watching," Sallie said, embarrassed.

"No problem at all," she lied, "I didn't really feel like watching TV anyway."

After an hour and a half of mundane small talk, Arianna politely, but firmly, escorted her outside and closed the door behind her. Almost immediately, the phone rang. "Hey babe!" is what Arianna heard when she answered.

"Uh Mike, this really isn't a good time," she said, feeling irritable and depressed.

"Listen Riann, I 'm going to leave the station early tonight. Why don't I come over and visit, and you can finally talk to me about what's going on?"

"OK, that's fine, I guess," she said. About a half hour later, Mike rang her doorbell. She answered it and he walked in and immediately wrapped her in a bear hug.

"Good to see …," she managed to squeak out.

Mike was wearing his policeman's uniform, which consisted of navy blue slacks, a light blue button down shirt, and his gold badge. He was looking very handsome, as usual. Arianna tried hard to recall all his bad qualities, like the fact that he was the clingy, affectionate type, and worst of all, prone to PDAs (public displays of affection). Unfortunately, he was wearing Antonio Banderas' "Blue Seduction" *eau de toilette*, her personal kryptonite. That scent was known to make her overcome with lust. She summoned up all her resolve and will power, not to jump his bones.

"All right Mike, sit down," she said, pointing at the couch, "before I tell you everything, I do have one question."

"OK, shoot!" he told her.

"Have you heard about any bad blood or fight between Jay Muster and Ron Dorchester recently?" she asked.

"No, I can't say that I have." "Is that what this is about?" He leaned forward on the couch. "Riann, I'm listening," he said impatiently. Arianna sat down on one of the chairs and spent the next twenty minutes filling him in on all the events of the past week. When she finished, she waited, but he didn't say a word.

"Well?" Arianna asked, "what do you think?"

Mike stood up. "What do I think? I think you and Sallie are both nuts, that's what I think."

"What?" Arianna stood up, "What are you talking about?" she asked in an offended tone.

"What am I talking about?" he asked incredulously.

"Will you stop repeating everything I say!" Arianna demanded.

"I'm talking about the fact that you would even think Ron's death could be anything but an accident. Riann, real life is not like TV. Murders very rarely happen in small towns, and when they do, they're domestic disturbances or the results of a bar fight - open and shut cases."

Arianna raised her voice, "I'm not stupid Mike, don't you think I know that?"

"And why," Mike asked, "would you ever listen to that dumb bimbo Sallie anyway?"

Arianna sighed and sat back down again. "I know Sallie isn't the brightest bulb in the box, but she has a strong intuition. She had a premonition something terrible was going to happen to me the other day, and then Susie moved into the neighborhood! Yesterday, her intuition told her that something very bad was going to happen, and now Gary's dead!" she exclaimed dramatically. Looking at Mike's face, Arianna knew exactly what he thought about her intuition, so she added, "Also, after learning what kind of man Ron was, it seems to me that a lot of people had a motive to kill him, and we know someone from the church made the call to change the catering order." Mike continued to look at her, shaking his head. "And what about Gary?" she asked.

"What about Gary?" Mike responded, "he had a heart attack."
"He had a history of heart trouble," he said, raising his voice.

"You don't think it's suspicious at all – two Council members dead within a couple of weeks?"

"No, I don't," he stated definitively.

"Well, you don't have to act so mean about it!" Arianna replied, her eyes starting to water.

Mike looked at her and said, "Oh I'm sorry baby, don't get upset."

"I'm not upset!" she cried, as tears streamed down her face, to her embarrassment. Mike always felt very uncomfortable when Arianna cried, but this time it worked to her benefit.

"C'mon Riann, please..," Mike begged.

"Mike, you know how hard it's been since the lay-off, Jesus, can you just give me a break?"

"Yes, yes." He walked over to her, pulled her up out of her chair and put his arms around her tightly, which only made her cry more. As mentioned before, he tended to overdo hugs, and she felt as if her heart would pop out of her chest, he was squeezing so hard.

"OK, OK, Mike stop, please!" she pleaded, as she managed to wrestle out of his bear hug.

"Riann, I'll help you any way I can, but you are not, and I'm going to repeat this, you are not going to accuse anyone of doing anything illegal until you talk to me first, understand?"

"Yes, Mike," Arianna replied, as she rolled her eyes, "I understand."

"Good. Hey, if you're really upset, I can stay here if you want," he offered.

"No thanks. I'm fine, thank you for listening." She rushed him to the door. Mike left and afterwards, Arianna leaned against the door for a minute. She took a deep breath. I guess I'm on my own, she thought.

***

Pastor Pete just hung up the phone. He had been talking to Gary Forrester's sister Rose, making arrangements for Gary's memorial service and funeral. "Ashes to ashes, dust to dust.." he recited, trying to remember what words were appropriate for a funeral. He decided he would consult his favorite book, <u>Ministering for Dummies</u>, which he kept handy on the table next to his bed. It had been extremely helpful to him over the years. He often wished they had a pocket-size edition. What a shame about Gary, he thought. The pastor really did like him. Even though he seemed pretty daft at times, Gary did manage to break up the monotony of the Council Meetings. Now, he thought, the meetings will be almost unbearable. He didn't think the Council should try and fill Gary's position. It was only logical that the less people serving on a committee or council, the shorter the meetings. It was Pastor Pete's fervent hope, that someday, the Council would whittle away down to six members. He yawned. He had done more pastoral work in the last two weeks, than he had in his entire tenure at St. James Christian.

He yelled into the next room, "It looks like I won't be home again for dinner tonight, Susan!"

***

Dick Anderson had met his wife, when she was a cocktail waitress at his country club. Her dad had run out on their family when she was in middle school, and her mom was left supporting Shelley and her two older brothers, as a kindergarten teacher. Shelley had a pretty tough life and got in with the wrong crowd when she was younger, especially the wrong men. She had driven her mother crazy back then with her rebellious nature, and Dick believed that Shelley overcompensates with her mother now, for the guilt she harbors over her behavior back then. She also wasn't able to go to college, but this was a subject that was *verboten* by unspoken agreement between the couple. Back when they had been dating, Dick had thought she was cute and liked the way she took charge. Of course, twenty-five years later, that take charge attitude was eventually reinterpreted as bossy. Shelley had just got off the phone with Jodi, her closest friend in the Women's Auxiliary Club, who had informed her of Gary Forrester's untimely death.

"Dick!" she called in a shrill voice.

"Hmmm," he answered from their living room, without taking his eyes off of CSPAN on their 60" wide, wall-mounted, flat screen TV.

"Dick!" she repeated. This time, Dick, dressed in a crimson-colored smoking jacket and holding a pipe, pushed down the recliner footstool with his legs and sat up.

"Yes, honey?" he asked, turning to look at his wife, who had just walked into their living room.

"Gary Forrester just died, apparently of a heart attack," she announced.

"Really?" he reflected for a moment and then said, "well, I bet you're relieved," as he turned back to look at the TV.

Shelley marched over to him furious. "What do you mean? How could you say something so cruel?"

"Oh c'mon darling, he annoyed you to no end, he was always driving you crazy." He looked at her pointedly.

Shelley stared back at him, shocked. "Well of course, Gary *could* be dreadfully tedious at times, but I was fond of him, and I certainly would not wish him dead!" With that, she stalked out of the room.

"Yes dear." Dick fumbled for the remote, switched the TV off and inhaled the smoke from his pipe deeply. It was going to be a long night.

***

Bob Grossman barged through the back door of his house like a wild bull. "Sheryl! Sheryl!" he yelled. He walked into each room looking for his wife, until he finally found her, in her long green and red flannel nightgown, lying on the bed in one of the guest rooms.

"Yes, what is it?" she asked, as she sat up alarmed.

"The Schultzs next door told me that Gary Forrester died!"

"What? How? When?" asked Sheryl, feeling disoriented.

"I don't know," Bob admitted. "They heard it was probably natural causes."

"What? Natural causes? Gary was younger than us!" Sheryl raised her voice, obviously upset.

"Well, maybe it was a stroke or aneurysm or something," he guessed.

"Oh my God!" Sheryl stood up with her hand on her heart, acting as if a stroke might befall her at any moment.

"Honey, please calm down," Bob said firmly, but gently. After a minute, she had calmed herself down and looked at her husband.

"Are you OK now?" he asked. She nodded slowly.

"Good! Now help me look for Pastor's cell phone number. I have some ideas about the readings for the memorial service," Bob said.

***

Ruth Williams was in her backyard, wearing a large straw hat with a white ribbon, a lime green sweater, baggy blue jeans, and green gardening gloves raking leaves. It certainly was a perfect day for it. It was beautiful out, almost like summer. She straightened up, hearing the faint ring of her telephone, and threw down her rake. Someday, she thought, I'm going to get rid of my phone, computer, and all contact with the outside world.

It had been Ruth and Roger's dream to retire to Sedona, Arizona and live in a "Seniors Only" trailer park, with no TV, radio, phone, or computer, and nothing but each other, to keep another company. Of course, that never materialized and Ruth hadn't even considered going ahead with that plan after Roger died. What's the use of anything anymore, she wondered. She managed to pick up the phone in her kitchen on the final ring.

"Yes?"

"Ruth, it's Thomas."

"Thomas, how are you?" she replied, taking her gardening gloves off.

"Fine. Unfortunately, this isn't a social call. I'm calling to let you know about Gary."

"Let me know about Gary?" Ruth repeated.

"Yes, he died yesterday, we presume of a heart attack," Thomas said.

"A heart attack?" Ruth asked, beginning to feel like an echo.

"Yes, Mrs. Cruxmore found him this morning," Thomas stated sadly.

"Well, that would explain why I didn't see him riding his bike today," reasoned Ruth.

"Right, I figure the memorial service might be on Sunday. If you'd like, I can come and pick you up."

"Umm, I guess that would be fine," she replied, sounding a little frazzled.

"OK then, I'll see you Sunday." Thomas signed off. Ruth hung up the phone, put her gloves back on and went back to finish raking her lawn.

***

After hearing about Gary's death, Hannah had decided to go for a long walk to clear her head. The cold air felt good to her today. She called Jay from her cell phone, and he picked up almost immediately.

"Hi Jay, it's Hannah, have you heard the news about Gary Forrester?"

"Yes, I have. One of his neighbors is a frequent customer of mine and he told me. I'm sorry to hear it, I didn't even know he was sick."

"Well, he wasn't really. He did have heart problems in the past, but he was taking medication for it, and as far as I knew, he was rather healthy," Hannah said, her voice cracking.

"Are you okay, Hannah?" asked Jay, sensing something was terribly wrong.

"No, I'm not. I rather liked Gary, even if he could be annoying at times. I'm already missing him."

"Well, I'm sorry. I know you've been through a lot lately," he replied. "Uh, hold on for a minute please, I'm getting another call." A minute later he came back on the line, "Hannah, can I call you back? Jeanne is on the other line."

"No need to Jay, I was just wondering if you knew about Gary, bye now." Hannah ended the call and slipped her phone back into her pocket.

It's funny, she thought, the people we take for granted, when they're gone, we realize how much they really mean to us, and the ones we think we'd be lost without, we find we can live very well without them. Life is full of irony. I went all these years to church, and yet when I ask myself, what do I really believe, I don't even know, she reflected. She wondered, where is Ron right now? Where is Gary? Are they in the same place? Does God really care what we wear to church? Does God even know who goes to church and who doesn't? What is God anyway? So many questions and no answers to speak of, thought Hannah. Sometimes I feel like a hypocrite, repeating by rote all these creeds and prayers, taking part in rituals, singing all these songs, and yet I don't even know what I have faith in. How could Jesus die for sins I hadn't even committed yet?

Hannah felt she had nobody to talk to about these matters. She had little respect for the pastor, which was one thing she and Ron actually agreed on, but he had come highly recommended by the lady bishop and the women at the church he presided over in Michigan. She had a feeling that these recommendations arose mostly because of his looks, and not because of any merit. Hannah felt he was talking out of his ass most of the time. What was life all about anyway? She thought a lot of people just went to church because they believed they were supposed to, and they were all just covering their asses. Others probably attended because it was their only chance for a social life. I think I'm going crazy, Hannah thought. It's probably best not to think of these matters. She took a deep breath and ran the rest of the way back home.

***

Arianna started pondering the case and quickly began to doubt herself, for her sense of self-esteem had not been the best lately. The reason she got laid off in the first place was that the company she had worked for, started a redistribution of all the departments, in order to save money. What that meant was, her department had been basically demolished. She and three other colleagues got let go and her supervisor was now managing another department. Even though her supervisor actually broke down crying when she had to let Arianna go, and everyone assured her it had nothing to do with Arianna's work, abilities or attitude, she had to admit it still hurt. She knew it had nothing to do with her and there was nothing that she could have done, but still... She had been an exemplary employee for twelve years and all she got for it was a three month severance package, now exhausted. Maybe this whole thing IS a total waste of time. Maybe I AM stupid for believing in Sallie's intuition, she reflected. Perhaps Mike is right, maybe she did watch too much TV. She decided to go get Ben and Jerry's "Americone Dream" from her freezer and break out Dame Agatha's, And Then There Were None. This was one of the only books that ever gave her nightmares as a child, and could still give her nightmares today. Even though she's read it numerous times, and of course knew who did it, that never prevented her from deriving enjoyment from it again and again. If intense fear and delicious ice cream couldn't bring her out of her funk, then she didn't know what would.

***

To all outward appearances, the cause of Gary Forrester's death seemed to be natural causes, but nobody would know anything for certain, until the coroner's report came back. Gary Forrester's friends, neighbors, and fellow Church members learned the cause of death was officially heart failure. He had problems with his heart a few years back and was taking Digoxin for it. He had the standard amount of Digoxin in his system, so there was no suspicion of overdose, accidental or otherwise. Foul play was not suspected in the slightest. Nearly everyone who lived in Meadowville knew Gary, including the Meadowville police, and it was beyond anyone's imagination that someone would actually do him harm. Anyone but Sallie and Arianna, that is.

Chapter 21 - Shelley (Thursday)

The next morning, it turned out that Agatha Christie and ice cream had done the trick. Arianna's depressed mood had dissipated and she decided she would continue on with the investigation after all. She drove to the Somerset Hills mall, which was packed, as it was the busiest shopping season of the year. Unlike most women she knew, Arianna hated shopping. She never tried anything on, hence most of her clothes never fit exactly right. They were either too tight or too loose. She despised dressing rooms. She hated the mirrors, the fluorescent lights, everything about them basically. She just greatly loathed having to change clothes in a public place, period. She also loathed large crowds of people, so she wasn't in the greatest mood that morning.

When she arrived, Arianna walked around the mall for five minutes and decided to purchase a Cinnabon and a *Pina Colada* smoothie. The smoothie was delicious, and the Cinnabon she decided, was possibly the most awesome thing she had ever eaten. Hmm, she thought, maybe malls aren't so bad. The glaze from the cinnamon roll got all over her fingers and she was in the process of happily licking them off, when she heard an imperious voice ask, "Aren't you Sallie's friend?"

She looked to her right, and of course, it was Shelley looking at her as if she were a leper. "Yes I am, and you're Shelley?"

"Mrs. Anderson," she answered firmly.

Arianna bit her tongue. "Well, nice to run into you Mrs. Anderson and I'm sorry for your losses."

"Sorry for my losses, what do you mean?" she answered, confused.

"Ron and Gary from St. James Christian Church," Arianna explained.

"Oh, oh yes, well, something was bound to happen with Ron being as heavy as he was. Some people have absolutely no discipline," Shelley said. Arianna was fervently hoping Shelley was the killer, for she was already disliking her intensely.

"And Gary?" Arianna asked.

"Yes, that was a shame," said Shelley, acting as if she didn't care at all.

"Were you close with either of them?" she asked.

"Oh, we served on Council together, I'm sure Sallie's told you, but not really." Shelley looked inside Macy's and said, "I don't see any big sale."

"Big sale?" asked Arianna.

"Yes, Sallie Rigelli told me there was a big sale here between nine and ten-thirty today."

"Oh, she must have been mistaken," answered Arianna.

"Obviously!" said Shelley, annoyed.

Arianna took a deep breath and reminded herself that violence is never the answer. "Have a good day Miss Archer," she told her, and before Arianna could respond, Shelley had walked away.

Chapter 22 - Hannah (Friday)

Arianna had picked Hannah to be the next Council Member she interviewed. She really hoped she had better luck with her than with Shelley. She felt her conversation with Shelley had been a total waste of valuable time. She knew Hannah would probably be immediately suspicious of her because of the whole Jay's Catering debacle, so she figured she'd go jogging in her neighborhood and accidentally run into her, literally, that way. Everyone in town basically knew what garbage day and time was assigned to each neighborhood in Meadowville. Arianna was aware that Hannah's was around 8:30 am on Fridays. Luckily for Arianna, residents were forbidden to put out their garbage cans the night before, as night critters such as raccoons and the like, would tear through everyone's garbage indiscriminately, wreaking havoc. Arianna was an animal lover, but she drew the line at raccoons. They had chewed through numerous pieces of expensive lawn furniture of hers, so she was not a fan.

She planned on getting up super early and jogging near her house at that time, hoping to catch her as she put her garbage cans out. She figured Hannah for a late riser, but she thought she'd get up at 6:00 am, just in case, and get over there at 7:00 am Friday morning. Arianna's alarm went off at 6:00 am, and for a second, she forgot she no longer had a job. For twelve years, she would start work every day at 7:30 am and got up at 6:00. However, now she wasn't used to getting up this early anymore and it was more difficult. It was also pitch black outside, not to mention freezing cold, which only increased her desire to huddle under the covers and fall back asleep.

"Oh fuck!" she said out loud. Arianna loathed cold weather. She believed she must have SAD, (Seasonal Affective Disorder), because she definitely became sadder and crankier during the winter months. She also despised any type of physical activity, except for swimming and bowling. She didn't mind walking, but for this to work, she had to appear as if this was a new jogging routine, and she HATED jogging. She truly believed that jogging caused all of your organs to jostle around, and that if you were a jogger, years later you'd discover that all your organs were in the wrong place. She limped out of bed and turned the heat up higher on the thermostat on her bedroom wall. She walked into her kitchen, made herself a cup of coffee and grabbed a raspberry danish out of the fridge.

After she ate, she washed her face and brushed her teeth. She would usually apply some makeup, even if it was only cover-up and mascara, but she decided if she was going to portray a serious jogger, she better look the part, so sans makeup it was. She opened up her closet and found an old aerobics outfit she wore many years ago, when she wanted to lose some weight. She had bought some VHS tapes of Richard Simmons' "Sweating to the Oldies" at the time, and used to wear that outfit when she worked out to those tapes. Because Arianna never exercised or was interested in anything related to exercise, she was a little out of the loop when it came to "fitness fashion". Consequently, she went outside looking like a much less attractive Olivia Newton John in the video of her 1981 hit song "Physical", complete with sweatband and striped leg warmers.

Arianna was also badly out of shape and became out of breath just from putting on all the layers of her jogging attire. She stood in her bedroom with her legs together and attempted to bend over and touch her toes, but unfortunately got only so far as her knees. Then she stretched her arms above her head and twisted once from side to side. Now that her warm-up was complete, she left the house.

The Dorchesters lived about six blocks away. Arianna planned to actually jog there so that her fake excuse would look more realistic, when she appeared all sweaty and red-faced. She took off jogging and after one block, she was out of breath. After two, her face was bright red. After three, she had worked up a copious sweat, and after that, she appeared as if her demise was imminent. She got about a half a block away from Hannah's house and stopped. Then she bent over, put her hands on her knees, and wheezed for about ten minutes. No sign of Hannah yet, but lots of other people passed by, walking to their cars on their way to work. They all stared at her as if she was an alien from outer space or something, which made her even madder.

After a group of teenagers walked past, looking at her and laughing, she yelled after them, "This will be you in fift, I mean, ten years!"

Eventually, she raised herself up and decided to run past Hannah's house for a half a block to see if she was there. She did that back and forth three times, when Hannah finally came out in a heavy black winter coat with hood. By that time, Arianna was about ready to pass out and almost managed to collide with her. Just in the nick of time, Hannah luckily stepped out of the way.

"Miss Archer?" Hannah said, surprised. Arianna stopped, but couldn't talk. Actually, she couldn't breathe either.

"Huh Huh Huh," she puffed, gasping for air. Shit, she thought, my plan worked and I can't even ask her any questions.

Hannah said, "Oh my goodness, come in the house. You look like you're going to collapse." She helped Arianna walk the footpath that led up to her front door.

"Come in," she offered, as she pushed the door open. Arianna had no choice but to follow her, as she was sure she was going to drop dead at any second. Some detective I am, she thought. Well, if she was going to die, she'd much rather it be in a nice warm house, than sprawled about a public sidewalk in the freezing cold. Hannah pushed her into a chair and pulled off her layers of jackets and sweat clothes. She walked quickly into the kitchen, came out and handed her a bottle of water.

Arianna gulped it down gratefully and managed to utter, "thank you." She really hoped Hannah wasn't the killer for two reasons: 1. She seemed to be very nice, and 2. If she was, then Arianna had played right into her hands, weak, defenseless, and breathless. Hannah could possibly knock her on the head with a frying pan, plunge a kitchen knife into her heart, push her into the fireplace or possibly even poison her... Oh my God she thought, the water! What if.....?

"Miss Archer!" Hannah repeated loudly. "Miss Archer are you okay?"

"Uh, yes I am," Arianna replied, as she was shocked back to reality. "Thank you, I guess I got over winded."

"Over winded?" she repeated incredulously. "You looked like you were going to die. Do you have asthma?" Hannah asked.

"Not that I'm aware of," Arianna replied.

"Well, what were you doing then, if you don't mind me asking?"

"Oh," she explained, "this is my new jogging routine." "I'm trying to lose ten pounds," she lied.

"Honey, maybe you should just concentrate on eating better and forget the exercise. Just a thought," she added.

"Maybe you're right," Arianna agreed. She looked around her. Hannah and Ron had a pretty nice house with a good sized living room, nothing too ostentatious though. She noticed an average sized kitchen with a blue and yellow theme. The living room featured a huge comfortable looking brown recliner with matching couch and loveseat. It also contained the aforementioned potential weapon, a fireplace which was ablaze with a nice, warm crackling fire.

"Well, I should probably go," Arianna told her, very embarrassed. She added, "I'm sorry, I heard about the death of Gary Forrester from Sallie." In response, Hannah looked extremely sad, as if she might burst into tears at any moment. "Oh I'm so sorry, I didn't mean to upset you," Arianna quickly stated, and patted her on the shoulder.

"That's OK, you didn't say anything wrong. His passing was just so sudden, I guess I've taken it rather hard."

"Well of course, coming right after Ron...," Arianna paused, "who could blame you for feeling upset?" "You've been through a lot."

Hannah wiped a teardrop from her eye. "Yes, I guess I have," she agreed.

"Sallie was rather fond of Gary as well," added Arianna.

"Yes," she smiled, "Gary was so child-like, it was hard not to like or at least get a kick out of him."

161

"I had only talked to him a couple of times," said Arianna. "Besides being child-like, what kind of man was he?"

"Gary was very innocent and naive. He only believed the best about people. Unfortunately, people like that seem to always get taken advantage of," Hannah answered.

"Hmmm, yes I would probably agree with you there." "By the way," she remarked, "I didn't even know Gary was sick, he looked pretty healthy to me."

"Well, he wasn't really. He did have some minor heart problems a few years back, and of course, his eating habits weren't exactly the best," responded Hannah.

Arianna recalled his shopping cart at Jewel's and nodded her head vigorously in agreement. There was an awkward silence. "Well, thanks again," Arianna said. They both stood up. She noticed a big picture of a good- looking blond boy on the wall. "Is this your son?" Arianna pointed.

"Yes!" Hannah beamed. "Toby's in college now. He's practically getting straight A's, and he wants to be an architect."

"How nice," Arianna replied with a smile. Hannah walked her out. Arianna thought, oh shit, now I'm going to have to walk the six blocks home. When all this is over, Sallie's going to owe me big time!

Chapter 23 - Bob (Friday)

When Arianna got home, much worse for wear, she jotted a few things about Hannah down in her notebook, took a long shower and then rested a while. Afterwards, she called Sallie. "Hey, can I come over now?"

"Sure, come on over. I have to warn you though, I look horrible. I haven't had a chance to put on makeup or anything."

"Don't worry about that, Sallie."

When she hung up the phone she thought to herself, finally I'm going to get to see Sallie looking less than perfect. When she arrived at her condo though, she was quite disappointed to discover that she barely looked any different than usual. On the other side of the coin, when Arianna one day made the mistake of not wearing makeup to work, half of her coworkers asked if she was exhausted, and the other half thought she had the flu. Life isn't fair, she decided. Arianna sat down at Sallie's kitchen table, which was small and round, and made of white painted wood. Her kitchen was also small, but it was very pretty and quite feminine. She wondered what her bedroom looked like.

"Sallie, I still need to talk to Bob Grossman. Where does he hang out?"

"I have no idea, let me think for a minute," Sallie said in response. After a minute she said, "Hey, why don't you have Mike fake arrest him for something, while you two are out on a date?"

Arianna looked at her, and replied, "Seriously? I don't think so. 1. Mike would never do that. 2. I would never ask him to do that, he's very annoyed at me as it is, and 3. If Bob were arrested, do you honestly think he'd calm down enough, that I could question him about Ron and Gary?"

"Yeah you're right, dumb idea," she answered crestfallen.

"Don't worry Sallie, we'll think of something," Arianna placated her. "Wait, I think I might have something. Can you get me Bob's phone number please?"

"Sure." Sallie went into her bedroom and came out with her Church Council list, handing it to Arianna.

"OK, here goes nothing." Arianna punched in his number on her cell. He picked up on the first ring.

"Hello?" he shouted. She moved the receiver a couple of inches away from her ear.

"Hello Bob?" Arianna asked cautiously.

"Yes?"

"This is Arianna Archer."

"Who?" Bob yelled.

"Arianna Archer," she shouted, "Sallie Rigelli's friend."

"Sallie who?" he yelled again.

"S a l l I e R i g e l l i," she shouted the name back slowly. "I met you the other day at St. James Christian."

There was silence on the other end of the line. "Oh yes, now I remember. Did you need something?" he asked.

"Well, I'm actually thinking of joining St. James."

"You are? Splendid!" he answered.

"Yes, umm I did have some questions though about the Church Council," said Arianna, thinking fast.

"The Council?" he bellowed.

"Yes, I was very active in my old church, and if I joined St. James, I might decide to run for Council. Sallie mentioned you have two openings."

"Yes, but you'd have to talk to the Chair, which is Hannah now, or," he paused, and said in a slightly aggravated tone, "the Vice-Chair, Thomas Manning."

"Yes, I know," explained Arianna, "but I was hoping to talk to someone on the Council to get kind of an impartial view of what goes on there, just to see if it would be up my alley or not." "I already have Sallie's take on it, but I was hoping I could also talk to you for another point of view. Sallie mentioned that you would probably be the most knowledgeable of the Council members," said Arianna, hoping to appeal to his vanity. Sallie shot her an affronted look.

"Well!" Bob exclaimed, flattered, "yes, that Sallie is a fine judge of character." "Sure, why don't you come on over in an hour? I'll bring my binder out. Sheryl is at her brother's house, so we won't have any interruptions."

"Sure," she was taken aback, "umm that would be great, what's your address?" He gave her his address and explicit directions, despite the fact that she told him she didn't need them, and that she was only a mile away.

After they hung up, Sallie looked at her and exclaimed, "What a bunch of BS!"

"Hey, sometimes you have to stretch the truth a little when you're a detective," she explained. "Now how do I find Thomas Manning?" she asked.

"I know Thomas goes to the Royal Pines theater every Friday night with his son, but I don't know which show they go to. Oh! I can call Allen and find out," said Sallie.

"Who's Allen?" Arianna asked, curious.

"Oh, he's my gay BFF," she replied.

"Well, how would he know Thomas's schedule? Oh my God, are you telling me Thomas and Allen are gay lovers?" exclaimed Arianna.

"No," she managed to sputter out, while laughing hysterically. "Thomas's older son Glenn is gay, and Allen knows Glenn, but Thomas doesn't even know Glenn is gay. I'll call Allen right now."

"OK, but don't tell him why we want to know."

"Don't worry, I'm good at lying," Sallie assured her.

She dialed his number and put him on speakerphone, "Hi Allen."

"Oh hi sweetie, I'm just about to leave for a hair appointment, so you're going to have to make it quick," he replied.

"I'm here with my friend Riann."

"Hi Riann!" Allen interrupted her.

"Hi Allen!" Riann shouted back.

"Allen, Riann and I are planning on seeing a movie tonight at the Royal Pines Theater."

"Oh, anything good playing now?" he asked.

"Yes, real good." Sallie looked at Arianna and shrugged. "Anyway, I remember you telling me that Glenn goes with Thomas to the theater every Friday night. Do you know what time they go? We really don't want to take a chance on running into them."

"Oh yes, they always go to the earliest evening show, because then Thomas only has to pay matinee prices. Plus, Glenn says his dad has a pretty early bedtime. You know how old people are."

"Great, thanks Allen. We'll be sure to go to a later show then. Have a good one!"

"Bye Allen!" Arianna yelled, but Sallie had already hung up. Since Royal Pines was a small local theater that only featured one film at a time, the women just looked up the showing times on the theater's website.

"It looks like there's a 5:45, an 8:00, and a 10:15 pm show," said Sallie.

"Well, 5:45 it is," declared Arianna. "Now, I think we should probably plan out how I'm going to run into Dick Anderson. What does he do in his spare time?"

"He's a golf fiend, from what I've heard," replied Sallie.

"Oh?" Arianna looked let down. "He's not going to be going golfing in November. Do you know what club he belongs to?"

"Somerset Hills Country Club," replied Sallie.

"Hmmm," said Arianna, appearing as if she was nurturing an idea.

"What?"

"I think I may have to pay a visit to the club," Arianna explained.

"Are you a member?" Sallie asked, puzzled.

"No, but I know someone who is." A minute later, Arianna pulled out her cell phone and made a call.

"Stevenson," he answered.

"Hey Mike, I need a big favor," she said sweetly.

"Wonderful, is that all you call me for? I'm beginning to feel used," he replied, pretending to sound victimized.

"I'm sorry Mike, please, this is important," Arianna pleaded.

"OK, what is it?" he asked warily.

"First, would you please call your brother Matt and ask him what days Dick Anderson goes to the Somerset Hills Country Club? It's part of my investigation," she added.

"Yeah, I gathered that. It shouldn't be a problem."

"Great! And there's one more thing," she paused.

"Yes? I'm waiting..."

"Once we find out, you and I need to go there as guests of your brother," she said meekly, afraid of his reaction.

"What?" he replied, sounding quite irked.

"Just please ask him for me? And please do this now, I'm at Sallie's and we're both waiting."

"Oh brother, you're going to be the death of me Riann!" He hung up. Five minutes later, he called back, just as Arianna was beginning to get impatient.

"OK, Matt doesn't know all the days and times he goes, because he's not a STALKER Riann," he told her pointedly. "However, he's definitely there on Saturdays at noon, because Matt plays racquetball at that time, and that's when Dick eats lunch," he added.

"Wow that's great, thanks Mike!" Arianna replied enthusiastically. Sallie listening, clapped her hands and smiled. "Umm OK, now can you please ask Matt if we can come as his guests, the next time he plays racquetball? You can just tell him I need to talk to Dick regarding church business."

"Geez Riann, how am I supposed to fit this little escapade into my busy schedule?" Mike whined.

"It would only be like an hour. We'll eat at the restaurant in the club, and then I can see Dick and talk to him." "My treat," she quickly added.

"You know perfectly well you can't afford to treat me and you know Matt will pick the check up anyway, so cut the bullshit," he replied.

"Well, it's not my fault the Stevenson men are so kind and generous," she answered him flirtatiously. Mike groaned in response.

Sallie whispered, "yay!" in the background.

"Listen hon, I really do have to get off the phone, gotta go process a B&E."

"OK, thank you! Go take care of your B&E. See you at 11:45 am tomorrow at the club then. Let me know if there are any problems," said Arianna excitedly. Mike groaned again and hung up. Yes, Arianna thought, as she put her cell phone back in her pocket, everything is coming together nicely. She looked up to see Sallie grinning at her mischievously.

Sallie asked, "B&E?"

"Breaking and Entering," she replied. "Now stop smiling at me, we've got work to do," she told Sallie sternly. "What about Sheryl Grossman? Do you know where I might run into her? I saw her at Jewel the same day I ran into Gary, and I was able to talk to her a little about Ron, but I'd like to hear her thoughts on Gary. Maybe we can find out if she has a set grocery shopping day?"

Sallie sat down at the kitchen table and thought for a minute. "Sheryl does go to the doctor a lot. I think she has migraines or something."

"Oh yeah, that's right. Do you know which doctor?" Arianna asked.

"Oh jeez, yes I do, it's just not coming to me, give me a minute."

"Don't worry about it," she said, "it'll come to you when you're not thin..."

"Dr. Halden," Sallie interrupted, "yes that's it."

Arianna pulled out her phone again. "Great, let me look him up on the internet. I hope there's not more than one in the area. Yay, we lucked out, there's one Dr. James Halden in Meadowville, a general practitioner. The number is 555-207-1685. I'll call his office now." She punched in the number.

"What are you going to say?" asked Sallie.

"Just listen," she whispered, as she covered the mouthpiece of the receiver. "Yes, hello. I'd like to see if I can get a later appointment, this is Mrs. Sheryl Grossman." Arianna tried to remember what her voice sounded like. She seemed to recall it was pretty nasally, so she pretended she had a cold.

"Sure," answered the pleasant receptionist, "is this for Dr. Halden?"

"Yes, it is," she replied. A minute passed.

The receptionist came back on the line. "Is this for your Saturday appointment?" she asked.

"Yes," said Arianna, holding her breath.

"Well, we have you down for 3:45 pm. That's the latest appointment we have, I'm sorry," she apologized.

"Oh, OK," she backtracked, "for some reason, I thought I had made an earlier appointment. 3:45 is fine, thank you." She hung up and high-fived Sallie. "Oh yeah, we struck gold! Looks like I'm going to the doctor," she told her, feeling victorious. "I'm off to Bob's now, thanks for all your help."

"Good luck!" Sallie wished her happily, as she walked her to the door.

A few minutes later, Arianna arrived at Bob Grossman's house. He was standing in the doorway, behind the screen door, already waiting for her. She sighed and thought, what am I in for? Bob and Sheryl Grossman lived in an average sized, middle class Meadowville dwelling. She noticed their shades were drawn on every window. Probably because of Sheryl's migraines, she figured. They lived on a corner, and so they had a pretty big side lot to their Georgian style house.

"Hello there, come in, come in," Bob said, welcoming her. He motioned for her to sit down on a rocking chair in their living room. Their living room had a lot of pictures of, what she assumed was their children, on the walls. He took a seat on the sofa and began pulling paper after paper out of his giant binder, which was lying open on their coffee table. Arianna breathed out slowly, and tried to mentally reassure herself that it wouldn't be so bad.[1] Unfortunately, Bob spent the next thirty-five minutes ranting about issue after issue, blaming Ron Dorchester most of the time for everything under the sun. Finally, when he paused a minute to breathe, Arianna took her chance.

"So, I'm gathering you didn't think Ron was a good Council Chair?" she asked.

"That's right. Look, I had nothing personal against the guy, he just made a lot of stupid decisions, that's all," he explained.

---

[1] She was wrong.

"Did anyone on the Council like Ron?" she asked. "Ruth? Shelley?"

"Ruth is crazy, all she cares about is that damn library, and no, I doubt she liked him. I doubt anyone liked him."

"I've heard that Gary was pretty easy to get along with though, is that right?" she asked.

"Oh yes, everybody loved Gary, except for Ron. Gary bugged him," he said.

"Bugged him?" Arianna repeated.

"Yeah, Gary was dumber than a box of rocks," Bob sneered, "if you don't mind me saying so, and Ron had no patience with him." "He was also very naive."

"How so?" asked Arianna.

"He was just so gullible, people could take advantage of him very easily," he explained.

"That's interesting. Well Bob, thank you so much for your time. I'm going to really think this over in the next few days, and hopefully make a decision soon." She stood up and he walked her to the door.

"OK, please feel free to call me. You have my number right?" Arianna nodded, not bothering to remind him she was the one who called him. She walked quickly over to her car. I'm going to need a stiff drink after this, she thought.

Chapter 24 - Thomas (Friday)

That evening, which was unusually cold and frigid, even by Chicago's standards, Arianna headed off to the theater. She wasn't too happy about it, since a really ridiculous horror movie was playing, but she decided that she'd take one for the team, so to speak. She got there pretty early so she wouldn't miss Thomas and his son, and ended up freezing her butt off in the process. She stood there waiting impatiently, hands deep in her coat pockets rocking back and forth, exhaling and watching her breath. A half hour later, the men appeared. Thank God, there they are, Arianna thought. She noticed Glenn was just a taller, younger version of his dad, poor guy.

She walked up to them. "Hello, aren't you Thomas from St. James Christian?"

"Why yes, you're Sallie's friend, right?"

"Yes, I am," she answered.

"Well, I won't hold that against you, ha ha," he said, chuckling. Glenn looked uncomfortable. "This is my son, Glenn." The two nodded hello at each other.

"So I see you're going to the 5:45 showing as well," said Arianna.

"Yes, why don't you join us young lady?" suggested Thomas.

"Oh, that would be great," she replied.

This is going to be easier than I thought, Arianna said to herself. Then she noticed Thomas smiling at her and nudging Glenn. Uh oh, he's going to try and get us both together, that's why he's acting so nice. Well, this might work to my advantage, she thought, but poor Glenn! They paid for their tickets, and sat in one of the back rows, with Thomas making sure that his son and Arianna were next to each other. There wasn't much time to chat before the movie, and the movie, as Arianna had expected, was horrible. Afterwards, they made their way through the crowd out of the theater.

"Well, that was fun!" Arianna lied cheerfully.

"Yes, it was," Thomas agreed.

Arianna took her chance and remarked, "I heard about Gary Forrester, what a shame."

"Yes, especially coming immediately right after Ron's death. It leaves two holes on the Church Council," he explained.

"Oh right, I guess it does," Arianna replied. Glenn appeared bored and kept looking around him, while the two were talking. "Were you close to Ron and Gary?" she asked.

"Of course, great men, the both of them," he quickly replied. "The church will sure miss them."

Arianna raised her eyebrows, looking surprised. "Really? I was under the impression from Sallie that Ron wasn't well-liked within the church." Arianna was really wishing the TV show, "Lie to Me" was still on the air. That show was very helpful when it came to figuring out if someone was lying or not. Oddly enough though, she really didn't need it with Mike. Even though he was a cop, he was pretty transparent. Hmm, maybe writing another letter to a TV producer is in order, she thought.

"Well, Sallie might not have cared for Ron, but that wasn't my experience," he replied, acting surprised.

"OK Dad, I think I better get you home now." Glenn started rushing him to the theater exit.

"Oh, I think we have some time Glenn," Thomas said, patting his arm. "Glenn works in the city as a financial analyst. He makes a good living," he commented, then nodded at Arianna.

"Dad!" Glenn exclaimed, embarrassed. Thomas ignored him. "He's a very good son and he'll make a great husband and father someday." Arianna started choking on some Jujubes she was in the middle of eating.

"Are you OK?" they both asked her at once.

"Yes, I'm fine," she said, while in the middle of a major coughing fit.

"As I was saying, he will make a great husband and father someday." Glenn now appeared mortified, and was slowly inching away from them.

"I'm sure he will, but I go to bed pretty early, so I really need to get going," said Arianna, feeling quite uncomfortable.

"Oh OK, are you in the phone book Arianna? Just in case one of us wants to call you?" Glenn was pretending not to hear his father, and was already walking swiftly towards his car.

"Uh yes I am, under Arianna Archer, excuse me have a great night!" she yelled, practically running to her car. She was afraid if she stayed one minute longer, he would start making arrangements for their wedding. Before driving off, Arianna took a minute to write down her impressions of Thomas in her notebook.

"Oh my God!" she complained to Sallie on her cell when she got back home, "that was brutal!"

"What happened?" Sallie asked eagerly. Arianna reported back everything that had occurred at the theater, to Sallie's amusement, resulting in a full two minutes of hysterical laughter, at Arianna's expense.

Chapter 25 - Dick (Saturday)

At precisely 11:45 am the next morning, Arianna drove to the Somerset Hills Country Club, wearing a red long-sleeved blouse with a couple of the buttons undone, to reveal a black cami underneath, paired with a black skirt and red slingbacks. To her surprise, both Matt and Mike were already there, standing in front of the club talking with each other. Matt and Mike had a very good relationship. Mike was the oldest of a family of four children, with two brothers and one sister. Matt was the second in line and had done very well for himself. He had become a dentist, married a wonderful lady, and had two lovely teenage daughters. He had been a member of the Somerset Hills Country Club for years.

Arianna noticed that Matt had on a nice pair of black slacks and a white polo shirt with black designer gym shoes. Mike, on the other hand, to Arianna's great dismay, was wearing a bright yellow T-shirt, very worn blue jeans, and a pair of old gym shoes. She was quite irked because she felt this was his passive-aggressive way of upsetting her, to get her back for all the stuff she had put him through lately, and she was not amused.

"Hey Matt, nice to see you!" Arianna exclaimed and hugged him. Matt and Mike looked absolutely nothing alike. Matt's light brown hair had no grey in it at all, and he was clean-shaven with brown eyes. The only thing similar between them was that they were both around the same height, six feet tall.

"Nice to see you too Riann!" Matt exclaimed. Arianna frowned at Mike while he smiled exaggeratedly at her. "So," Matt asked, as they all walked inside the club, "you have some business, I gather from Mike, with Dick Anderson?"

"Yep, that's right," said Arianna, with a guilty look at Mike.

"Did you ever think of just calling him?" asked Matt with a grin. Mike shot her a self-satisfied look.

"Um, well it's complicated," she explained.

"I guess so, well come along then." "Richard," Matt said to the young gentleman standing at the front desk when they walked in, "please put down Mike Stevenson and Arianna Archer as my guests today. They will be dining in the Chamber Room at noon."

"Oooh the Chamber Room," Arianna whispered to Mike, as he made a face.

"Why certainly," Richard replied, with a smile.

"And make sure their lunch goes on my bill," Matt added.

"Will do," said Richard.

"Why that's so nice and generous of you Matt, thank you so much," Arianna said in her sweetest voice possible.

"No problem, just keep my brother out of trouble," he told her, as he winked and walked away.

"Thanks Matt!" Mike shouted after him. As soon as he was out of earshot, Mike turned and imitated her, "'Why that's so nice and generous of you!'" in a *falsetto* voice.

"Oh shut up, you're getting a free lunch out of it too, so don't complain. See, who says there's no such thing as a free lunch?" she added cheerfully. Mike groaned and followed her to the entrance of the Chamber Room.

The restaurant was furnished with beautiful dark wood-paneled walls and crystal chandeliers hanging from the ceiling. Every table had fresh flowers, a white linen tablecloth, red linen napkins, and crystal goblets for water and wine. Soon the *maitre d'* escorted them both to a big comfortable-looking booth, which faced huge arched windows, providing a view of a beautiful lake surrounded by giant oak trees.

"Isn't this magnificent?" Arianna gushed. Mike made a "hmmph" sound in reply. As they perused the menu, she suddenly exclaimed, "There he is!"

Mike turned around to see the sophisticated-looking, tall and thin man with graying hair and glasses.. "So what are you going to do now Columbo?" Mike asked her.

"Columbo? Why don't you try entering the twenty-first century and compare me to a detective who's still relevant?" she said sarcastically. "I am going to pretend I just noticed him and walk over to his table. You stay here," she ordered him firmly.

"Aye aye Captain," he saluted her, and turned his attention back to the menu.

She walked over to Dick's table. "Hello, aren't you from Sallie Rigelli's church, St. James Christian?" she asked.

"Yes I am, young lady," he replied, as he put out his hand, "Dick Anderson at your service." Dick was wearing a white polo shirt with a beige sweater wrapped around his neck, beige pants and brown designer loafers.

"Oh yes, Dick, I'm Arianna Archer, I met you Sunday."

"Of course," he said smiling. "I'm dining alone today, would you care to join me?" he gestured to one of the open chairs.

"Well sure, I am with a friend of mine though." She pointed to Mike. Mike waved dramatically at them, to Arianna's chagrin.

"Oh," he answered, appearing slightly let down. "Well, yes please feel free to have him come over as well."

"Wonderful! I'll go get him," she exclaimed. She quickly walked over to Mike and practically dragged him over to Dick's table, while whispering, "be nice and stay quiet."

"Yeah, yeah," he replied. "

Dick," Arianna gestured, "this is my friend Mike. Mike, Dick." The two men shook hands.

"Sit down," Dick said to both of them. "Do you two belong to this club?" he asked.

"No," Arianna answered, "Mike's brother Matt does, we're his guests for the day. He's playing racquetball right now."

"Oh, are you Matt Stevenson's brother?" Dick asked. Mike paused, and looked at Arianna as if he was asking for her permission to speak. She shot him a dirty look.

"Yes, Matt's my younger brother," he told Dick.

"Oh, nice man, I've talked to him a few times. He's a chiropractor isn't he?"

"Dentist," Mike corrected him.

"Oh, that's right," he replied. The waiter came by and Arianna told him that he and Mike were moving to Dick's table and to make sure that their lunches were on Matt. Dick quickly said, "Oh no need, just put them both on my bill."

Mike spoke up, "That's very generous of you, but my brother owes me big time for a bunch of old childhood pranks, so I'm going to make sure he will be paying the bill." They all laughed. Arianna took advantage of the free meal, by ordering a *filet mignon*- medium, a baked potato - loaded, a side of corn and a Caesar salad with a chocolate shake. Mike shot her an amused look as she ordered, but wisely said nothing.

"So," Arianna broached the subject, "I heard about Gary Forrester's death, I'm so sorry."

"You did? Oh I suppose Sallie told you."

"I'm sure it was quite a shock,..." she said, trying to lead him.

"Yes it was, but frankly, if you're a man over fifty you have to get used to friends dying unexpectedly." Mike, being fifty-one, had a disconcerted expression on his face, which Arianna admitted she took some delight in.

"Was he sick at all?" she asked, pretending to be concerned.

"Not that I was aware of. If he was, he never talked about it," he replied.

"I'm sure, especially coming right after Ron's death, it must have been upsetting to everyone."

"Well, the reactions to each of their deaths were much different," explained Dick.

"What do you mean?" she asked.

"Ron was not well-liked," he explained.

"Oh? Any particular reason?" she replied, trying to sound surprised.

"He was," Dick paused, "a man of very low-caliber." Mike and Arianna looked at each other and waited. "Ron easily rubbed people the wrong way. He knew exactly what would anger or upset a person and he would needle them by pushing those buttons," he explained. "Ron liked to play with people's minds. Sometimes he'd say things, just to see their reaction. For example, he'd threaten to do things to get people upset, but wouldn't go through with them. He liked to make people squirm."

"It seems like he was quite cruel," said Arianna.

"He was just emotionally immature. I felt sorry for him most of the time," he replied.

"Sorry for him?" she repeated.

"Why yes," Dick said, "he obviously felt the only way he could get any attention was to be nasty. He probably had a second-rate upbringing, in my opinion."

Arianna couldn't think of anything else to say without arousing suspicion, so she let Mike and Dick talk about the economy, a subject she found incredibly boring. It ranked right up there with sports, in her opinion. About twenty minutes later, their food had arrived and the conversation ceased. She thought she'd died and gone to heaven, it was the best steak she ever had. It was obvious Mike loved his well-done prime rib, sans mushrooms, as well, because he was smiling and making "mmm" noises while he was eating.

When they finished, Dick asked, "Will you be having dessert?"

Arianna was just about to say yes, when Mike cut in, "No, we can't, unfortunately there are criminals that need catching."

"Oh?" he replied, startled, "are you a policeman?"

"Yes, he is," said Arianna, shooting Mike a dirty look, as she stood up. "It was so nice to see you Dick, maybe I'll see you at St. James Christian again sometime."

"That would be nice," Dick replied, while standing up and shaking their hands goodbye.

"Why did you do that?" "I wanted dessert!" she said, quite upset, as soon as they were out of earshot.

"Yeah I know, but I only have so much patience. Geez Riann, you owe me big time!"

"Yeah, yeah, it sure looked like the free meal was torture for you, especially while you were eating your ginormous prime rib!"

He ignored her comment. "Well, did you get what you needed?" he asked.

"I suppose so, I'm at least forming better impressions of everyone anyway." "Did Matt drive you here?" she asked, as they walked through the parking lot towards her car.

"Yes, I told him you would be happy to drive me home," he replied, grinning.

"Oh you did, did you?" Arianna was afraid of that. She did not want to be invited in, because she was trying to resist the temptation of something starting up between them again. She had enough problems right now. Although, to be honest, his attire was such a big turn-off, that she didn't think she had to worry about it too much.

As she was driving him home, she complained, "Oh by the way, I'm so glad you decided to dress up for the occasion. Seriously though, did you have to wear that crappy outfit?"

"Do you know who you're talking to young lady? I'll have you know I am CHIEF of Police, show a little respect!" he jokingly replied. Arianna just sighed and shook her head with exasperation.

Ten minutes later, she pulled up to his little red brick ranch house. Mike's home was pretty small - two bedrooms, one bathroom, and no dining room, just a kitchen. It was nice; nevertheless, and he kept it relatively clean, or to be more accurate, the young Russian girl who came in periodically did.

"Thanks again Mike, for everything," she said, turning her head to look at him.

"Don't mention it, you wanna come in?" he offered.

"I'll take a pass today, maybe next time," Arianna declined.

"OK then, see you later," he said, as he shut the car door and walked away. Arianna reached into her purse and retrieved her notebook. As she jotted down her impressions of Dick, she shook her head and thought, poor guy, he gets to go home to Shelley.

Chapter 26 - Sheryl (Saturday)

A few hours later, Arianna drove her Cavalier up to a big brown medical building on the corner of Oak and Pine in Meadowville. She

182

walked up to the door and scanned the building directory. Dr. Halden was on the first floor. Thank God, she thought, after that jogging fiasco, I don't want to have to exert myself physically for at least a month! She had decided to get there at 4:00 pm and lurk around the outside of the office, waiting for Sheryl to come out after her appointment. At 4:30 pm precisely, Sheryl exited the doctor's office, wearing a soft pink babushka over her shoulder-length blonde hair, which happened to match her heavy pink coat and gloves nicely.

"Sheryl!" she tried to sound surprised, "you go to Dr. Halden too?"

"Uh yes," Sheryl seemed slightly disoriented, "I'm having problems with vertigo at the moment."

"Oh, what a shame," Arianna replied, "I'm having problems with ummm, gout." Arianna, wishing again that she had thought this through and decided on a malady ahead of time. Mike suffered with gout every so often, and so that was the first thing that popped into her head.

"Gout? Aren't you a little young for that?" Sheryl asked quizzically.

"Yeah, well you would think so!" Arianna replied, attempting to sound annoyed and in pain, "It's driving me crazy, my toe is killing me!" She raised up her right foot convincingly to make the point. Arianna always believed the theatre lost out on a great star when she decided to go into the book distribution industry instead.

"Well yes, I've been coming to Dr. Halden for many years. I don't think I've ever seen you here before," said Sheryl.

"I'm a new patient. I had my appointment earlier, but I lost one of my gloves and I just wanted to see if I left it here."

"Oh, well you better go now, they're closing soon," replied Sheryl.

"I will. By the way, I'm so sorry about Gary. Sallie told me," she explained.

"Yes, it's a real tragedy. Gary was a long-time church member and much beloved by the community," she said, looking upset.

"I know, what a shame. He certainly didn't look sick when I met him."

"Yes, you would have thought Gary could have lived forever," said Sheryl, in a far-away voice.

"You were pretty fond of him then?" asked Arianna.

"Of course, who wasn't fond of him?" asked Sheryl, looking surprised.

"Right, well I better go back and ask about my glove," she said opening the door.

"I've got to get going as well." "I hope you feel better," Sheryl said, as she fumbled in her purse for her car keys.

"Feel better? Oh yes, my gout, thanks!" replied Arianna, as she walked into the doctor's office, waited a minute and walked back out.

Hmm, she thought, as she made her way to her car. Sheryl appeared to be genuinely fond of Gary, as did most of the Council Members. This case is proving to be quite difficult. Now that I've talked to all of them, I really need to try and determine if Gary's death really was due to natural causes, or if it was helped along by someone. I really need to get a hold of his medication. Arianna's face suddenly lit up. I think I know just how to do that.

Chapter 27 - The Brunch (Sunday)

On Sunday, five days after Gary's death, his sister Rose held a brunch at Gary's house, immediately after the memorial service. It was NOT provided by Jay's Catering, whose business, not surprisingly, had severely dropped off since Ron's death. The brunch was very well-attended, and as expected, all the Church Council Members made an appearance.

Sallie was dressed in black, appropriate for the occasion, and her dress was actually a conservative length, which was quite the rarity. The fact that her neckline was so low; however, combined with the success of the push up bra she was wearing, ensured that her cleavage was center stage. This unfortunately deflected from the rest of her attire. As soon as she got there, she found Arianna and gave her the copy of the church finances that she had asked for. Now she was sitting on Gary's couch, drinking a glass of *Moscato d'Asti*, her favorite wine. Gary's sister sure has good taste, she thought.

Meanwhile Arianna, dressed in a long-sleeved black casual dress with a silver belt and two silver barrettes pinning her hair up and back on the sides, was thinking the same thing. This is one awesome spread. Shrimp cocktail, lots of deli sandwiches, including; ham, roast and corned beef, slices of turkey breast, an assortment of cheeses, angel hair pasta with choice of *alfredo* or meat sauce, green salad which included; romaine lettuce, red cabbage, carrot shavings, plum tomatoes, and red onions, mixed with what appeared to be balsamic vinaigrette dressing, and fresh bread on the side. For dessert, there was cherry pie and fudge brownies. Arianna, in seventh heaven, was rapidly filling up her plate, but couldn't help also noticing the giant bowls of candy sitting on Gary's coffee table. Thank goodness I'm wearing a dress with deep pockets, she thought greedily.

Shelley and Dick Anderson sat off by themselves in a corner of the dining room, looking quite bored, especially Dick, who could think of at least ten places he'd rather be than there. Hannah was standing nearby, looking pensively out a lovely bay window in the dining room. Rose Forrester, Bob, whose clothes actually matched,[1] and Sheryl Grossman, sporting a black babushka over her blond hair, were talking to one another in the kitchen.

Actually Bob was talking, Sheryl and Rose were pretending to be listening. Sheryl's mind was quite preoccupied at the moment. The two recent deaths made her painfully aware of her own mortality. She also felt a tremendous sense of guilt. She believed that she should have made much more of an effort to be friendly to Gary. True, she was always nice and polite to him, but she felt she always, like most of the Council, treated him like a nuisance, rather than a "friend in Christ Jesus", as Pastor Pete would say.

At the same time, Pastor Pete was looking quite dashing in a grey suit with a silver and blue striped tie. To all the ladies' dismay, he had brought his wife, who was wearing a very pretty purple maternity dress and sporting a cute little baby bump. Craving sweets, she had her hand wrist deep inside a bowl of black licorice. The couple was in the middle of a conversation about everything baby with Gary's next-door neighbors, who were also with child. Lorraine and Ruth were standing awkwardly next to each other in the hallway, evidently trying to escape the crowds of people hovering about in the living and dining rooms.

Lorraine looked over at Ruth and said politely, "The St. James Library looks wonderful, by the way."

Ruth glowing, replied, "Yes, thank you. Roger would be proud." Ruth then felt obligated, so she asked Lorraine about the Sunday Church School.

[1]Everyone assumed (correctly) that he had allowed Sheryl to pick out his attire that day.

186

"Well," Lorraine began, "we are knee-deep in Christmas play rehearsals and it is NOT going well, I tell you." "We have no money in the budget for decent costumes. The sheep costumes cost too much, so we've had to resort to pasting cotton balls all over the preschool children." She sighed and threw up her hands, looking disgusted.

Ruth said, "Now that Ron is gone, why don't you just ask the Finance Committee to reconsider the budget?" "All you would have to do is convince Pastor and Hannah, and you'll get your money."

"Oh, is that all?" asked Lorraine sarcastically. "I am not going to beg," she added. "It'll just be evident to the parents, how little St. James Christian cares about their children!" declared Lorraine triumphantly, as usual deriving pleasure out of being a martyr.

"Will you excuse me?" asked Ruth in response, successfully making her escape, as she walked through the dining room over towards Hannah.

"How are you doing dear?" she inquired, placing a hand on Hannah's shoulder. Hannah turned to face her.

"Oh hello Ruth, I'm doing all right. Of course, sometimes it's easy to forget that Ron is gone."

Ruth sighed in response, and said, "Yes, I know very well what that's like." The two of them stood there together for a while enjoying the silence, and watching the last of the beautiful red, brown, and amber-gold leaves drift down from the Maple trees in Gary's front yard.

Meanwhile, Thomas Manning was in a very good mood. The fact that he was now Vice-Chair filled him with a sense of power that he never had before. Oh I wish Wanda was alive to see this, but such a shame about Gary of course, he thought. He was always so full of life, such a shock to see him lying there in that royal-blue, satin-lined casket so, so.. lifeless. Thomas was in the buffet line filling his plate. His glasses kept sliding down his greasy nose and so he pushed them back repeatedly with his right index finger. He looked up to see Sallie Rigelli sitting on the couch resembling, in his opinion, the Whore of Babylon. Noticing him staring at her, she waved exaggeratedly at him. He ignored her, looking down at his now overflowing plate. *Sallie certainly likes to dance with the Devil, doesn't she? Well, at least now that Ron is gone and I'm Vice-Chair, I might have another chance to motion for the Dress Code to be reinstated again*, he thought optimistically. Thomas smiled, he was imagining how wonderful it would be when he was no longer subjected to such filth during the weekly Sunday Church Service.

At the same time, Arianna was taking, probably the only opportunity she would ever have, to snoop around Gary's bathroom, which incidentally had a plethora of very interesting reading material in it. A basket full of National Enquirers, Stars, People Magazines, Weekly World News and other tabloids sat next to the commode. The bathroom also featured a beautiful lion claw bathtub that she'd kill for. Unfortunately, Arianna had a mission to accomplish, specifically to search Gary's medicine cabinet, otherwise she'd be locked in there taking advantage, and perusing through the latest gossip. Luckily, she quickly found his prescribed heart medication and slipped it into her purse. Afterwards, she went to find Rose to thank her for her hospitality, and again offer her condolences.

She left Gary's house and made her way quickly to her Cavalier. When she got home from the brunch, the first thing Arianna did was look through the church financial report that Sallie had given her. After about fifteen minutes, she threw the file on her dresser and came to the conclusion that was a total dead end. Next, she searched her bookshelves for her giant Physicians Desk Reference (PDR), which she originally bought to look up various medications and poisons that were featured in the murder mysteries she read. She flipped through numerous pages, until she found Digoxin. Then she poured Gary's pills out onto her bed. She looked first to make sure the pills were all the same, which they were. *Hmmm, yes they all appeared to be Digoxin as well. Guess that theory's shot to hell*, she thought. She lied back on the bed and sighed, but then remembered, candy! She sat up and emptied her pockets onto the bed and looked over her booty.

Arianna was suddenly struck by an idea. She thumbed through the PDR again, until she found what she was looking for, and then shut it and put it away. Then Arianna took out her notebook, in which she had recorded her impressions of all of the suspects, and the results of all the background checks. She sat down on the antique rocking chair in her bedroom, which had once belonged to her great-grandmother and read through the entire notebook. Then she closed her eyes and put her hands together in front of her chest, making a triangle with the fingertips of each hand touching the other. She rocked back and forth in silent meditation. The rhythmic sound of the rocking chair lulling her into a calm, peaceful state.

Fifteen minutes later, she abruptly stopped rocking. "Yes," she said aloud, opening her eyes, "of course!" Her face broke into a wide grin.

***

Lorraine arrived home after Gary's memorial service and brunch, absolutely exhausted. The events of the last two weeks had definitely taken their toll on her. Ralph was at work and so Lorraine decided that now was a good chance to catch up on her e-mail, as most of the time when Ralph wasn't monopolizing the television set, he was hogging their computer. She only had three e-mails, and on all of them the subject line read, "LORRAINE DO YOU WANT A LONGER STRONGER PENIS?" Sometimes, she thought Thomas was right, this world has gone insane. She decided to log onto Facebook. Her two daughters had accounts there, and sometimes that was the only way she knew what was going on in their lives, She saw that Bethie and a good-looking boy named Andrew had just broken up. Bethie didn't seem to be too upset about it, as she just posted several pics of her and her girlfriends partying it up at some nightclub. All of a sudden, Lorraine felt very sad and lonely and wished Ralph wasn't so cheap, so they could go and visit the girls.

Her daughters were always extremely close, and when they were younger, it was their dream to move to California someday. Tessa was always a good singer and had hoped she would make it big out there, but since hundreds of other girls with good voices were hoping the same, she ended up going to beauty school instead. Now, she was doing hair during the day and working singing gigs at night. Bethie worked as a dental hygienist in a small dentist's office in West Los Angeles. Lorraine had been out there twice to visit them. They had a very small apartment together, and so Lorraine was forced to stay in a cheap motel both times she was there. Well, at least I'll see them at Christmas she thought, her mood brightening considerably.

She noticed she had a Facebook message and that it was from one of the SCS teachers, Linda. It said: "Lorraine I'm sorry, but this is a very stressful time of year for me, and I don't have the time or energy to attend another SCS meeting this month. Can we please postpone these until after the first of the year? Thanks!" Lorraine was livid. She already had to cancel the one in October, because only one SCS teacher, Marcia had shown up. Lorraine believed in having a meeting every month, so the fact that Linda wanted to go three months without one, drove her up the wall. Seriously?, she thought. Sometimes Lorraine wondered why she even bothered. She logged off and decided she'd take a nap, and then probably go to the church later and check to see if they had enough supplies in all of the classrooms. She kicked off her shoes and headed for her bedroom, her head throbbing. Right then, the telephone rang. Oh this is just great, what is this, she thought, more bad news?

"Hello, this is Lorraine," she answered, with a slight tinge of irritation.

"Hello Lorraine, this is Rose Harmon, Gary Forrester's sister," she paused, "you were just at my brunch."

"Yes of course, is something wrong?" Lorraine asked, confused.

"No, not at all, I was just wondering. My brother left a cat Snickers and unfortunately, I'm allergic to cats, and I really don't want to have to put him in a shelter," Rose said.

"OK, I'm not sure I understand," she replied.

"I was hoping that perhaps you wouldn't mind taking him. You seemed like someone that I could trust with him. There are a lot of people who don't like animals, but you didn't appear to be one of those people," she explained.

"Oh, well yes, I mean, we had a cat for many years, Moonlight, but he died from renal failure a few years back. We don't have any pets now, but I still have all his stuff down in the basement....," her voice trailed off. "Sure, I can do it," Lorraine said firmly, with a tinge of joy in her voice.

"Wonderful! I have your address from Gary's Church Council Contact List, so if it's all right, I can come over now. I can even bring the cat food and kitty litter that Gary had left over in his pantry."

"Now? Uh yes, sure that would be fine, thanks!" she said. Lorraine hung up, and with a burst of excited energy, ran down into the basement to look for Moonlight's feeding bowls and kitty litter box.

***

Thomas dropped Ruth off at home after the memorial service. As soon as she walked into the house, a teardrop trickled down her face. She had almost started crying in the car, but she managed to keep it together long enough to get home first. She didn't feel comfortable crying in front of Thomas. She was afraid he'd start talking about the devil or spouting some other nonsense. Ruth could tell he wanted to be invited inside, but she wasn't in a talking mood. Plus, she was sick of hearing him bad mouth Sallie Rigelli all the time, a major obsession of his. She was also tired of him complaining about his son Kenny, who literally drove him crazy on a regular basis. To be honest, Thomas just gave her a headache period. Ruth truly believed silence was golden and hated the idea of talking, just for the sake of talking.

Also, wakes and funerals always depressed her, especially the older she got. She was seeing more and more of her friends and relatives pass away. Ruth was very much going to miss Gary. She found him quite amusing at times, he was so like a little boy at heart. She recalled the time the church had one of those chocolate fountains purchased for some shindig they were hosting. The fountain was surrounded by strawberries, honeydew melon, cantaloupe, pineapple, and grapes on individual skewers, where you were supposed to take a skewer and just dip it in the layers of chocolate flowing down, but Gary put his mouth under it instead and grossed everyone out, especially Ron. He innocently explained to Ron that he didn't like fruit and he really only wanted the chocolate, so he didn't understand why everyone was making such a big deal about it. Boy was Ron ever pissed, she chuckled, remembering that day.

She knew that Gary was leaving a lot of friends behind, but she couldn't think of anyone who would really mourn Ron, except for Toby, and maybe Jay. She didn't even think Hannah was that fond of him, but had unfortunately, been trapped in a loveless marriage. Simply put, Ron was a nasty man. Roger never liked him either, and Roger was an excellent judge of character.

She had noticed Sheryl was looking unwell at the brunch, more so than usual, and had overheard her telling Bob she felt dizzy and sweaty. Ruth had approached her and told her to elevate the lower half of her body as soon as possible, as it sounded like classic low blood pressure. I hope she or her idiot husband listens to me, Ruth thought, as she retired to her bedroom to take a nap.

***

Pastor Pete and Susan also went straight home after the brunch. Susan was feeling slightly nauseated, and so she went right to bed, wisely placing a garbage can on the floor where she could have easy access to it, should the need arise. Pastor Pete went into the kitchen and turned on his lap top. He logged onto Facebook, a site that he despised, but Ron had mandated that all the Council Members "enter the 21st century" and sign up for an account. Ron had liked to communicate through it a lot, and so the pastor was forced to log on at least once a week, if he didn't want to incur his wrath. He had one message from an old friend Keith up in Michigan, who had put feelers out for him about potential job opportunities. Keith had written that he did hear of one church in Minnesota where the pastor there was planning on retiring at the end of the year. Pastor Pete sent a message back thanking him for looking into it, but that he's decided he'll stay here at St. James for a while.

Before he logged off, he noticed he had ten "pokes". He didn't know what a "poke" was, and he wasn't sure he wanted to know either. He recognized all of the Facebook friends who poked him as his female parishioners, and saw he had the option of "poking back", but he figured he better not take the risk. If he "poked back", they may re-"poke" him, and he didn't need the stress of deciding who and when to "poke". He also noticed a lot of posts on his wall, as of late, which he also ignored. When he first established a Facebook account, he made the mistake of liking and commenting on people's posts on his wall, and in return, he received a barrage of more comments and posts, so much so that it made him dizzy. He had decided he would make the announcement to the congregation next Sunday morning, that he would be disbanding his Facebook account, citing the fact that he's too busy with "pastoral duties" to give the Facebook account all the attention it deserved. Pastor Pete took a deep breath, life was finally good.

***

After Thomas dropped Ruth off, he also went straight home. He had received an email before the brunch from Kenny, requesting that he join Facebook. Fat chance of that, Ron couldn't even persuade him to get a Facebook account. Thomas had explained to him that Facebook was just another invention of Satan's, and that he would have no part of it. It was very disconcerting to Thomas, just how many people would be going straight to hell after they died. He had tried repeatedly to get others to change their ways, especially within the church. He had recommended they all read another classic book by Dr. Rottenhell, How to Pack for Your Trip to

<u>Purgatory</u>, but as far as he knew, nobody ever did. He didn't know why Ruth was so standoffish sometimes either, he really wanted to be invited in, so he could talk to her about Satan's grasp on Kenny and what he was putting his father through. Thank God for Glenn though, at least I have one bright star in my life, he thought.

***

Meanwhile, over at Jay's Catering, Jay Muster was in his office looking over his finances, and he was worried for a couple of reasons. For one, business had dropped off considerably since the clam sauce debacle. He still didn't know what to make of that, for he could hardly believe someone would deliberately harm Ron. He was certainly aware of course, that Ron was difficult to deal with and could be mean, cranky, and bossy at times, but for somebody at the church to do that, was just incomprehensible to him. Jay had a father who was very similar to Ron in temperament, and so he was used to dealing with that sort of man. Therefore, he learned a long time ago how to handle Ron, which was to basically give whatever he dished out, right back to him.

Hannah seemed like she had a lot on her mind lately and he was a little worried about her. He hoped she was doing all right under the circumstances. Another reason Jay was worried, was now that Ron was gone, he was afraid he wouldn't get the church business anymore. He knew Hannah was only going to stay on Council for another year, and without Ron there making all the executive decisions, who knows what might happen. St. James Christian may start exploring other options. Unfortunately, all of this happened at the worst time. Jay had recently remodeled the kitchen in the restaurant to allow more room for cooking, and it ended up costing him an arm and a leg. Also, because the economy was so bad, more and more people were doing their own cooking. He suspected the TV industry with all their fancy cooking shows had something to do with that as well. Damn that Rachael Ray!

***

A couple of hours later, Arianna rang Sallie's doorbell outside her condominium. Nobody answered, so she rang it again. Her white Volkswagen was sitting in the driveway, so Arianna was pretty sure she was at home. After a minute or two, Sallie finally buzzed her in. Arianna walked up the three flights of stairs until she reached Unit #303. She didn't have any fear of elevators per se, but was always scared that the elevator would stop, and she'd be stuck there for an hour or two. Then of course, she would have to go to the bathroom, and would have to resort to going on the elevator floor, and she really didn't want to have to be rescued in a puddle of urine. Arianna was very "bathroom conscious". When going anywhere, she always had to make sure there was a bathroom nearby. She had a very tiny bladder, so in any foreign country she visited she always made sure she knew how to ask, "Where is the bathroom?" before learning anything else. She knew how to ask this in Spanish, Greek, and Italian.

She also never entered any kind of moving vehicle, without first emptying out her bladder. Who knows what could happen if she was stuck in a traffic jam? A couple of years back, people were stuck on Lake Shore Drive for hours after a record-breaking blizzard hit Chicago. If that had happened to Arianna, at least she wouldn't have to worry about dropping her pants in public to relieve herself, and possibly getting frostbite in a sensitive area. Or God forbid, while relieving herself, she have a stroke or something, and then a most innocent bystander happens to come upon her dead, face down in the snow, her naked butt in the air.

Arianna tried to always be prepared for anything. That is why she also always had water and food in her purse and car. If she was going to die of anything after being stranded somewhere, it certainly wouldn't be of thirst or starvation, she'd make sure of it. She also always carried Band-Aids, Kleenex, and Wet Ones, not to mention aspirin and ibuprofen in her purse. The ibuprofen was for her, but the aspirin was just in case, Mike or some other old person, happened to have a heart attack right in front of her. She was very proud of her preparedness, and believed her friends and family were extremely fortunate to have her in their lives.

She knocked on Sallie's door and heard a faint giggling sound from inside. Nobody answered and so she knocked a second time harder.

"Oh, hi Riann! What are you doing here?" Sallie asked, after finally making it to the door. Her hair was tousled and her makeup smudged. She was wearing a long, very sexy, black nightgown, adorned lots of feathers and lace.

"Hi Sallie, would you please send an email today to all the Church Council Members and ask them to come to the church tomorrow night at 7:00 pm. You can tell them you have an important announcement," Arianna said, and started to walk away.

"But why?" called Sallie after her, confused.

"Don't worry about it," she yelled over her shoulder. "You just get back to your uhh," she paused, "date." Arianna smiled to herself as she got into her car, picturing in her head the embarrassed expression on Sallie's face.

A few minutes later, Arianna entered the Meadowville police station, which wasn't exactly abuzz with activity. In fact, most of the policemen on duty looked bored out of their minds. Arianna was wearing a very pretty black sweater with black fur on the collar and cuffs, and tight black jeans with big silver hoop earrings hanging in front of her long blond hair. John, the policeman who sat closest to the door, smiled at her as she walked towards him.

"Looking good kiddo, looking good!"

"Hey John, how's it going?" Arianna always got treated very well at the station. They all knew about her and Mike's mercurial relationship, but they never took sides, which Arianna always greatly appreciated.

"Can't complain, are ya here to see the boss?"

"Yes, is he available?" she asked.

"Sure, you can go on back," John replied, as he stepped aside for her. She made her way to the back of the station. Mike's office door was wide open, and he was sitting at his desk eating a huge cheese danish. He looked up, and upon seeing her, waved her in. She entered his office, took a deep breath, and closed his office door all the way behind her.

Chapter 28 - Conclusion (Monday)

The Monday night Church Council Meeting began with Arianna and Sallie waiting patiently in the church basement for all the members/suspects to arrive. Arianna had strategically placed twelve chairs in a circle in preparation for the meeting. She intended on being the focus of attention in the center. Arianna wanted very much to be taken seriously that evening, so she had spent a long time deciding what she was going to wear. First, she was thinking about renting a tuxedo so she would resemble Agatha Christie's famous Belgian detective, Hercule Poirot, but decided she really couldn't be spending that kind of money, now that she wasn't working. She also considered possibly wearing a tweed skirt and jacket to look like Miss Marple, another of Christie's famous detectives, but she found the clothes extremely uncomfortable and itchy. Finally, she settled on an outfit that she was quite happy with, paying homage to another one of her favorite detectives.

However, as luck would have it just as she was about to leave her house, her mother stopped by. She took one look at Arianna's houndstooth coat, deerstalker hat and pipe, and remarked, "I thought Halloween was last month?" Taking this as a sign that she might have gone too far, she went back in the house, took off all her clothes, and put on a pair of jeans. Unfortunately, almost all of her tops were in the laundry, so she was forced to wear her grey "Better Call Saul" T-shirt, which was a reference of course, to one of her favorite TV shows, "Breaking Bad". Sallie, on the other hand, in a long tight red dress that hung far below her knees, and two-inch high, sparkling red, open-toed heels, looked exactly like *Miss Scarlett* from the board game Clue. All she needed was a long black cigarette holder to complete the look.[1]

The Church Council Members arrived all at once, almost as if they were waiting outside the church for each other to arrive, and decided to come in as one unified group. It was a little intimidating, Arianna admitted to herself. They walked in with questions written all over their faces. Thomas came in complaining, "This is highly unorthodox Sallie!" Then he saw Arianna and stopped. "Well hello there, nice to see you again. Has Glenn called you at all?" he asked Arianna hopefully. Sallie laughed, and quickly put her hand over her mouth. Arianna shot her a warning look.

"Uh no, he hasn't," she replied.

"Well, he's pretty busy. Did I mention he's a financial analyst downtown?"

"Yes, you did," Arianna replied, walking away quickly, but Bob swiftly blocked her path.

"So, is this meeting about you joining the Council?" he asked, curious.

---

[1] and possibly a candlestick from the Conservatory.

Arianna replied, "You'll see, why don't you take a seat. Why don't you all please take a seat," she told everyone. Lorraine sat down nervously, crossed her legs and began biting her nails.

After they were all seated, Shelley broke the ice by standing up and asking in a very angry tone of voice, "Why ARE we here? Why did you call this meeting Sallie? I have much better things I could be doing right now."

Dick was standing up, his hands in his pockets jiggling his car keys. "Yes," he agreed, "I am also quite busy on Monday evenings and I don't appreciate this little surprise gathering." "Couldn't you have made your announcement via email?" Dick spent Monday nights with old business acquaintances he had made over the years. Besides the country club, he also belonged to a private men's club whose primary goal, it seemed to be, was to sit around in big soft easy chairs, smoke pipes, and talk about how much the federal government was ruining people's lives. Dick very much resented missing that this evening.

Arianna stood up and stated firmly, in an authoritative voice, "Please everyone sit down. I asked Sallie to call this meeting because I have something to say to all of you." Dick and Shelley sat down looking extremely annoyed. Pastor Pete kept looking at his watch. Thomas wasn't sure if it was his imagination or not, but it seemed like Sallie was grinning at him in a strange way. Arianna noticed this and shot Sallie a look that clearly said, "cool it". The others all managed to look both curious and wary at the same time. Arianna stepped forward into the circle and faced the Council.

"Ladies and Gentlemen, Sallie Rigelli called me a few weeks ago, because she wanted me to investigate a death that had occurred at your church, and which appeared to be an accident. A death that was caused by an ingestion of clam sauce by a man who was severely allergic to shellfish." Hannah looked down at her hands. Arianna continued, "Sallie obviously did not believe Ron's death was an accident. She got some vibe or some type of intuitive knowledge that told her something was off. I did not take Sallie very seriously at first, but I agreed to look into this matter for her, primarily because I didn't have anything much better to do at the time, I must admit." She made a feeble attempt at a laugh while glancing over at Sallie. "However, after visiting your church a few times, observing everybody, and watching months' worth of Council Meetings, a task by the way that I wouldn't wish on my own worst enemy..." Hannah looked at her sympathetically. "I have concluded that," she paused for effect, "Sallie Rigelli was correct. Ron's death was no accident!" she said, her voice rising dramatically.

"What?" asked Pastor Pete, "that's crazy!"

"No, it is not crazy," Arianna replied, walking over to the pastor. "It is NOT crazy at all!" she said as she stabbed her finger at him. "It was clearly a case of deliberate murder, a murder most foul," she added, in what she hoped was a frightening voice. She was beginning to really feel like Hercule Poirot and she was starting to enjoy herself. She wondered if exclaiming, "Mon Dieu!" every so often, would be considered over the top.

"Let us start at the beginning, shall we?" She walked back and forth in front of the group, with her hands clasped behind her back. "The day of the Annual Autumn Banquet, a day quite frantic and busy with preparations. A few days before, Hannah Dorchester placed the order at Jay's Catering, like she had done for the last fifteen years. She, like so many times before, ordered the entire dinner, including linguini with *puttanesca* sauce, did you not?" Arianna looked over at Hannah. She nodded her assent. "Then according to Kevin, a young man at Jay's Catering, a few hours before the banquet began, he received a phone call. This call, according to their Caller ID, originated from inside the church, by what he thought was a woman, but couldn't be absolutely sure. This was a pity, as that would have narrowed down our suspect field considerably. Anyway, this person of unknown sex, knowing that there was a big Culinary Expo that day and Jay would not be there to interfere with their diabolical plan, called in a minor change to the order. This person requested that the red clam sauce be substituted for the *puttanesca* sauce." The Council erupted into noise, but Arianna ignored them, raising her voice. "Anyone familiar with Jay's Catering knows the *puttanesca* and the clam sauces look very similar, and Ron didn't seem to be a picky eater, so it's doubtful he would have noticed the difference."

"Picky eater, Ron? Now that's a good one," said Bob, folding his arms over his chest. Sheryl shot him an embarrassed look.

Arianna continued, "Now, I interviewed Kevin myself, and considering the fact that he was a kid who didn't even know the victim, and that he seemed genuinely upset, I immediately surmised that he was telling the truth. Kevin was just an innocent pawn in this deadly game of murder." "I also did some uh, research of my own about Jay, knowing he was very close with the deceased, but I could find no evidence of any bad blood between them."

Hannah made a noise and murmured, "Of course not."

"I also suspected that maybe you Hannah, and Jay were having an affair, since it seemed you two had a close relationship as well."

Hannah looked at her coldly. "That is simply ridiculous, I was not..."

Arianna interrupted her, "No Hannah, you weren't. By all accounts, Jay is a happily married, family man, who frankly even if he had the desire to, he would have absolutely no time at all to carry out an affair, which means....."

"Someone in the church is a murderer!" shouted Sallie, with excitement.

"Yes Sallie, not only a church member, but specifically a Church Council member, as they were the only ones there at the church the day of the banquet," revealed Arianna. The Council Members all looked at her with mild skepticism. "But the question remained, who killed Ron and why? We already knew how the murder was accomplished. After becoming acquainted with all of you, it was immediately apparent that you all had a motive to commit this crime."

"Except for me of course," laughed Sallie, flipping her long hair back away from her face.

"Even you, Miss Rigelli!" Arianna shouted, as she walked towards her.

Sallie went pale. "What do you mean?" she asked.

"I mean," she continued, "you were having an affair with the deceased, weren't you??"

"Riann stop, you're scaring me," cried Sallie, nervously playing with her right earring.

"Answer the question!" barked Arianna.

Sallie took a deep breath. "Yes, it's true," she admitted, with a guilty look on her face. She hung her head in shame.

"Eww!" Lorraine squeaked, wrinkling her nose disdainfully. Everyone stared at Sallie in amazement.

"Figures," Thomas mumbled under his breath. What do you expect from a Jezebel, he thought.

"Really?" Dick asked. He looked down at Arianna through his spectacles. "I cannot believe Ron was even capable of having sex, his stomach was so huge." He looked over at Sallie, "How is that even possible? How exactly did you two...?"

"Enough!" cried Shelley, "do we really need to air all their dirty laundry?" She gave Arianna an icy glare.

"How did you know?" Sallie asked, very surprised.

"It wasn't difficult to figure out. Knowing you and your tendency to always have a love interest, I couldn't believe you would take time out to serve as a member of the Church Council, unless there was some sort of romance involved. After viewing the videotapes, I could see how Ron looked at you, and you even admitted Ron was the one who asked you to serve on the Council. You also seemed to be taking his death especially hard, and obviously cared enough to have asked me to investigate it. Also, when I asked you to tell me about Ron, you seemed to cast him in a particularly favorable light compared to everyone else."

Sallie nodded. "One night after a Council meeting about a year and a half ago, I had a date planned with a man I really liked and he stood me up. Ron knew something was going on because he had overheard part of my phone conversation and saw I was really upset. When I explained to him what happened, he told me the guy had to be an idiot to stand me up and he made me feel a lot better. I was really vulnerable and so one thing led to another and well...." She looked over at Hannah. "I'm so sorry Hannah, I know this must come as a big shock, and I hate to do this to you so soon after Ron's death," Sallie said sincerely, appearing very contrite. Hannah looked up, but didn't say anything.

Arianna said, "Sallie, Hannah already knew, didn't you Hannah?" Hannah nodded, to everyone's amazement.

"How did you know that?" Sallie asked Arianna.

"Hannah is smart, and a smart woman always knows when her significant other is cheating on her," she explained. Arianna gleaned this, after watching all six seasons of "The Sopranos", by how Carmela always knew about Tony's infidelities, even when he thought he was being careful. Again, just another way all my TV watching has come in useful, Arianna thought smugly.

"But what does this have to do with Ron's death?" asked Sallie.

Arianna said, "Perhaps you wanted him to leave Hannah, and he wouldn't?"

Sallie shook her head vigorously. "No, I didn't want him to do any such thing! We only slept together a handful of times, well, I shouldn't say sleep together, it was more like....."

Shelley interrupted by blurting out, "Ugh, how very repulsive."

"Positively vomitrocious," said Thomas, nodding in agreement.

"Don't worry Sallie," Arianna said, "I know you, and I ruled you out as a suspect a long time ago. You wouldn't want one man on a permanent basis, and if he did something to upset you, you would just move on to the next guy."

"Yes, thank you!" said Sallie, visibly relieved. It took more than a few seconds to realize Arianna wasn't exactly casting her in the most favorable light.

"Now, that brings me to Hannah. Ron's unfaithfulness definitely gave her a reason to commit this crime." Arianna turned and walked back and forth in front of her, while Hannah stared blankly in response. "But I don't think Hannah cared enough to hurt Ron, did you?" she guessed.

Hannah grimaced and steely replied, "I did not kill my husband."

"This is absurd! What is this?" demanded Shelley, "some murder mystery game you're playing Miss Archer?" "If so, I am not going to take part in this." She picked up her purse, obviously intending to leave.

"Stop!" ordered Arianna. "Sit down Mrs. Anderson." Shelley paused, and then took her seat. "You also had a motive."

"Well, I I I never," stammered Shelley.

"When Ron began his latest council term, he decided he would do background checks on everybody to make sure nobody convicted of any crime would be given a position of authority in the church. Interestingly enough, he discovered you had something to hide, Mrs. Anderson." Shelley grew pale. "As a young woman, you were arrested on possession of illegal narcotics!" The Council members gasped in unison, as they all looked at Shelley.

Sallie sprang from her seat crying, "Just Say No!" as she shook her finger in Shelley's face.

"I was with my boyfriend at the time, and unbeknownst to me, he was carrying a great deal of cocaine on his person," Shelley said, shaking. "I didn't know he had been in trouble before and that he was on the police's radar." She looked at everyone pleadingly. "Anyway, yes Ron found out and made a few snide comments about it to me after the Council Meeting, but I wouldn't kill because of that! Dick already knew all about it, but thank you for briefing the whole town on my personal affairs Miss Archer. How did you find out anyway?" Shelley questioned her nastily.

"Oh, it was on a hunch after watching the video of the last Council meeting that Ron presided over. Mr. Manning neglected to turn the recorder off and it caught Ron on video asking to meet with you privately after the meeting. When you two were finished, Ron looked gleeful but Shelley, you appeared enraged. I figured he had some dirt on you, so I had Sallie "borrow" Ron's Council background check records, and they confirmed my hunch," explained Arianna. Pastor Pete shot a suspicious glance at her. "You definitely had a motive for keeping this information hidden, and so I couldn't rule you out as a suspect, OR your husband for that matter." She looked at Dick menacingly, as the Council collectively raised their eyebrows. "You could have killed him on behalf of your wife, out of your intense love for her," reasoned Arianna. Then she looked at the two of them, "although, that is HIGHLY doubtful," she added, while walking away from the couple. Shelley opened her mouth and then closed it. "Not to mention the fact that Ron had embarrassed you in front of all your golf buddies, including one of your oldest and dearest friends," Arianna said, looking back at him over her shoulder, as Dick stared at her in surprise. "Yes, Mr. Anderson, Arianna Archer knows all." She tapped her forehead with a self-satisfied smile, channeling Hercule Poirot as best she could.[1]

"And Bob," Arianna swung around and addressed him, "you also had a motive."

"Whhaat? Why would I kill Ron?"

"Maybe you thought that with him out of the way, you could finally have a say in how this church is run?"

Bob looked around incredulously. His wife sat open mouthed, staring at him. "Sheryl, tell them how crazy this is!" he demanded. When Sheryl didn't say anything, he looked at her and said, "Sheryl! You don't think I did this, do you?"

She hesitated and then quickly answered, "of course not." Her husband remained in his seat, looking at her stunned.

"The zame goez with her, maybe you did theeze Sheryl zo your husband could finally get what he alwayz wanted," accused Arianna, moving her face uncomfortably close to Sheryl's. Sheryl gave her a weak look as everyone else scoffed. "Nah, evenz I have to eedmit," Arianna waved her hand, "zhat theory iz pretty ridiculezs!" Sallie quickly raised her hand.

Arianna, annoyed that she broke her rhythm, condescendingly asked, "Yes?"

"Why are you talking in a French accent?" responded a confused Sallie.

---

[1] Unfortunately, everyone was just left with the impression that she was strange and had a huge ego.

"Ize am not zpeaking weeth a French., I mean.. I am NOT speaking with a French accent!" she replied, blushing furiously. Arianna then spoke the following words carefully, "But of course, Mrs. Barger also had a motive!" She swung around and looked intensely at Lorraine, who was sitting at the edge of her seat transfixed by the proceedings.

"Me?" she asked, shocked.

"Of course, you had a very open argument with Ron over the Sunday School budget."

"Oh, that?" replied Lorraine. "Yes, but you can't imagine," she swung around quickly in her chair. "You don't think??" she stopped when she noticed everyone looking at her suspiciously.

Arianna ignored her reaction, walked right past her and suddenly stopped in front of Thomas.

"Mr. Manning!" she said loudly.

Thomas looked petrified. "Yes?" he asked with hesitation.

"After Ron died, you ran for position of Vice-Chair did you not?" asked Arianna.

"Well yes, along with Bob Grossman," he responded defensively.

"Isn't it true that you had been asking the Council to vote on reinstating the Church Dress Code for years, and every single time Ron convinced everyone to shoot it down?"

"Yes," Thomas yelled, "but I wouldn't be petty enough to kill someone over a dress code!"

"Maybe not," acknowledged Arianna, "but when there's a crime, we always look first to see who profits from that crime." "Maybe the

idea of power was so overwhelming that you couldn't help yourself?"
Sallie stared wide-eyed at Thomas.

"Oh my God, that is just absolutely not true!" he denied it
loudly. Thomas looked around, "It isn't!" he repeated for good
measure. Sallie continued to frown at him, and it looked more and
more likely, that there was a chance he was going to throw up.

"Let's move on now to Pastor Pete," said Arianna, to Thomas's
relief. "Pastor Pete, you haven't had a raise in three years, and with a
baby on the way, maybe you needed to make sure you got that raise?"
she yelled in the Pastor's face rather obnoxiously.

"I..., I am not even going to dignify that with a response," he
stated and looked away in the opposite direction.

"Well then," continued Arianna, "let's move on to Gary, which
was the second death to befall a St. James Christian Church Council
Member within a month."

"But," raising her hand, Ruth spoke up for the first time, "that
wasn't a murder, surely?"

"Hold on Mrs. Williams, everything will be explained soon
enough," answered Arianna. "One Sunday morning during Coffee
Hour, Mr. Forrester happened to overhear a conversation Sallie and I
had with Hannah, about Ron's death possibly not being an accident.
He was standing nearby when we were discussing specifically, how
Kevin at Jay's Catering said someone from the Church had called the
restaurant changing the order the day of the Banquet. The Council
Members were all there early that day helping set up. Later,
something must have clicked in Gary's mind and he remembered
hearing someone on the church phone the day of the banquet. I am
guessing he overheard the person say something like, "a change in the
order", which meant nothing to him at the time, but now it became
obvious that this person he had overheard might be accused of
murder. Poor Gary was very naive, he could not imagine this person
in his wildest dreams ever killing anyone. Therefore, he automatically
just assumed that this person didn't know about Ron's allergy and

changed the order because of a personal preference. He called this person, let's just refer to him as, 'the killer', shall we? He called the killer on the phone and asked to meet him, so he could talk about the conversation he overheard.

Afterwards, this is what I believe happened. Once they met, Gary told the killer, who as I mentioned, he completely trusted, about hearing him change the catering order and about the conversation he had overheard at the Coffee Hour. He told the killer that he thought he should just go to Hannah and explain what happened. The killer went along with what Gary assumed, that he hadn't known about Ron's allergy, but had changed the order because he disliked the olives in the *puttanesca* sauce, or something to that effect. He pretended to feel horribly guilty for accidentally causing Ron's death, and convinced Gary not to say anything. Later, the killer was forced to act quickly. He knew it was only a matter of time before, given Gary's proclivity for talking, he divulged the truth to somebody, not so naive. The killer knew someone would figure out that he had to have known about Ron's allergy, after having served so many years on the Council with him, and having attended so many of the Autumn Banquets. The killer also was aware that Gary was regularly taking Digoxin and that he had a major sweet tooth. Consequently, within the next twenty-four hours, he brought over a large bag of black licorice for Gary. We saw evidence of the licorice during the brunch at..."

Sheryl raised her hand and Arianna paused mid-sentence. "Yes, Sheryl?" Arianna asked in a steely voice.

"I need to use the restroom," she whined.

Arianna groaned, "OK just go, we'll wait." She scampered quickly towards the women's bathroom. An uncomfortable long silence lingered over the group until she came back.

When she returned, Arianna continued, "As I was saying…", then she became embarrassed because she lost her place.

Luckily, Thomas rescued her by interrupting, "We saw evidence of the licorice…"

"Oh yes, thank you," she said, and in a louder voice repeated, "we saw evidence of the licorice during the brunch at Gary's house." "However, what none of us knew but the killer, was that mixing Digoxin with licorice is extremely dangerous, and in many cases even fatal." The Council Members gasped. "Unfortunately, as we know the killer's diabolical plan worked and poor Gary bit the dust," recounted Arianna. Hannah whimpered slightly.

Sallie raised her hand sheepishly. "What now?" Arianna asked.

"May I use the restroom?"

"No, you may not!" Arianna yelled, losing her temper. A stunned Sallie crossed her legs, looking quite uncomfortable. "Now, where was I? Oh yes, now when going through Ron's background checks, besides discovering Mrs. Anderson's sordid past as a drug fiend," Shelley shot her a nasty look. "I also found out that one person on the Council had a medical background, providing this person with enough knowledge to not only know about the severe effect anaphylactic shock would have on a man of Ron's weight, but how dangerous it would be for a man Gary's age, eating copious amounts of licorice, while at the same time, taking Digoxin. This person was also very familiar with Ron's eating habits and knew he would take a giant helping of the sauce, which was chock-full of clams, at the Banquet. The effect would be much greater than if he had just taken an accidental bite of shellfish. This person, as mentioned before, was both aware of the medication Gary was taking, and his penchant for sweets. He knew that he would be sure to gorge himself on the licorice he brought him."

"And this person is," Arianna paused, observing that all the Council members were staring at her expectantly, and wishing she had thought ahead of time and had Sallie purchase a drum for the requisite drum roll, "RUTH!" she swung around and pointed at her.

"What? Oh my God!" the crowd erupted into noise.

"No, I don't believe it!" Sallie cried.

"Believe it!" continued Arianna melodramatically, "according to the background checks Ron initiated, Ruth was a nurse many years ago at Maguire Hospital in Chicago, before she was married to her beloved Roger. But sadly, as you all pretty much suspected, she became unhinged after Roger's death. Sallie had told me that he suffered a heart attack and died right here while in the middle of building this library. The library they spent months dreaming up, designing, and building."

Arianna walked over to the library. "Ruth privately blamed Ron for her husband's death. The couple had asked for help with the library using church funds, at a Council Meeting a couple of months prior to Roger's death, and Ron had denied their request. Consequently, Roger had to do a lot of the physical work himself. Ruth felt that if they had that help, Roger wouldn't have exhausted himself mentally and physically, and would still be alive today. However, she recently gave Ron a chance to redeem himself by asking for the utilization of church funds to hire a handyman to finish the library, and to purchase a memorial for Roger in the form of a gold plaque. After Ron's last Council Meeting, the videotape revealed Ruth asking to meet with Ron alone. She must have asked him for the help and memorial plaque then but Ron refused, and that made Ruth angry and frustrated enough to kill him. Ruth knew this library meant the world to Roger, and she was going to see to it that it was completed, AND that he got the credit for it. She also expected that with Ron dead, Hannah as Chair would grant her request. Ruth and Hannah always got along very well, but Ruth knew Hannah would never oppose Ron while he was still alive." Arianna looked over at Hannah, who appeared very sad, twisting her wedding ring back and forth around her finger.

Sallie was staring at Ruth who was sitting extremely still and expressionless. "So you mean she killed Ron out of love, love for Roger?" Sallie asked incredulously.

Suddenly, Ruth leapt from the chair and screamed, "My husband DIED for this library, for this church, IN this church!" Everyone sat back shocked. "Not only did Ron refuse to hire someone to finish the library, and then deny me the memorial plaque and acknowledgment for Roger, he told me that he never approved of the library in the first place. That now that Roger was gone, the first thing he was going to do in 2014 was get rid of it! He was an evil evil man and because of him, Gary had to die, he had to die!!! ohhhh!!" she screamed and moaned.

The Council sat there speechless, mouths agape. Arianna put two fingers to her mouth and whistled very loudly. Suddenly, the Chief of Police appeared seemingly out of nowhere, with two other policemen. He walked over to Ruth and proceeded to read aloud her Miranda rights, while the other two men cuffed her. The rest of the Council members were talking to each other excitedly. This was the biggest thing that had ever happened in Meadowville, let alone St. James Christian, and they were all reeling from the shock.

As the policemen made their exit, Mike Stevenson winked at Arianna and said, "Nice job sweetie, give me a call soon." Arianna nodded and blushed, as everyone turned to look at her. Sallie smiled and shot her a knowing look.

Several minutes later, Pastor Pete quickly walked out of the church. Susan is NEVER going to believe this, he thought. Then he began to worry, now I'm probably going to have to change my sermon Sunday to something involving murder. Hmm, Cain and Abel might work... Thomas left looking devastated, darting mean looks at both Sallie and Arianna as he walked by.

Shelley slipped on her short mink jacket and exited the church whispering to her husband, "I think we need to find a new church, I don't want to worship in a place where there are dangerous killers lurking left and right."

Dick nodded in agreement and replied, "The church's reputation is definitely shot."

Bob Grossman stopped in front of Arianna. "It seems there's a third opening on the Council, we'll really need someone now, are you game?"

Before she could reply, Sheryl interrupted, "I don't think she's planning on joining the Council, Bob." She looked over at Arianna.

Bob looked confused. "Oh? OK well, thank you young lady, great work! Of course, if I had been Chair none of this..."

"Let's go Bob," his wife cut him off, taking his hand and pulling him away, for which Arianna was grateful.

Lorraine stopped as well. "Thank you Arianna, you have quite the brain. In fact you would make a wonderful teacher, have you ever considered ....?," Arianna smiled and then quickly walked away from her.

Hannah was the last to leave and Arianna approached her. "You knew it was Ruth, didn't you?" Arianna asked her gently. "I didn't know for sure," replied Hannah, "and I certainly didn't know or suspect that Gary's death was anything but natural." "Ron had told me how he had responded to Ruth, in regards to the library, that evening of the Council Meeting. I told him that what he was doing wasn't right, but he didn't listen to me. " She paused for a second and went on. "He never really ever listened to me or anyone else," she added. "Ruth just wasn't the same," Hannah shook her red curls and continued, "after Roger died." "I could tell she wasn't, but I thought it was just grief, and it would pass, but obviously," she sighed, "it didn't." "Goodbye Miss Archer," she said, extending her hand. After shaking Arianna's hand, she nodded at Sallie and said, "Sallie." Hannah then walked out of the church into the blustery autumn evening, a strong wind howled, pushing her forward as she opened the door.

Only Sallie and Arianna were left. "Riann, I'm glad that we found out who killed Ron, but it makes me sick to my stomach that it was Ruth, and worst of all, that Gary had to die because of her craziness. How did you know for sure it was Ruth?" she asked.

"Well, the videotape revealed Ruth asking to talk to Ron after the Council Meeting, and a couple of days later he was dead. I felt like something might have been said in that conversation, that could have been the key to Ron's death. By all accounts, Ruth was never right in the head after her husband's passing, and it was obvious after watching the videotape, that Ruth knew what she was doing when caring for Lorraine's wounded knee. This led me to suspect she had some sort of medical background, which of course was verified later in Ron's background checks. I also noticed her appeasing Gary with Hershey's Kisses at a few of the meetings, so I deduced she was quite aware of his addiction to candy. She was the only Council member who not only had the opportunity to kill both men, but the medical knowledge to pull it off," Arianna stated with confidence.

"However, I must admit that at first I thought it was highly unlikely a sweet old woman could be a killer[1], but then I remembered that looks can be very deceiving. You can never really know anyone, no matter how close you are to them. In the TV show, "Breaking Bad", Walter White's own brother-in-law, a DEA officer, never suspected him of being a drug lord because Walt was a meek, respectable, middle-aged, married, high school science teacher with two kids. Because Hank had underestimated Walt, he unfortunately ended up meeting his demise," Arianna explained.

"Wow! The way you also figured out the whole heart medication and licorice thing was pretty genius as well. Thank you so much Riann, I'm really grateful that you took a chance and trusted me," Sallie thanked Arianna profusely.

"No problem Sallie," she said in reply. The two women hugged.

"You know Riann, you should really think about doing this kind of thing for a living. This could be your calling," suggested Sallie.

---

[1] especially an Agatha Christie fan, so sad!

"Oh right," laughed Arianna, "like there's just tons of murders around Meadowville waiting to be solved by yours truly!" "C'mon let's get out of here and get something to eat, I'm starving, and needless to say Sallie, dinner's on you!"

Epilogue - One Week Later

Arianna woke up to the sound of someone ringing her doorbell. She groaned as she stretched her arms above her head. The doorbell kept ringing. "Alright already, I'm coming, I'm coming!" she yelled out. She walked over to her front door in her soft pink Scooby Doo pajamas with feet. She looked through the peephole and yanked open the door.

"Mike, what the hell? Do you realize what time it is??" She paused and looked at her cuckoo clock, which hung on her dining room wall. "It's....oh, it's ten o'clock. Wow, I must have been really tired," she said, as he walked past her, looking her up and down while doing so.

"Yeah, must have been," he remarked sarcastically. "Um, what the heck are you wearing?" he asked, looking amused.

"What? These pajamas are very warm and comfortable, I'll have you know," she replied defensively.

He took a seat at her dining room table and she sat down next to him. "OK Mike, why are you here?"

Mike said, "Rose Forrester called the station last night. She was going through Gary's things and she found this." He held out a big baggie that had a label on it that read, "Evidence #10305."

"What's that?" Arianna asked, very curious.

"It turns out Gary kept a journal, Riann."

"Is that so? I thought only women did that," she said.

"Well, I guess Gary was pretty unique," he replied. "Rose was going through it and she came across some incriminating evidence against Ruth. It turns out if she hadn't confessed, we'd probably have enough here to convict her anyway."

"Really?" Arianna asked excitedly.

Mike took out two pairs of plastic gloves from his coat pockets. He handed one pair over to her. "Here, put these on," he ordered her.

"Ooh, this is awesome! I feel like Catherine on "CSI"," exclaimed Arianna, slipping on the gloves.

"Who?" Mike asked.

"Never mind," she replied with a sigh.

"Well there are some interesting passages here. I can't leave this here with you since it's evidence, but I can wait until you finish reading the sections that are pertinent to the case," he told her, as he handed over the baggie.

Arianna pulled the journal out of the baggie and flipped it open. She took a deep breath and began reading.

Monday, September 9, 2013

Hannah Dorchester looks so sad now that Toby's gone. Maybe she should adopt a kid, although I can't see any adoption agency giving them a child after meeting Ron. Ruth has also looked so sad since Roger died and Lorraine has acted depressed ever since her daughters moved to California. I am so lucky, I have Snickers and my sister Rose and all my St. James Christian friends to make me happy.

Arianna felt a lump in her throat. Poor Gary. She skipped ahead until she reached the beginning of the November entries.

Tuesday, November 5, 2013

I need to remember to get Snickers her favorite kitty treats when I go to Jewel today. I meant to a few days ago, but forgot. I lent Sallie a book on VD. I pretended like it was mine, and that I just thought she might like to read it, but I really bought it for her. She's dated a lot of men lately, more so than usual. Jerry Springer had a show about these men that had been with hundreds of women and all the STDs they carried. I was telling Thomas from church about it and he said Jerry was Satan in disguise. I asked him if Satan could be disguised as anyone, why would he choose Jerry Springer, and not some beautiful woman or something. He said Satan wears many masks. I have no idea what that means.

Sunday, November 17, 2013

Today was a pretty good day, even though at church this morning Sallie and Hannah were arguing. I don't like it when people fight. Sallie was talking about how someone purposely killed Ron. I don't know how she could say such a thing. Ron could be nasty but nobody at St. James Christian would ever do something as horrible as that. Something she said though got me worried. She said somebody called Jay's Catering to change the pasta sauce, so that Ron would have an attack. When I got home, I remembered something about the day of the banquet, when everyone kept kicking me out of the kitchen, because they said they had everything handled and didn't need my help. Shelley had told me that if I really wanted to help, I could just sit on the back steps and keep out of everyone's way. So I sat by myself and was about to turn my iPod on, when I heard Ruth calling Jay's to change the order.

So I called Ruth to let her know what Sallie said, and I told her she should just call Hannah and explain everything, so that they know nobody tried to kill Ron. I knew she either didn't know about his allergy or that she had forgotten about it. (she is over sixty-five, after all) I didn't want anyone to think someone from St. James Christian could do anything like that.

Ruth was very grateful that I told her. She said that she really didn't know about Ron's allergy. The marinara sauce hadn't agreed with her stomach at the last St. James function, because of all the garlic in it. She didn't think anyone would mind if she changed the sauce. I told her I knew it had to be something like that. Garlic doesn't agree with my sister's stomach either. I don't think there's anything that doesn't agree with my stomach. She said that she always thought I was very smart and that she was glad she had me as a friend. That made me feel good.

Monday, November 18, 2013

Late last night Ruth stopped by and dropped off a humongous sack of black licorice whips. She said there was a two for one sale at Target, and she couldn't eat that much. I thanked her for thinking of me. I am so lucky to have such nice friends at St. James Christian! I ate about a third of it already. I'm going to try and save some for later. I don't want to get a stomachache like I did last week when I ate all those boxes of Nerds at one time.

"Wow!" Arianna looked up, "thanks Mike for bringing this over." She put the journal back into the bag, took off her gloves, and handed them back to him.

Suddenly looking serious, Mike suggested, "Riann, maybe you should try out for the police force?"

Arianna, quite shocked, stood silent for a moment, then asked, "Umm, don't you have to pass a physical exam for that?"

"Yes, of course," he replied.

"Then yeah, that's not happening," she answered, sounding a little gloomy. Her face suddenly brightened, "Hey, maybe you could use me as a consultant?"

"A consultant?"

"Yes, don't cops hire psychics sometimes?" she asked.

"Yeah, but Meadowville doesn't, and besides, you're not psychic."

"I know that, obviously, but I could be like Patrick Jane," she suggested.

"Who?" he asked.

"Never mind," she replied, irritated once again, by his ignorance about the things that really mattered in life.

"I better go then," Mike said awkwardly. Arianna noticed he was acting a little strangely, looking almost like he was at a loss for words. Suddenly, he leaned in closer to her and said, "I'm proud of you Riann." He then gently stroked her face and kissed her passionately on the lips. Afterwards, he got up and walked out the door, leaving Arianna stunned and speechless, but smiling.

The End

ABOUT THE AUTHOR

Karen Berg-Raftakis lives in Brookfield, Illinois with her family and two cats. She holds a B.A. in English from the University of Illinois at Chicago and has published poems and articles in various e-magazines and websites. This is her mystery novel debut.

Made in the USA
Charleston, SC
11 July 2015